EVERY
LITTLE
LIE

BOOKS BY LESLEY SANDERSON

The Orchid Girls

The Woman at 46 Heath Street

The Leaving Party

I Know You Lied

The Birthday Weekend

EVERY LITTLE LIE

LESLEY SANDERSON

bookouture

Published by Bookouture in 2021

An imprint of Storyfire Ltd.
Carmelite House
50 Victoria Embankment
London EC4Y 0DZ
United Kingdom

www.bookouture.com

ISBN: 978-1-80019-995-8
eBook ISBN: 978-1-80019-994-1

To Anne – for being such a great friend, and for introducing me to Shrewsbury!

PROLOGUE

The houses in this street sell for not far short of a million. Know where to look online and you can see exactly how much they were bought for and when. You can snoop around the rooms, examine the carefully selected photographs – angled to make the rooms look bigger than they really are – see the double bed where the occupants sleep, compare your kitchen to theirs. Most houses have a floor plan too. If you're really lucky, you might even get a virtual tour. Their house is one of those.

You might think I'm a burglar, but I have no desire to enter the house in the non-virtual world. My own reality is going to be far more interesting.

The outside of their house is even more familiar to me now. It's one of those picture houses children draw, painted white with a red front door and four neat windows, two up, two down, stepping-stone path snaking through the square of grass in the front garden, neat little brick wall securing the property. Or so they think. Sometimes a cat even obliges and completes the picture by sitting on the front doorstep.

They have the same routine every day and I know it off by heart now. He leaves first in the morning, gets into his shiny gas-guzzling statement car and drives to his office in the centre of town. I say town, but Ludlow feels more like a village to me compared to the London sprawl I've left behind. I followed him at first, got to know his routine before I focused on my main object of interest. Jogging along beside the stream of traffic, it was easy for me to keep up with him; he didn't seem to realise he'd be better off on foot. Selfish, that's what he is. Fifteen minutes after he leaves, she walks down the path holding the child's hand and takes her to school.

I prefer those times when I focus on her, watch her as she leaves the house, her slim figure in expensive jeans and pale jacket, blonde hair loose down her back, so straight compared to the girl's tight curls. On those days I follow them a few paces back; she's so absorbed in the child that she doesn't notice anything that is going on around her. Dangerous, that is. It makes her vulnerable. Makes it easier for anyone wanting to take advantage of that vulnerability. Someone like me.

When she reaches the school, I slip into the café opposite and position myself in the window. I'm such a regular now that the owner has my coffee ready for me each morning. Flat white, one sugar. I sip it and watch her squeeze the child tight as if she doesn't want to let her go. She always waits until the girl has crossed the playground and is swallowed up by the building with all the other children, a mere dot amongst the sea of navy blue.

I can't always be there after school, when the mothers congregate on the pavement outside like a load of birds chirping and flapping their wings. She's always one of the first, her gaze trained on that exit even when she's twittering with the others, her little group of friends. If only they knew.

Her clique stands out from the other mothers, those who arrive last minute in their tracksuit bottoms, carpet slippers on occasion, these harried parents always in a hurry, unconcerned with how they look on the morning school run, just wanting to offload their kids for the day's reprieve. In contrast, her group doll themselves up to look smart, as if they are heading to the office afterwards. Some of them will go straight on to work, but she doesn't have to be anywhere to earn her keep. She'd tell you she runs her own business, but it's nothing more than a hobby as far as I can see. She's like a fifties housewife, flitting around the house all day with a feather duster, making everything gleam for her husband when he gets home.

He will be the first act; she will be the second. Before I move on to the main feature, he needs a little help to see his wife for what she really is. Once that is complete and he can gaze into the dark depths of her soul, I will hit them where it hurts. I've made my first move and I can't tell you how good it makes me feel to see them whirling out of control like spinning tops before crashing to the floor. They have no idea what is about to hit them. I'll split up the unit they think they've created, open the cracks, let them look inside and see that their whole life is built on an illusion, leaving them with nothing.

I'm enjoying working out who will be more devastated by this, him or her. I know who my money is on, but what about yours?

CHAPTER ONE

ANNA

From: AnnaJForrester@sewsew.com

To: Wilbraham Road Group

New Wilbraham Road WhatsApp group!

Hey everyone, Anna from number 7 here. So many random goings-on in our street lately so I thought we could do with a messaging service to keep everyone informed. I don't know about you lot, but personally I find emailing cumbersome, so I'm setting up a WhatsApp group so we can message each other. Drop me your number if you want to be part of it, and let anyone I've missed out know about this. I'll send out invites to everyone who responds. I don't want it to be too formal but have drawn up some basic guidelines (taken from the Neighbourhood Watch guidance for social media groups) so we can keep it nice and friendly. It's so important to respect one another in this crazy world we live in.

Evie hands Anna the letter at the school gates.

'What does it say, Mummy?'

'It's about the school fete. We went last year with Granny, though I don't expect you remember. There were lots of stalls set out and you played with Sam in a big green bouncy castle. And Granny dropped her ice cream.'

Evie giggles, putting her hands over her mouth.

'Silly Granny.'

'*Poor* Granny, it was an accident. Ice creams melt in the hot sun and it was very hot that day. I seem to remember you having sticky fingers too.' Anna chuckles to herself at the memory – Marion jumping to her feet in alarm as the dollop of ice cream melted on her red top.

Evie shrugs. It's her new favourite move. 'Can we go to the fete, Mummy?'

'Of course. I'm going to run a cake stall. People will make cakes and bring them to me and I'll sell them to raise money for the school. I'm hoping you'll help me.'

Evie nods and jumps up and down. 'I want to make a choco-late cake, Mummy.'

'The fete isn't for a couple of weeks yet, but we can practise when we get home. Would you like that?'

'Yes, yes, yes.'

AnnaSews@no7: Welcome to the Wilbraham Road group. To those of you whose kids attend Greenside: as you will know if you've had the letter, the new date for the school fete is Saturday 20 July. I'm running the cake sale with Gemma and Kate. If any of you fancy contributing your baking delights, let me know so I can arrange to collect them early that morning or the day before. Proceeds go towards school funds – a very good cause obviously.

Gemma@no19: Letter!! What letter? Little wretch never gives me anything.

AnnaSews@no7: They were given them today.

Gemma@no19: Found it! Scrunched up at the bottom of Sam's bag along with a chocolate wrapper.

Tim@houseonthecorner: Nice.

Jennybrown: I'll make my trusty Victoria sponge.

AnnaSews@no7: Great!

Tim@houseonthecorner: I won't offer to bake – ask my wife if you want to know about my prowess in the kitchen.

Sadie&Ali: Thanks, Anna – again!! Is there anything you can't do???!

Jennybrown: Maybe you could run a time management course for us? I don't even have kids and I don't get time to do half the things I want to.

AnnaSews@no7: You should see my to-do list. It's all a sham!

Evie stands on a plastic stool so she can reach the counter, and whacks flour in a bowl with a wooden spoon, which looks huge in her hand. White clouds puff into the air, making her cough.

'It's dust, Mummy.'

'It isn't dust, you're stirring too hard. Let me show you.'

Together they hold the spoon, and Anna guides Evie to gently fold in the flour.

'I want lots of chocolate, Mummy.'

'Of course. We use chocolate powder to make a cake. You can put some in with this teaspoon ... Not that much!'

Too late, Evie has spooned a mound of chocolate into the flour.

'Whoopsadaisy. This will be very chocolatey. Now let me show you how to add the butter.'

She places her hand over Evie's, which is hot and sticky, and together they beat the golden butter, already softened by Anna in the microwave. Evie is concentrating hard and breathing through her mouth. Anna moves a curl that is dangling in front of Evie's eye and causing her to blink furiously.

'There,' she says. 'Now we're ready for the eggs.'

She loves these moments when it's just the two of them, doing something as simple as baking. As long as she has Evie, she is happy; that's all she needs in life, just her and her daughter – and Seb, of course, their happy little family unit. Her friend Kate would give anything to have an au pair and be able to go back to her job instead of being a stay-at-home mum. Anna feels a pang of sympathy whenever she thinks about Kate – Benjamin is such a difficult baby. She wonders how she would feel if Evie hadn't been so good, but she can't imagine feeling any different. She's been through a lot to get to where she is now, but it's all been worth it. She can't imagine not wanting to be a mother.

Thinking of Kate reminds her of her old friend Susan. The two women are of a similar type. It's been several years since she heard from Susan – no, that's the wrong way to put it. Anna was the one responsible for letting the friendship slide. Susan left voicemails, messages she didn't answer. She sighs, wondering if she'll ever stop feeling bad about it.

'Mummy, you're hurting.'

She hasn't realised how hard she is gripping Evie's hand, and relaxes.

'I'm sorry, darling. Mummy was daydreaming.'

She hopes Susan understands how difficult it was having a young child to contend with by herself, how time slipped by, making it awkward for her to pick up the phone to her oldest friend. She wonders what Susan is doing now, whether she has a partner, a family. People move on, she tells herself, have different friends at different stages of their lives. But she can't entirely convince herself not to feel guilty. Losing Susan was totally down to her, and not entirely accidental.

Seb arrives home as she's checking the new WhatsApp group. Nearly everyone in the street has signed up.

'Anything interesting?' he asks, kissing her before he shrugs off his jacket and slumps onto the sofa.

'Just the Wilbraham Road WhatsApp group.' She tells him about the school fete. 'I'm running a cake stall.'

'Great. Talking of cakes, I can smell something rather delicious.'

She grins. 'Evie wanted to make a cake straight away.'

'Of course she did. I'd better eat a large chunk to see if it's any good.'

'I thought you might say that. I'll put the kettle on. Evie, Daddy wants to try your cake. Hey, did your mum ring you?'

She changes the subject, a mischievous smile on her face.

'Oh yes. Don't worry, I took your side.'

Marion was miffed when Anna refused her offer to collect Evie from school on Monday, when she had a dental appointment.

'I told her that it was on your way back from the dentist, and that anyway you needed to speak to Mrs Gold. Don't take any notice of her. You know how easily offended she is.'

· · ·

That evening, after Anna has bathed Evie, helped brush her teeth and tucked her into bed, she stands on the landing and listens to Seb as he reads her 'Sleeping Beauty', which is the only story she will let them read at the moment. She likes to copy the pictures of the sleeping princess and the wicked queen, who she colours in green. Anna goes into their bedroom and stands by the window, looking down into the silent street. Light spills from the street lamp onto the front garden, making Seb's new yellow car – his pride and joy – gleam, and she takes a moment to feel grateful for everything she has, her family and her home, as the low rumble of Seb's reassuringly familiar voice forms a soundtrack to her contented thoughts.

Rubywiththegingercat: Hi, Anna, thanks re the cake stall – I'm selling second-hand books. If anyone has any donations, drop them round to no. 14. I'll leave a box in the porch.

AnnaSews@no7: Great!

Tim@houseonthecorner: I'll hire a truck for all the wife's Mills & Boons.

Rubywiththegingercat: Bit sexist, Tim ...

Tim@houseonthecorner: Soz. It's sad but true – she can't get enough of them.

Pedro55: That says something about you, mate.

Rubywiththegingercat: I'm happy to make cakes, Anna, but I haven't any tins. If anyone can lend me some I can come and collect them?

*AnnaSews@no7: Cheers, Ruby, I'll drop some spares over –
and a few books.*

CHAPTER TWO

ANNA

Anna is always the first to arrive at school pickup. She waits over by the tree, same position every day. It gives them a good vantage point to spot the children as they come out. Gemma strolls along a few minutes later in her denim jumpsuit and dark glasses, looking effortlessly cool. Kate is last as usual, in her expensive leisure wear, fussing over a screaming Benjamin, his chunky legs kicking at the covers of his pushchair – also usual, unfortunately. Kate's face is almost as red as his. She throws Anna a despairing grimace as she parks the buggy and sticks the brake on with her foot.

'Hi, Kate.'

'Anna,' she says. 'I don't suppose you want a baby, do you?'

'No more babies for me.' Anna gives her a sympathetic smile. 'Let me hold him for a bit, see if I can get him to quieten down.' The warm bundle of Benjamin is thrust into her arms, and she coos and clucks. As usually happens, he settles immediately.

'I wish I had what you have,' Kate says. 'He's the same with my mum, stops hollering the minute she looks at him.'

'Don't beat yourself up,' Gemma says. 'It's the novelty of a different person. Sam used to do it with her dad. Drove me utterly bonkers. Especially when Dave rubbed it in, swaggering about with a smug grin on his face. I'd like to see him spend all day looking after a two-year-old like I do, instead of working at his cushy job.'

'I wouldn't call decorating cushy,' Anna says. 'Give me a room full of children any day.'

'Please no,' Kate says, pushing her too-long fringe out of her eyes. 'Roll on the day when they're both heading off for school.'

'It's cushy when you love every second of it,' Gemma says.

'You know, if there's anything I can do to help ...' Anna repeats the offer she's made several times before. Kate gives her a tired smile.

'I know. You and Gems have both been great. But I'll manage. Mum's only working one day a week now, so she's going to come over more. We'll probably drive each other mad, but ... Oh look, here they come.'

Shrieks and excited chattering shatter the relative quiet of the road as the school doors are flung open by Mrs Gold, who steps aside with practised dexterity as the mass of small children swarm past her, some running, some walking, some in a world of their own. Evie stands out to Anna in her blue uniform dress, her small legs pumping as she races to beat Sam, both girls arriving with their parents at much the same time. Evie hurls herself at Anna and Sam barrels into Gemma. They all laugh, and Anna loses herself in Evie and wills her to stay little forever, so she never has to grow up and leave her. She's sure Gemma is thinking the same thing; they've had this conversation many times, wanting to preserve the moment so that time doesn't pass by without them noticing. Not that Anna stops appreciating the moment anyway – most people haven't been through what she and Evie have.

'Good day, darling?'

'Yes, Mummy. Mrs Gold says I did the best painting ever.

It's me, you, Daddy, our house, Daddy's new car and ...' She hesitates. '... a cat.'

Kate catches her eye and grins. Anna can't help laughing. 'Nice try, little one. You know Mummy is allergic to cats.'

'But you could take special medicine.'

'I wish. If there was a special medicine, I promise I would. But until some clever scientist discovers one, we'll have to stick to just being the three of us for now. And that's not so bad, is it?' She ruffles her curls and Evie turns to Sam, Anna forgotten. Kate's Daniel dawdles across the playground, lost in his thoughts, his round glasses wonky on his nose. Kate straightens them as she takes his bag, tucking in all the stuff spilling out of it, and sticks it underneath the pushchair, where Benjamin is now absorbed in the attention of his brother and his classmates.

'I saw your message about the cake stall,' Kate says, looking less flustered now that her children are occupied for a rare moment without her. 'Mum loves to bake, if you let me know what you need. Her cakes are delicious. Have you had many offers?'

'A few, but it's early days. I've made a list of suggestions and added some simple recipes. I'll email it to you all later if you like.'

'Why don't we have a coffee and chat over it instead?' Gemma suggests. Kate nods eagerly.

Anna is pleased that Kate's mother is stepping in, but her selfish husband should do more. Kate won't hear a word said against Michael, although from what she says he never seems to be at home. His job in travel takes him all over the world. Anna is thankful Seb's job doesn't require any nights away. Running his own business is a definite plus – not that he doesn't work hard, and the last few months have been tough, with the business doing so well since they won the award and Seb having to put in more late nights, but he makes being around for Evie a priority.

'Great idea,' she says. 'In the next couple of days? Wednesday morning, maybe?'

'Sounds good,' Gemma says, and Kate agrees.

Anna's attention returns to Evie, who is squealing loudly at something she's spotted on the ground. Most likely a worm, or a spider; insects are another of her current obsessions.

Evie swings Anna's arm as they walk home, chattering about her day. Seb calls as they're turning in to the crescent, their house the one right in the middle where the road bends, nicely placed to see the whole street. They've never lived in such a friendly place before. Anna is kept busy, what with the Neighbourhood Watch she's been running for the last few months, and the school committee. To think she was worried she'd be bored not going back to an office job when Evie started school. She still has to pinch herself that doing what she loves is earning her money.

'Do you fancy going out for something to eat after I finish work?' he asks.

'Tonight? You know I can't leave Evie just like that.' Getting a babysitter needs to be planned.

'The three of us is what I mean – burger and chips. I'll finish up early, say around six, and meet you there.'

She's smiling when she ends the call. Of course Seb wouldn't expect her to leave Evie at the drop of a hat.

'Was that Daddy?' Evie asks.

'Yes, he's got a surprise for us. That's nice of him, isn't it?'

'I like surprises. He's a good daddy,' Evie says. 'And he likes cats.'

'Mummy likes cats too, Evie.' Anna ruffles her daughter's hair, suppressing a smile.

'Not as much as me and Daddy do.'

'Don't you want to know what the surprise is?' Anna is used to moving on from the cat subject.

Evie nods furiously.

'We're going out for burger and chips.'

'Yes!' Evie says, jumping up and down. 'But I haven't got my new shoes on.'

'We're not going straight away. Daddy will meet us there in an hour. So plenty of time for a change of shoes – and if you hurry up, you'll be able to watch *Penguin Parade*,' she says, turning her key in the door.

Evie squeals as she charges into the living room, and the jolly tune of the Penguin March fills the house, joined by the ringing of the house phone. Anna walks into the open-plan kitchen diner, picking up the phone as she dumps her bag on the island. Seb created the kitchen exactly to her specifications, and it still gives her a thrill every time she goes into it. Everything about Seb makes her want to pinch herself. He's her soulmate, best friend, a fabulous lover ...

'Hello.' She doesn't usually answer withheld numbers, rarely in the mood for an automated voice telling her she's wanted by the taxman, or been left a fortune by an unheard-of relative overseas, but nothing can spoil her good mood today.

There's a beat, a split second before a voice speaks, unfamiliar, feminine.

'You destroyed my life. Now I'm going to destroy yours.'

She's gone as fast as she arrived.

Anna was wrong about her mood: it plummets like a falling stone, and she sinks onto a chair to support her trembling legs. Who is this woman and what does she mean? Could the message really be aimed at her? After all this time? No, it has to be a wrong number, it means nothing, it can't possibly be intended for Anna. She wills herself to calm down, look at this objectively. The caller didn't ask for a name – she wonders if they would have left a message for whoever answered the phone. She sits for a moment steadying her breath. Evie has her back to her, oblivious to the switch in her mother's mood, caught up in a world of cute penguins, where everything is fuzzy and happy. Her dark curls bounce as she laughs with delight.

'Are you watching, Mummy? The penguins are being so naughty. One of them is climbing up the side of the house.' She looks back at Anna, her eyes lit up, her gappy smile still a surprise since she lost her first tooth. She frowns. 'He won't get hurt, will he?'

'No, he won't get hurt,' Anna reassures her. *And neither will they.* She hasn't come this far to let a mystery caller threaten her family. 'The penguins always get a happy ending, don't they?'

Evie nods gravely and switches her attention back to the screen. Questions dart in and out of Anna's mind, and that was all it took: one call to make her second-guess everything she thought she knew.

CHAPTER THREE

SEB

'You are wonderful. Love you.'

'Love you too.' Seb puts the phone down.

'You look pretty pleased with yourself,' Tina says, looking over from the desk opposite. It's not easy to escape Tina's notice. With only three of them in the office, they're a tight-knit unit. Jamie is off in Majorca this week, leaving Tina to cover for him, as well as her usual role of general assistant and unofficially acting as Seb's PA when required. Winning the Best New Small Business award last year has finally allowed him to relax more and trust that the others can cope when one of them needs time off.

'I'll be leaving early tonight, taking the family out to eat.'

'You spoil them,' Tina says.

He shrugs. Evie grins at him from the photo on his desk; not that he needs a picture to visualise her cornflower-blue eyes with the twinkle of mischief in them, the tiny mole, her engaging smile. He wonders if Anna's noticed how Evie has started mimicking his mannerisms – it's unbelievably cute.

'And why not? They deserve it.'

He turns his attention back to the screen and continues

with the website design he's doing for a photographer, enjoying the beautiful images he's working with. Maybe she'd do a shoot for his family. Anna would like that. Both his girls are so photogenic.

Finishing work on time is satisfying. The days of getting home late from work are behind him, and he feels a rush of guilt when he recalls how frequent it became for a while. Anna was right to pull him up on it, though she thankfully never questioned why his job had become so much more demanding. She didn't doubt him for a second – as far as he knows.

He's on his way down to the ground-floor exit, taking the steps two at a time, when he sees her pass by. A flash of blue – he'd recognise that jacket anywhere – and he curses himself for forgetting she always leaves work at this time. Working on the same street isn't great when you're trying to avoid someone. She has her back to him, but he daren't linger in case she turns, afraid of her reaction, so he goes back up the first flight of stairs and waits a moment before deciding it's safe to leave. Seeing her has reminded him of a time he'd rather forget, and he's even more pleased he's taking his family out for dinner, to show them how much he loves them.

Anna and Evie are already seated when he arrives.

'We got a little room, Daddy,' Evie says.

'So I see. It's called a booth.' They try to take Evie out to eat around once a month. The Big Burger is her favourite. He kisses them both and sits down opposite, the seat squeaking loudly under him.

'Was that a mouse?' he says to Evie.

'No, Daddy, it was the seat.'

'Are you sure?'

'Seb, stop teasing,' Anna says, laughing. 'Idiot.'

'Have you ordered?'

'Not yet, I wasn't sure what time you'd arrive.' There it is again, that reminder of a time when he might have been late, chased by the inevitable pang of guilt, which he erases with a smile.

'Great.'

Evie chatters and he listens as he tucks into his burger, delighted by her habit of giving lengthy accounts of everything she does, taking an age to eat her food in between chatter. Anna always eats more slowly than he does, and today she leaves most of her chips.

'Don't you want those?'

'No, I'm full up.' She pushes the plate towards him, smiles. 'Go on, I know you want them.'

'Everything OK?' Now that he's stopped to study her, she looks tired, not her usual sunny self. Her optimistic disposition is one of the things he loves about her. When he first met her, he admired her fierce independence, never bemoaning her lot as a single mum but embracing any challenges that came her way. And her daughter came first in everything. She didn't need to make that clear to him when their feelings for one another became apparent. He loved the summer evenings they spent together, playing with Evie in the garden and reading her stories – such a delightful little girl and so easy to get along with. Once she'd gone to bed, they'd share a bottle of wine out on the small terrace, which Anna had made beautiful with flowers of all colours, the doors wide open behind them so they could hear Evie should she call. At that time, Anna had only just begun her own business, making bespoke children's wear, and the shelves behind her sewing machine were rammed with fabric, ribbons and cotton reels. When she was working, she tied her hair up with colourful scraps of leftover fabric, usually matching whatever piece she was currently engaged on.

She nods, her hair pulled back with a clip this evening,

glancing at Evie, who is creating tomato sauce patterns on her plate with a chip.

'Eat properly, Evie.'

'I'm drawing.'

'You look tired,' Seb says.

'My tooth aches.' Anna rubs her gum. 'I'll put some clove oil on it when we get home.' She removes Evie's plate and stacks it onto hers. 'She's exhausted. Shall we get the bill?'

Seb carries Evie from the car and takes her upstairs, telling Anna to relax while he sorts her out for bed.

'Is she asleep?' Anna asks as he comes back into the kitchen.

'She didn't even protest,' he says. 'Went straight off.'

'What have we done to deserve such a sweetie?' She looks wistful.

'What's up?' he asks. He still worries she might know something, and the thought of it breaks his heart. He can read her so well, as she can him, which is why the last few months have been hard. He's forever grateful that she never found out about his terrible error of judgement, and a rush of love overtakes him as she sits down heavily as if she's carrying a massive rucksack that has suddenly become too much for her slender frame. 'Here, have some wine.' He pours two glasses from the bottle of white he's just taken from the fridge, and sits down at the table with her. 'Is it your tooth?'

'No, that's a bit better now.' She touches the wooden table as she always does when she needs luck, then takes a sip of wine and twists the glass between her hands. 'Something happened today. It's probably nothing, but ...'

'Tell me.'

CHAPTER FOUR

ANNA

Anna takes another sip of wine, her hands trembling just thinking about the phone call. Seb's expression is hard to read. 'It has to be a joke, right?'

'I'm sure it is. It was definitely a woman?'

'Yes, the voice sounded strange, as if it was put on, but it was definitely a woman.' She tries to recall the exact timbre, the slight huskiness of a smoker perhaps, or was the rasp in the tone an attempt to hide the caller's identity? No accent that she remembers.

'Was it directed at you specifically? Did she say your name?'

She frowns. 'No, nothing like that. I can't stop her words going round in my head.'

'Listen.' He takes her hands, so petite in his own large ones, the protectiveness he feels whenever she's upset surging inside him. 'Can you think of any reason why someone would threaten you? Have you fallen out with anyone lately, anything at all that you can think of? Not upset any of the neighbours?' He winks, but she doesn't react to his feeble attempt to lighten the mood.

'No.' She looks baffled. 'I've thought of nothing else all afternoon.'

'OK. Then if I ask myself the same question, and my answer is no too, then it has to be a wrong number, or a prank call, kids messing about. Me and my mates used to do that all the time when we were younger. We'd just pick random numbers, say something stupid and hang up. We thought it was the funniest thing ever. That's what it will be. The telephone version of a troll.'

'You could never be a troll. You and your friends were kids messing around. Trolls know who they're targeting. This wasn't a child, although the voice sounded distorted. It felt directed, vindictive. She wanted to hurt me.'

'Hurt *us*,' he says, still holding her hands. 'We're a team, don't forget, the three of us. These people want to cause unease, it makes them feel powerful. Don't give her the satisfaction, eh? We've established it isn't meant for us.'

'You're right,' she says, relaxing, her mind eased.

Wednesday soon comes around. Anna showers and gets ready to meet her friends in town. She puts on a flowery dress and pulls her long blonde hair into a loose ponytail, applies some light make-up and sprays herself with a citrusy perfume.

The sun is already shining, but despite Seb's reassuring words – that the call was a harmless prank and doesn't deserve a minute more of her thoughts – a sense of unease undermines the delight she'd normally take at the feeling of warmth on her skin. An unease that was once all too familiar to her.

Kate is standing outside the café, casual in hooded sweat-shirt and jeans, waving at Anna as she spots her coming towards her. There's something different about her friend, Anna thinks, then it comes to her: no pushchair, no Benjamin, and her face looks less strained than it usually does. The recent weight loss makes her beautiful facial structure stand out, her cheekbones needing no artificial highlighting. Anna smiles widely at her, masking her relief. Kate's attention won't be divided for once, and time to herself with her friends is exactly what she needs.

'My sister has got Ben,' Kate says as if she can read her mind. 'She's taken him out for the day. Asked did I mind – as if! He's been so difficult this last week. Nice to see you, by the way.' She kisses Anna on both cheeks.

'Perfect,' Anna says. 'As it's so warm, shall we take our coffees into the park?'

'That's a lovely idea. We can have a bit of a walk. I barely get a chance to exercise. You don't know how free I feel. Even not having the pushchair makes a difference; you wouldn't believe how heavy it is.'

Anna laughs. 'Oh, I would. You always have so many bags crammed underneath. That must be exercise enough. You've lost weight, you know.'

Kate sighs. 'I know. My parents have been on at me. I'm pretty sure they put my sister up to offering to take him out. She's never done that before – she's always far too busy in her so important job. I mustn't be ungrateful, though; she's done me a huge favour. And Mum's coming over next week to help out.'

Anna is nodding, but she's aware of how different the two of them are. She finds it impossible to relax if anyone else takes Evie out; in fact she rarely allows it to happen. It's one of the few things she disagrees with Seb about. His mother, Marion, would have Evie far more often if Anna wasn't so 'uptight', as she overheard her tell Seb once when she thought Anna was out of earshot.

'Let's get the drinks and Gemma should have arrived by the time we've done that. She's running here,' Kate says. She rolls her eyes and they both laugh. Gemma's sportiness puts them both to shame.

Sure enough, Gemma soon arrives in a white T-shirt and black running tights, face flushed from exertion. She gulps down water from her fancy bottle.

'First time it's been just the three of us for ages,' she says. 'It's so weird not to have any children around, isn't it?'

'I'm making the most of it,' Kate says.

'That's why we need cake, to celebrate. Largest slice is for you, Kate; you've not been looking after yourself lately.'

'I don't know how you two manage,' Kate says as they head towards a bench overlooking the pond.

'Don't make comparisons,' Gemma says. 'You have two children under five and Ben has a lot of needs. And no offence, but your husband could muck in more. Anyway, we all know Anna is super-mother, so don't even think about measuring up to her.'

'Hardly,' Anna says, looking pleased despite herself. 'Hey, did you notice that man waiting outside the school yesterday? I've never seen him before.'

Gemma takes a huge mouthful of cake. 'The one with the flat cap? I don't mean an old-man cap, more of a hipster vibe. Quite a catch, actually, if that's your thing. He's Charlotte Rivers' dad – you know, the girl who moved here from Manchester last term.'

'Oh yes.' Anna is relieved. She likes to know who people are.

'Don't tell me you fancy him.'

'Of course not.'

'Are you mad, Gemma? Anna only has eyes for her Seb. And I don't blame her.' Kate winks ostentatiously.

The conversation moves on to the cake stall for the fete, and once the logistics have been sorted, Anna heads off home. She suspects she'll end up doing most of the work herself, but she wouldn't have it any other way. She likes to be occupied while Evie is at school.

She's so engrossed in running through the list of ingredients she'll need for the three cakes she plans to bake that when she careers into a woman coming in the opposite direction, she jumps so hard she immediately feels ridiculous. She apologises profusely and vows to pay attention to her surroundings after that.

The morning out with her friends has buoyed her mood, and she hasn't given the phone call any more thought. But as she lets herself into the house, she hears the phone ringing and experiences a sense of déjà vu. She makes a dash for the receiver, skidding slightly on the polished floor, but she's too late to pick the call up. She dials 1471 and learns that it was from a withheld number. That's all it takes to set her mind racing again. A red flash indicates a voicemail and she plays it back.

'I'm watching you all.'

It's the same voice, and she's back on that treadmill again, dread pooling in her stomach, mind whirring as she contemplates what this could mean if the threat is genuinely directed at her family.

AnnaSews@no7: Anyone been getting crank phone calls?

JackieC: Tell me about it. I've been in a lot of accidents lately LOL.

Tim@houseonthecorner: Apparently I've been left some money in New York, just need to send over a small fortune to secure the deal. I'm tempted.

Gemma@no19: Everything all right, Anna?

AnnaSews@no7: All OK, just checking.

CHAPTER FIVE

SEB

Seb looks at the photo of Evie on his desk. It was taken that first summer, when he was getting to know Anna, already falling in love with her although they hadn't even kissed at that point. He picks up the other framed photo he keeps at work, the one of Anna laughing, her hair blowing in her face. They'd gone for a picnic on the beach at Southend, their first day trip together. He'd just got a new car and wanted to take it out for a spin; it was a good excuse to spend more time with Anna, and Evie would love the beach – what child didn't? He was surprised at how quickly he'd become fond of the little girl. He hadn't really considered whether he wanted children at that stage in his life. His previous girlfriend had wanted three, but he hadn't been sure enough about the strength of his feelings to commit, and they'd ended up drifting apart. It was a stage in life he imagined would happen when he met the right person, when he felt ready. As soon as he met Anna, he knew she was that person.

He took the picture of Anna on the seafront. They'd bought ice cream cornets with Flakes from an old-fashioned van that played a tinkling tune, and sat on the wall looking out at the beach. Anna had sand on her cheek, and he brushed it off without thinking. She didn't object. 'Let me take your photo,' he said. 'Your hair is lit up against the blue sea.' She didn't object to his flirting either. He took out his phone and pressed the camera button, and she laughed as he did so. He wonders if she remembers that moment as clearly as he does. It was the moment he fell in love with her, the sea sparkling behind her smile.

Evie wasn't difficult to love either. Both of them were such easy company. Once he'd got to know Anna, he realised he was the first partner she'd introduced into Evie's life. Despite their instant attraction, it had taken her a while before she really let him in, but after they'd had several of those new relationship heart-to-hearts where you want to know every single detail about the other person, he understood why she was guarded. She told him her whole history with Luke, her ex, Evie's father, and how important being a mother was to her. And he found that he didn't mind not having any more children. Once he understood that she couldn't conceive without risk to her health, he honestly came to see Evie as his own. Luke being out of the picture suited him. Anna had looked fierce when he'd tentatively suggested Luke might feel differently knowing he had a daughter, and he'd asked her to forget he had ever uttered such a suggestion.

Soon they were spending most evenings together. He loved being in her flat. She had such a creative eye, and the place was so cosy; she'd painted the walls in vibrant colours, and the small log burner became the focal point of the room in the colder months. As it got warmer, they migrated to the small patio area, a delightful space decorated with plants and flowers. Once Evie was in bed, they'd sit up talking until late in the night. Kissing her for the first time happened out there on the patio, and after that they were inseparable.

He wasn't even nervous the first time he took Evie out on his own, one Saturday morning when Anna had an order to complete. He'd suggested taking the little girl swimming. He could see Anna was anxious, but he loved her for trusting him with the most precious thing in her life. They both had so much fun it became a regular outing, giving Anna quality time alone to do whatever she needed to do without having to worry about deadlines. He thinks back to last week, how he and Evie emerged from the leisure centre, skin tingling and alive, after an hour thrashing about in the water with large inflatables. Evie had managed to swim a whole width – with floats, of course – for the first time, and they couldn't wait to tell Anna. Anna isn't a confident swimmer, and he wants Evie to share his love of the water. This summer he's determined they must get away somewhere hot for a much-needed holiday, where he will teach Anna to swim in the sea.

The warm glow these memories give him fades when he turns his mind to the phone call. Anna was clearly worried, and he did what any decent person would do to reassure her, but was it enough to reassure himself? Chances are it was exactly what he said it was, some moron having a laugh at whichever mug picked up the phone. Even without asking her, he knows Anna doesn't have any enemies; she's the focal point of Wilbraham Road, she's popular at school and she's just one of those people that everybody likes, friendly and funny and good-natured. It could make a person jealous, he supposes, but threatening phone calls, really?

He lets out a sigh. Across the small office, Tina raises her head, and he makes out that he's yawning, chastising himself for letting this get to him. He likes to set an example at work, and he's usually so laid-back. Tina knows him well enough to suss if he's worried, and if he were to tell her it was all over a dodgy phone call, she would think he was being ridiculous.

But is he? As soon as Anna mentioned that the caller was female, he had a sense of foreboding, a churning in his stomach. She wouldn't, would she?

CHAPTER SIX

ANNA

Anna is earlier than usual to meet Evie from school. Her daughter skips across the playground, full of her day's news, and Anna takes her straight home, telling her friends she's going to make a start on the cakes. She isn't in the mood for chatting. On opening the door to her house, she stops dead when she notices the answerphone flashing a message, and Evie cries out as she bumps into her legs from behind.

'Sorry, darling, silly Mummy,' Anna says, helping the little girl out of her coat and shoes. A stone lodges itself in her belly. Evie runs off to play and Anna psychs herself up to listen to the message. First, though, she sets out everything she needs to make a lemon tart – Seb suggested baking might help to take her mind off the calls. Everything ready, she goes back to the hall and plays the message. She puts her hand on the wall to steady herself as the rasping voice fills the air. It's a variation on the previous threats, and fear trickles through Anna's veins. She unplugs the phone from the wall.

Seb is in a meeting when she rings him at work, and she doesn't want to bother him with a message, making inane small talk with Tina before ending the call. Back in the kitchen, she puts away her recipe book and mixing bowl, no longer in the mood for baking. She's too distracted to get on with the dress she's making for a client and doesn't know what to do with herself. Evie is sitting at the table concentrating on a drawing, so Anna flicks through the free local paper, hoping something will catch her attention. Unable to concentrate, she glances at what Evie is doing, colouring Seb's latest car a lurid shade of yellow. Once she's finished that, she starts on a red car with a woman sitting in the driving seat.

'Who's that?' Anna asks.

'The watching lady,' Evie says.

'What do you mean, the watching lady?'

'She's watching me drawing her. Shall we show her my drawing?'

Anna goes to the window, keeping out of sight, and looks at the car parked outside the house. It doesn't belong to any of the neighbours, as far as she knows. The woman glances her way and starts her engine, pulling away from the kerb. She turns her head to look out of the rear window, and all Anna can see is a dark head of hair, shaped into a bob.

'Shall we, Mummy?'

'No, we don't know who she is and it's not good to talk to strangers. You know Mummy's always telling you that.'

Evie nods and abandons the drawing, wandering into the kitchen. Anna stares out of the window.

Seb thought she was mad when she raised the idea of setting up a Neighbourhood Watch group for the street. Since her sewing business took off, surprisingly and wonderfully, two years ago, she's been incredibly busy. What started as a hobby, making clothes for Evie, has developed into a lucrative business, firstly through word of mouth until eventually she asked Seb to build her a website. The work takes up a lot of her time, and Seb expressed surprise that she wanted to take on other 'unnecessary' projects. Beneath his surprise was admiration, though, and he laughed, ruffling her hair and pretending to roll his eyes.

'Little Miss Perfect' is his nickname for her, and he's bought her a mug to match. Anna doesn't mind his harmless teasing – why do something if you can't do it properly? She knows one or two of the mothers at the school gate think she's a bit of a meddler, one of those over-zealous middle-class mothers who are caricatured on sitcoms, but it doesn't bother her. Most of the Wilbraham lot are grateful to her for doing something they wish they had time for.

Anna would rather have too much to do. It's when she has time on her hands that she gets into her head too much and worries about silly niggles, blowing them up out of proportion. Like fussing about school security when she trusts the school completely. Since Evie started school, she dedicates her time to her sewing business during the day, devoting herself entirely to Evie when she's at home. She allocates an hour each day to community business, equally important in her eyes – doesn't everyone want a safer, healthier environment for their family to grow up in? Most of the houses in Wilbraham Road are inhabited by families of varying descriptions, and most have allocated one member to the WhatsApp group. Which proves her point. The neighbours want to know that their street is a safe place to bring their children up. The woman in the red car is probably nothing; she's being vigilant rather than paranoid.

After bath time and a story, with Evie tucked up in bed, she's preparing the evening meal when Seb texts to say he's on his way. She switches the oven on low and makes room for the salad in the fridge, then decides to change her top, and goes upstairs. She's closing the shutters in her bedroom when she notices a woman down in the street. The street lights are on, but it's still fairly dark. The woman looks at their house as she passes, and Anna steps back, not wanting her to sense she's being watched and look up. She closes the blind. She's especially jumpy this evening, making sure the front door and the French windows at the back of the house are firmly locked. When she's feeling like this, she wishes she had curtains to pull across and shut out the dark garden, which looks ominous at night-time, bushes making large shapes as they move with the wind.

Seb texts that he's five minutes away, and she turns up the heat for the casserole in the oven. Soon the smell of chicken fills the kitchen, but Anna has no appetite. She pours herself a glass of water, but her hands are unsteady and she spills some on the floor tiles. A memory flashes through her mind of an earlier clumsiness, knocking into a woman when she was hurrying back from coffee with Gemma and Kate, and she thinks how that woman was wearing a similar jacket to the woman she noticed outside earlier. She rushes upstairs to look out of the window again. What if somebody is following her, this unknown woman at the end of the phone; what if she knows where Anna lives and the calls *are* aimed at her; what if this person really does want to ruin her life?

Seb's key sounds in the door and she rushes out to the hall and into his arms, unable to contain her fear.

'Hey, what's up?' he asks, shrugging off his jacket and hanging it on a peg.

'We've had another message. Same person.'

'You're joking?' His face is anything but amused, a deter-mined expression taking over his features. 'Let me hear it.' He presses play on the answer machine and the throaty voice echoes in the high-ceilinged hall.

'Shit,' he says. He looks shattered.

'Come and eat,' Anna says. 'We can talk about it over dinner.'

Seb chews slowly at his meal, mulling over the phone call.

'Do you still think it's a prank?' Anna asks, pushing a piece of chicken around her plate. Her stomach is a knot, but she doesn't want Seb to know she's having doubts when only a couple of days ago she was convinced it was no more than a joke.

He nods. 'I do, and I really don't want you to worry about it. We could get rid of the landline – I've been thinking about that for a while. We hardly use it, and we get a lot of nuisance calls – apart from these ones, I mean. We both use our mobiles, so we don't really need it.'

'True. If it hadn't been here when we moved in, I doubt we'd have bothered getting one.'

He nods, finishing his food. 'You haven't eaten much. Are you still worried?'

'A bit. I can't help it.'

'If you want, I can report it to the police.'

'Maybe.'

'Let's sleep on it, see how we feel in the morning.'

They clear the table together and he gives her a big hug.

'You know I would never let anyone hurt you or Evie,' he says.

Gemma@no19: Has anyone noticed that car hanging around our street? It's a red VW Golf and it's been there a few times this week. Driver is a young woman, maybe thirties. I went out to speak to her on Friday afternoon but she saw me and drove off. #abitweird

Tim@houseonthecorner: MI5?? AC-12??

Gemma@no19: LOL.

Jennybrown: I saw it last night. No idea. Maybe it was a taxi? Or a driving instructor?

Gemma@no19: I suppose it could have been, but it didn't have a company logo on it, or learner plates.

AnnaSews@no7: It was there last night at 7 p.m., gone by 8.

Tim@houseonthecorner: A stalker?

Sadie&Ali: Be serious, Tim.

JackieC: Tim doesn't know how to be serious. Not seen any unusual car, sorry.

When Anna opens this latest thread on the Wilbraham Road WhatsApp group, it's hard to ignore the little voices that whisper to her, as if they are in competition with Seb's attempts to reassure her.

CHAPTER SEVEN

SEB

Seb hates seeing Anna like this, how seriously she has taken these calls. He wishes he could tell her that he is the one who should be worrying, should be working out whether he has upset anyone in the last few months. But he doesn't even need to ask himself that question, because he knew instantly who this was, despite the attempt to disguise her voice. The vitriolic message may not be directed at Anna, but unless he puts a stop to this, she will be collateral damage.

He lies on his side, staring towards the window, sleep evading him, despite his desperate desire to switch off both mind and body. He is unable to get Anna's description of the mystery woman out of his mind. After she'd read Gemma's message, she told him about a woman she'd bumped into, and a woman Evie had noticed outside their house. The description fits, but it's pretty generic and could be applied to any number of the female population, and both encounters were fleeting. If it is her, why now? He thought it was in the past, that he'd smoothed things over – after all, he made his position clear. She said she understood – she'd known all along he was married.

Anna's breathing is the only sound he can hear, and he's

grateful that one of them at least is getting some sleep. Although she tried to hide it this evening, he could tell she was anxious – frightened even. Could she sense his own fear, could she tell he wasn't being sincere with her? His hands are clenched into fists as he replays the phone messages in his head. He turned her down and now she's out to get him, simple as that. He would never leave Anna; he loves her deeply. He imagines the gossip circulating around the coffee machine at work if his colleagues were to find out what he'd done, and once again tightness strains his chest.

He's worried about her. He shouldn't even have said hello to her. If only he'd never decided to go to the pub that particular day.

He knew he was taking a risk when she caught his attention across the bar. He was exhausted after a day of difficult meetings and having to chase a client who was evading payment. He'd handled it well and the client had paid up, but Seb carried the emotion inside him and needed an outlet for it, not wanting to take it home, risk taking it out on Anna or Evie. He'd gone to the pub, the local used by his office, hoping to run into a friendly face and offload his woes. At first glance he couldn't see anyone he knew, so he perched on a stool at the far end of the bar and ordered himself a pint.

The pub was fairly quiet that early in the evening. A couple of women were sharing a bottle of wine at a table in the corner, and every now and then they'd guffaw with laughter. He'd never been one to laugh like that, with such abandon. 'Sensible Seb', they'd called him at university. A group of builders in paint-spattered trousers and fluorescent jackets stood around drinking pints, and a woman sat alone by the window. He'd been there a while before he really looked at her and saw there was something familiar about her. She had a dark bob and was wearing a suit, as if she too had come straight from work. She was watching something on her phone, a tall glass full of ice and a slice of lemon in front of her.

He ordered another pint and tried to think how he knew her, and it came to him as he was pressing his card to the contactless machine – she was the woman he saw in the coffee shop some mornings on his way to work. She was friendly and had good dress sense. Seb always noticed what people wore – he liked to think he looked good in his clothes, and always made an effort. He hadn't realised he was looking at her until she raised her eyes from her phone and smiled at him, no doubt recognising him too.

'Join me,' she mouthed, raising her glass, and in a moment he's regretted many times since, he hopped off the bar stool and sat down opposite her at the small round table. Her perfume gave off a musky fragrance, and up close he saw how pretty she was, wearing light, natural make-up in a way he appreciated.

'Fancy seeing you here,' she said. 'Regular latte man. Sebastian, is it?'

'Seb. Observant, aren't you?'

She shrugged, smiled. 'I like to know what's going on. My job is all about people. I'm Jo.'

'What *is* your job?'

'I run a hair salon just a few doors along.'

'Snap, my office is along this street too.' Anna had used that salon in the past, but something stopped him from mentioning that.

'And what do you do?'

'I run a website design company.'

'Nice. Would you like another drink? I've been watching you and you look like a man who's had a hard day. I reckon you need one.'

He hesitated. He liked her London accent, the slightly deep tone of voice, and her face was friendly. But she was also attrac-

tive, and alarm bells were ringing. He should drink up and go –
go home with a takeaway and watch something mindless on
Netflix. She had a wicked gleam in her eye as she watched him,
twirling a strand of hair around her finger, her carefully mani-
cured nails catching the light.

'It was a pretty crap day,' he said.

'I'm a good listener.'

'Go on then, just one.'

'What can I get you?'

She was right about being a good listener. It helped that he
didn't know her. He imagined this was why people went for
therapy: an outsider with no ulterior motive, no divided loyal-
ties, enabling them to give objective advice and allow the client
to come to their own conclusions. Jo, thankfully, had good
insight. Despite the difference in their fields of work, they were
both managers responsible for a team, and she made him laugh.
He was able to forget the stress of the day, enjoying this conversation with somebody new. It had been a while since he'd done
that.

'You need to lighten up,' she told him. 'Try not to take
worries home. That's a rule I live by when I'm at work. Once
I'm out of that salon, anything job-related stays at my desk.
Home time is chill-out time.'

'What do you like to do to chill out?'

'This.' She raised her glass, grinning. 'Drinks, meals,
watching crap TV.'

'And where is home?'

He was curious as to whether she lived on her own, but
didn't want to ask. He surreptitiously angled his wrist so that
the digital time glowed on his smart watch. Anna would be
wondering where he was. He should be getting home, not
asking dangerous questions of an attractive woman in a pub. He
glanced around, checking that nobody he knew had come in
without him noticing while he'd been enjoying himself with a

stranger. He'd hate to be the source of office gossip; he prided himself on his good reputation. *Sensible Seb.*

'Just off the marketplace,' she replied.

He drained his pint. If he stayed, he'd divulge where he lived, and he didn't want to get into that. But the truth was, he didn't want to leave either. There was a connection between them – she had such a warm smile, with perfectly formed lips that he'd love to kiss ... *What am I thinking?* He jumped to his feet, knocking the table, and she grabbed her glass to steady it.

'Got to be somewhere?' she asked.

He picked up his phone, and his wedding ring glinted as it caught the light. Of course, she'd have noticed his ring; besides, they'd been primarily chatting about work. She wasn't interested in him in that way. He needed to calm down.

'I have to get home.'

'Shame,' she said, her eyes on his. 'We should do this again.'

'Look,' he said, shoving his phone into his pocket, 'it was great meeting you. But my wife will be wondering where I am.'

'Shucks. I was rather hoping you were divorced.' Their eyes met and his stomach flipped.

'See you around,' he said.

He picked up his jacket and she stood, touching his arm, cool fingers on bare skin.

'I hope so,' she murmured.

He hurried from the pub, out into the cold evening, his arm tingling where she'd touched it.

Sleep is impossible. He rolls onto his back, suppresses the urge to sigh aloud, fearful of waking Anna, wishing he could block his mind from recalling how Jo made him feel in that split second, and how he hoped she felt it too.

He climbs out of bed and creeps from the room, placing his feet carefully on the bare wooden stairs to avoid making them creak. In the moonlit kitchen, he drinks a glass of water, before going back to bed. His every instinct cries out against it, but he'll have to make contact with Jo, make her see that she has to stop. Of course he runs a risk of setting her off again, rekindling her feelings, but he'll have to take that chance. He hates himself for it, but he still finds her attractive. It is basic chemistry. Round and round go these thoughts, and at three o'clock, he is still awake.

Tim@houseonthecorner: Watch out, guys, the suspicious car is back this morning. I'm here with my telescope.

JackieC: Anyone in the driver seat? I can't see it from this end of the street and I can't be bothered to go out. And I've got my PJs on.

Gemma@no19: LOL.

Tim@houseonthecorner: Nope. Agent is on Special Branch business.

AnnaSews@no7: Somebody must know her?

Sadie&Ali: Not necessarily. Probably works in the area. Shouldn't we be talking about the rubbish collection that didn't happen this week?

Tim@houseonthecorner: Now you're talking rubbish ... Sorry. Car's gone now BTW. We can all sleep safe in our beds tonight.

CHAPTER EIGHT

ANNA

Anna sends Evie upstairs to brush her teeth, then watches from the front window as Seb heads off to work. He tightens his cotton scarf as he crosses the road, then hesitates and she sees him stiffen. It's her, the woman from last night, standing outside number 15, directly opposite their house. She walks away, fast, as if she doesn't want him to see her. Interesting. If she is hanging around, what does she want? Or is Anna being completely paranoid?

She doesn't have time to dither. Their morning routine runs on a tight schedule, and she calls up the stairs to Evie, telling her to hurry up. Then she grabs her cardigan and keys from the table. The idea of being late is anathema to her.

'Are you cross, Mummy?'

'No, darling, not with you. Mummy got distracted. I don't want you to be late, that's all. Got everything?' She checks Evie's bag and helps her put it on. 'Good girl.'

The house is too quiet when she gets home after dropping Evie off. She can't help thinking back to those early days when she was so anxious about being a mother. How would she know what to do? Her every waking moment was spent with Evie.

She'd sit by the pram in her small courtyard and watch over her as she slept, marvelling at her tiny hands and feet, the silky softness of her skin, the startled expression when she opened her eyes before kicking her legs with joy at being awake. She soon learnt to decipher the meaning behind the nuances of her cries, more desperate when she was in need of a feed, screwing up her face and bellowing when she was in pain.

In those days, it was just the two of them. Anna had been working in an administrative role for an employment agency when she found out she was pregnant; as soon as she'd gone on maternity leave, she knew she wouldn't be going back. She also knew that Luke would not have a part in this pregnancy – he'd already made his priorities clear when he hooked up with his new partner and posted everything they did on Facebook. She didn't want to miss a second of the mothering experience. She'd wanted to be a mother since she was a little girl, and found that she loved being pregnant. Colleagues told her she was blooming, and that was how she felt: more alive, and as if she had discovered her true purpose in life. Her skin glowed and her hair shone. She spent hours poring over websites, following baby bloggers and reading books on pregnancy. She shunned alcohol and ate the best pregnancy diet she could find. On visits to the doctor she made notes, making the doctor smile at her excitement, but she wanted to absorb as much from the experience as she possibly could. The bigger her bump got, the prouder she felt. She spent the earlier months doing up her tiny spare room as a nursery, and had her three-month scan blown up and framed, hung it on the nursery wall. She was in a secure flat rental, had been there for a long time, and her landlord assured her he was happy to extend her tenancy for as long as she wanted.

Seb didn't come into her life until Evie was two. Their first encounter was in the park, when she was consoling Evie after she'd stumbled when dismounting from a swing. She'd managed to calm her down and had sat her in her pushchair, where she was dabbing her grazed leg with a tissue. Hot, sweaty and flustered, she was startled when a male voice spoke to her from behind, and she turned to see him holding two coffees.

'You looked like you could use this,' he said. The usual caution she felt when being approached by a stranger didn't kick in; she was so grateful for the kindness that tears had sprung to her eyes. It was a cold morning and the coffee was exactly what she needed in that moment. Besides, he was friendly and good-looking. His blonde hair was cropped short at the back, with a slight curl at the front, and his black-rimmed glasses made him look academic. He was well dressed in checked scarf and bomber jacket, narrow dark jeans. Evie seemed transfixed by him and rewarded him with one of her best smiles, hurt knee forgotten.

He introduced himself and told her he was happy to leave her to drink her coffee in peace, but she asked him to stay and they sat on a bench and chatted as if they'd known each other for ages. Afterwards, they walked back through the park together, and when he asked her out for a meal and she explained that she couldn't afford a babysitter, he promptly invited both of them to lunch at the weekend. Right from the start, he understood that they came as a package, one that he gratefully received. The relationship developed quickly; soon he was spending weekends at Anna's flat, which extended into weeks, and it seemed logical to move in together. They bought their first house together after a couple of years. She had persuaded him to try a different area, to make a completely fresh start for life as a family, and the day he proposed was the happiest of her life.

She takes herself out to a café and spends a couple of hours logged on to the Facebook page she set up for the neighbourhood. The posts are mostly photographs of watercolours of the area painted by a prolific local artist, and offers of items for sale

– nothing that requires following up, like broken street lights or any of the other issues that Anna enjoys occupying herself with, giving her a sense of purpose. She knows it's a long shot, but she hoped somebody else might have reported abusive phone calls, but nobody has. She can hear Seb's voice in her head telling her she's overreacting, and she thinks back to his attempts to reassure her, which sounded to her like he was trying to convince himself. She woke at around three this morning to find the bed covers flung back beside her, and no Seb. She could hear him moving around downstairs, which was unusual for him, but she fell back to sleep and he rushed out to work before she'd had a chance to ask him about it. Clearly he had something on his mind. Most likely he was worrying about her.

Evie comes out of school clutching a piece of artwork in her hand, and Mrs Gold beckons Anna over.

'Show Mummy your drawing,' she says. Evie gives her the painting and Anna feels uneasy as she looks at the picture of a woman in a red car beside a house. Mrs Gold says quietly, 'We always ask the children what their pictures mean to them, and Evie says this lady has been following her. I'm sure it's nothing, but I thought it best to draw your attention to it.'

Anna experiences a trickle of alarm, but she has no intention of discussing her private fears with the teacher, especially as they are most likely unfounded.

'I know what this is. It's nothing to worry about; a friend of mine was waiting outside the house, and Evie's got a thing about drawing cars at the moment. You were right to bring it to my attention, though. Did you think we had a stalker?' She fakes a laugh, then drops the picture quickly into her bag so that the teacher won't notice how her hand is shaking.

On the way home, she asks Evie about the picture.

'You told Mrs Gold this lady was following you. That isn't true, is it?'

'She was watching outside the house.'

'She wasn't watching *us*, it just looked like that. She was waiting for someone.' Anna doesn't sound convincing even to herself. 'You haven't seen her anywhere else, have you? In the playground?' She can't think of any other places Evie would be without her. 'The park?'

Evie shakes her head and skips ahead. Anna takes her time, reluctant to get home, where the threat of more phone calls lurks. Her biggest fear is that, heaven forbid, someone is threatening to get to her through her daughter. Her pulse quickens at the terrifying thought. If that were the case, she would grab Evie from school and keep her safe at home forever. And if the phone calls are directed at Seb? Her stomach clenches at the thought, because an angry woman can only mean one thing – that he's been having an affair.

CHAPTER NINE

ANNA

AnnaSews@no7: Update for parents at Greenside School – side gate issue that was concerning some of us is now resolved.

Kate: Cheers, Anna. What would we do without you?!

AnnaSews@no7: And don't forget it's the school fete this Saturday, raising proceeds for school funds. Thanks to all those who have volunteered. See you at our delicious cake stall!

Anna visits the supermarket to stock up on baking ingredients and bumps into her mother-in-law in the café. She manages to keep her on the topic of the garden centre where she works part time and off the subject of collecting Evie from school. Once she's dropped the groceries at home, she walks round to the school in time for pickup.

The iron railings run the length of the building and the gate is locked. Firmly. Anna checks, shaking it with her slender hand, satisfied at the clanking noise it makes. A man clad in utility trousers and jacket appears from the playground, the huge bunch of keys that hangs from his belt smacking against his thigh as he approaches, his heavy boots thudding, and she scurries off, not wanting him to see her face. No doubt the head, Mrs Thomas, will have spoken to him about her concerns that the open gate wasn't supervised at certain times of the day. 'Of course, Mrs Forrester,' she said when Anna raised the issue, 'I understand,' but her eyes were saying, *neurotic, overprotective.* Still, she promised to investigate: 'All concerns are taken seriously and investigated accordingly, Mrs Forrester, you can rest assured.' That made Anna laugh. Obviously the woman doesn't have children, doesn't – cannot – know what it's like having something so precious that at times it stops your breath. *Rest assured* just doesn't cut it.

She is updating the others on her meeting with Mrs Thomas when the school bell rings and the children hurtle out. Evie skips towards her.

'Come, Mummy.' She takes Anna's hand. 'Mrs Gold wants to speak to you.' She pulls her across the playground.

'Slow down, darling, there's no need to rush.' Anna wonders if it's to do with the side gate issue, Mrs Gold wanting to reassure her.

'Mrs Gold, Mrs Gold, here's Mummy,' Evie says.

Mrs Gold has delicate features and long brown hair. Evie adores her and is always drawing her. The teacher smiles in every picture and her cheeks are always rosy.

She says goodbye to a little boy who is hanging back. 'Off you go, Jacob, your nan is over there, see.' She points towards the gate, where an elderly woman waits behind an old-fashioned shopping bag on wheels, and presses lightly on his back. Jacob sniffs and wanders off as if he doesn't want to leave. Anna can understand. Mrs Gold is young and pretty, and Evie isn't the only one who worships her.

'Thanks for coming back, Mrs Forrester. I just wanted a

quick word. I wasn't sure it would be you who was collecting her. I hope everything is OK?'

Anna frowns. 'Why shouldn't it be?'

'I'm afraid we couldn't allow Evie to be released from school early today. I hope it hasn't caused you too much inconvenience.'

'I'm sorry, I don't know what you're talking about. Are you sure it's me you want to speak to?'

Mrs Gold nods, looking slightly put out. She isn't known for making mistakes. Unlike Mrs Abbott, Evie's former teacher. The parents heaved a collective sigh of relief when she left. All sorts of chaos prevailed last term. Lost notes, messages sent to the wrong child. The parents' WhatsApp group was always buzzing. No doubt Mrs Gold will be aware of this.

'Of course,' she says. 'Let me explain. The office informed me that earlier this afternoon Evie's aunt called to tell us she'd be picking Evie up and needed to leave slightly before the end of the day. I'm afraid she's not on your approved list of people with permission to collect Evie, so we couldn't allow it. If you want to add her, it's not a problem – I can take the details and pass them on to the office. As long as we know in advance next time, the issue won't arise.'

Anna stares at the teacher, her hand tightening round Evie's, her mouth slightly open. She wants to speak but can't quite find the words.

'Mrs Forrester? Are you feeling all right? You look very pale.' Mrs Gold looks as though she expects Anna to pass out on the spot. Anna is surprised she hasn't. Evie's hand wriggles inside her own and she realises how hard she is squeezing and loosens her grip. 'Mrs Forrester, can I get you a glass of water?' Mrs Gold touches her arm. 'Please tell me what's wrong.'

'Evie doesn't have an aunt,' she says. 'That's what's wrong.'

. . .

Mrs Gold takes command and ushers Anna and Evie into the school reception. She pours Anna some water from the dispenser and gives Evie a carton of juice and a comic to look at. 'I'll fetch Mrs Thomas.'

'No,' Anna says. 'There's no need.'

Mrs Gold stops on her way to the door. 'But we have to inform her about this situation. I imagine she will want to report it to the police.'

Anna's mind is working furiously. Fear is making her skin prickle. Both she and her husband are only children, and they have never bestowed the title of aunt and uncle on any of their friends. From the office, a telephone rings, and for a crazy second she thinks it's the phantom caller from home. Would she go as far as harming Evie? She threatened to destroy their family, and Evie is the jewel in their crown. She's not sure it makes sense, but nothing makes sense right now. Mrs Gold is hovering in front of her, her rosy cheeks now hot with conster-nation, her face looking strained, her eyes full of concern.

'No need for that either,' Anna says. 'I've realised who it was.' She lets out an exaggerated breath. 'That gave us a scare, didn't it?' She gets to her feet, desperate to go home now, to talk to Seb, to get to the bottom of this. She doesn't want to take it to the head or the police; they'll ask Evie questions and worry her unnecessarily.

'Thank goodness,' Mrs Gold says, although she looks perturbed by the sudden change in Anna's energy.

'Yes, I'd completely forgotten. My cousin mentioned taking her out after school, but if I'd known she wanted to collect her early, I'd never have said yes. It most certainly wasn't a definite arrangement. I'm so sorry.'

'Are you sure you don't want me to get the head?'

'No.' Anna's voice sounds sharp. 'Sorry, I'm still a bit shocked. I'm such a bird brain.'

Mrs Gold laughs shakily. 'That's not how I would describe

you, but of course you'd be shocked. Anyone would be. Do you want to call your cousin and check?'

'No, it's fine. I'll wait until we get home. This is exactly the kind of stupid thing she would do. She's a lot younger than me.' Anna has no desire to see Mrs Thomas after the meeting the other day. No doubt it will just convince her that she's completely neurotic. 'But thank you, Mrs Gold. You've reminded my why we chose this school for Evie. Imagine if you let just anyone in – what might have happened.'

'It's school policy. I followed procedure. Any member of staff would have done the same.'

Anna nods. 'I know. I'd like to stress that only myself, my husband and my mother-in-law, Marion Forrester, are allowed to collect Evie. It will mostly be me.'

'I've only ever known you to pick her up.'

Anna nods. 'That's right. I enjoy collecting her, seeing the other parents. And I would always let you know even if one of the other two were to be coming, just out of courtesy.'

'You don't need to do that.'

'But I will. Thank you again, Mrs Gold, and I apologise for making you stay late.'

'No trouble at all.'

She pulls Evie close to her, strokes her hair. 'Let's get you home, poppet.'

CHAPTER TEN

ANNA

Anna asks Evie if she wants to watch cartoons and Evie doesn't need to be asked twice. Being encouraged to watch television does not usually happen. Anna observes her from the doorway. As always, Evie sits bolt upright, concentrating firmly on the pictures dancing around on the screen. Every now and then she chuckles, or gasps, fists clutched to her mouth. Instead of the warmth she usually feels watching her daughter, however, a chill runs through Anna's veins.

She sits at the kitchen table. Seb is not due home for a couple of hours and she needs time to think. Hopefully Evie will get off to bed early. She runs her finger over the patterns in the wood and goes over the conversation with Mrs Gold. Nausea rises in her throat. She fetches a glass and runs water from the tap until it is cold, then takes small sips, steadying herself. Since the phone call, anxiety colours everything.

The moment has finally arrived.

She's known for years this was going to happen, the realisation hitting her like a bolt of lightning every time she pictures the scene, keeping her awake at night. She's taught herself techniques to empty her mind of unwanted thoughts, and as each year has gone by, she's dared to believe that they won't come for her, that she'll be OK, that the life she's built up is the one she deserves. Sometimes weeks go by, months even, when she sleeps through the night, and she throws herself into activities, always the first to volunteer to help out, to organise, anything she can do to benefit the local community, wanting to be the good person she knows she is. She shakes her head at her own stupidity, at even thinking she could get away with it.

Now that the truth is staring at her, she'd almost prefer the calls to have been directed at Seb, meaning he'd been unfaithful. That would be easier to cope with than knowing Evie is in danger. Her child comes before her marriage. She imagines she's not alone in that thought; what parent would not put their child first?

So this is what it looks like, her downfall, here now, at the kitchen table. A pleasant day in July, the evenings are lovely and warm, not the raging storm she imagined would accompany this moment, with dark skies, pounding rain and thunder, wind blowing tiles from roofs and sending them clattering into buildings and cars, leaving debris all around. This pleasant summer day is the cruellest of deceptions, and the inevitable blow has crept up on her unawares.

She grips her arms around herself in an attempt to warm her body, which is cold and trembling. What is she going to say to Seb? How can she possibly tell him that their life is under threat? That she has always been justified in throwing a protective ring around Evie, panicking at the slightest divergence from a routine, at anything out of the ordinary. If she'd been able to explain it to him, she would have done, but to do so would have brought about her downfall even faster. And so she has plodded on, each step taking her closer to this moment.

Obviously she can't tell him the truth. Maybe one day she will have to, but she isn't there yet. Her eyes stray to the kitchen noticeboard, where notes are stuck under magnets, ordering her weeks, her days, mostly in the form of lists. That's what she needs now, a list, a plan of action. This is how she has always dealt with her life, and this coping strategy will help her now.

She tears a piece of paper from the pad on the table and fetches a pen from the kitchen drawer. First she needs to confirm who is doing this: track down the person who is making the phone calls, check that her suspicions are right and that it is the same person who called the school. Hope flickers for a second – if only she has got this wrong and it's an innocent mistake. That way there will be no threat to her family and she can go back to the life she has created. The threat of revelation will always be the dark cloud behind her, but anything would be better than the truth. She hopes none of the other parents get to hear about what has happened – the fewer people who know about it the better. Somehow she also needs to warn Marion to be even more vigilant, but already her mother-in-law thinks she is way too protective, and this is going to make it worse. This is the real reason why it would be so much easier to stick to just her and Seb having responsibility for collecting their child, but she's never been able to justify herself.

She writes *Marion* on her list with a question mark. Next she writes *Seb*. Writing makes her feel calmer, and she drinks some more water, her hand no longer shaking. He needs to know about the woman ringing the school. *Tell him???* she writes.

Yes, that's the answer. Tell him what happened and let him know she's dealing with it. Come up with an explanation – the wrong child was asked for, something like that. To cover herself, just in case Mrs Gold mentions it to him. He's not the hot-headed kind of husband who would charge down to the school and raise hell. If he was, he'd have been in uproar about the side gate, whereas he wasn't really interested. He's had a lot on his mind lately with work and doesn't have time for this. Besides, she always deals with the school side of Evie's life, so why change that now. She's confident he'll come round to her way of tackling this.

Her phone beeps: a message from Seb. *Going to the gym, back at seven.* She checks the clock, having lost track of time. Plenty of time to get Evie fed, bathed and into bed before he arrives home.

'Evie,' she says from the living room door, making Evie jump.

'Mummy, you scared me.'

'Sorry, poppet.' She knows how that feels. 'Tea in ten minutes, OK.'

'Is it fish fingers and baked beans and toast?'

'If you like.'

By the time she hears Seb's car outside and the creak of the garage door being pulled down, Evie is in bed, having fallen asleep halfway through her bedtime story. Seb's dinner is in the oven – some leftovers reheated from last night, as she hasn't the energy to cook anything from scratch. Besides, she wants to be able to talk with him, not faff around cooking. She doesn't have the patience for that right now.

He opens his post while he eats and she waits until he's finished before joining him at the table.

'I bumped into your mum earlier, had a coffee,' she says.

'Hope it wasn't too awkward after the other day.'

'It was fine. You know what she's like. She had a bit of a grumble, but I managed to get her off the subject.'

'Good move,' he says. 'I did tell her to back off, you know. Have there been any more phone calls?'

'No,' she says. She double-checked the machine before he came in, and dialled 1471 as well. 'But something else has happened.'

He puts his cutlery down.

'Do you fancy a drink?'

'Sounds ominous. Am I going to need one?'

She doesn't answer, but brings the bottle and two glasses back to the table.

'Your hand is shaking,' he says, taking it in his own. 'What's up?'

With Seb sitting in front of her, her earlier resolve disintegrates. This man who has been so good to her and who loves Evie as his own deserves only the truth, but she can't figure out a good way to put it. Instead she tells him what Mrs Gold told her.

He looks pale in the kitchen light, his eyes tired. He rubs his face with his hands. 'Oh God. Thanks goodness the school were on it.'

'I reiterated that only the two of us or Marion is allowed to pick Evie up. They know I always notify them even when it's going to be you or Marion instead of me.'

'What about the police?'

'I told her not to call them just yet.'

'Why ever not?'

'Because I wanted to speak to you first.' His brow furrows in consternation. 'I think this is related to the woman calling the house. Think about it. She said she's going to destroy our lives. Hurting Evie is the worst thing that could happen to us, isn't it? At first when it happened, I assumed it was someone who wanted to cause trouble between you and me. Maybe they were jealous of our lifestyle, the nice house, the car, the beautiful child. I know Evie's your stepdaughter, but I forget that. To me you're her father. Another parent mentioned just the other day how much she looks like you. I always assume people know, but of course they don't unless I've actually told them. I forget we moved here after you found us.'

Anna is surprised but relieved that he isn't straight on the phone to the police. He looks as if the news has taken his energy away. She has to tell him the rest, but she can't bring herself to say the words.

He drops his head into his hands. 'I don't know what to do.'

'What do you mean?' She thinks about the way he reacted to the phone calls, his preoccupation. What if ... 'Do you know something about this? What aren't you telling me?'

'Nothing. I don't know. I mean ...'

'Spit it out, Seb. Evie has been threatened here.'

'You don't know that.'

'Of course I do.' She pulls his hands away from his face. 'You're scaring me.'

'Don't be scared. I think we should go the police, but there's something I want to check out first.' He picks up his glass and fiddles with it. 'We had a client who was unhappy with our services and caused a bit of a stink. It's highly unlikely she has anything to do with this, but I want to make sure.'

'Tell me the details. This is Evie we're talking about. I want to know anything that will help us find out who this is.'

'No,' he says. 'You have to trust me. If I tell you, you'll rush off and try and deal with it yourself. This woman is still a client, and I don't want to make an almighty mess if she isn't the one who's behind all this. Just give me tomorrow to check it out, and if we haven't got anywhere with her, then I promise you we will go to the police.'

He looks surprised when Anna agrees. She knows he expected her to explode. She acquiesces because she doesn't want to go to the police either if they can avoid it. Her revelation can wait. She's still hoping to put off the inevitable.

CHAPTER ELEVEN

SEB

At work the next day, Seb finds it hard not to worry about what might have happened at the school. It's all very well the staff there being vigilant, but what if it happens again? What if the woman who pretended to be Evie's aunt is the same woman who has been calling the house, determined to hurt them? He has to find out for sure whether Jo is behind this.

Late morning, fate plays into his hands. He's about to pop downstairs to pick up a sandwich and a coffee. He glances through the window to the square outside and sees Jo sitting on a bench, holding a large drink with a straw in it. She's reading on her Kindle and looks unaware of anything going on around her. Her hair is pulled back into a sleek ponytail.

'I'm going out for a moment,' he says to Tina, who nods absent-mindedly, without taking her gaze from her computer screen. He hurries down the stairs, knowing he has to do this but hoping it isn't going to undo the last few weeks, where he has finally managed to convince her that he has no intention of going back on his word.

As soon as he's outside the building, he sees that she's gone. How can he have missed her? He takes the stairs back up slowly, ignores the confused look from Tina when he goes back to his desk. By the end of the afternoon, he's convinced himself he's had a lucky escape. Speaking to Jo is not the brightest idea – if it is her, he has a problem, and confronting her will only make it worse. He needs to have evidence. Accusing her of calling the school is serious, and he shudders at the thought of getting it wrong and stirring everything up again.

His phone rings, a welcome distraction until he hears his mother's voice.

'What's wrong, Mum?' It's not unknown for her to call him at work, but it's unusual, and his first instinct is to worry. Since his father's death, he's tried to be a good son, although she has lots of friends and is in robust health.

'Nothing's wrong, son.'

'You don't usually ring me at work, that's all.'

'Am I disturbing you? If you're busy ...'

'No, Mum, it's fine.' He welcomes the distraction from Jo and his near faux pas at lunchtime.

'I had coffee with Anna yesterday.'

'Yes, she told me.' His mother and his wife aren't the best of pals, and at times he feels like a mediator, trying to maintain the balance.

'I bumped into her at the supermarket. I'd just finished my shopping and there she was in the café, all alone, poor thing. I do worry about her.'

Seb rolls his eyes. Tina looks over and raises an eyebrow. 'Anna is fine, Mum, she enjoys her own company. She was on her own for a long time before she met me. I expect it was a nice break for her without Evie.' He's doing Anna a disservice when he says this; she never begrudges time with Evie. Her selfless devotion to her daughter is one of the reasons he loves her. 'Did you have a nice chat?'

'Yes, actually. But she looks tired, she does too much. That's why I'm ringing. I tried to talk to her about letting me pick Evie up from school, but she said no, as usual. Can't you have a word with her? I want to see more of my granddaughter. If I looked after her, it would give Anna time to look for a job.'

'She doesn't want a job. How many times do we have to have this conversation? Her business is doing well.'

'Business! It's a hobby, Seb. As soon as her friends' kids grow up, they won't want any more of her cute little dungarees and she'll have wasted this time when she could be getting experience, having a career. I'm a great believer in women working as well as having children; you know I had my part-time job when you were little. It's so important to have a life outside of the home. She focuses too much on that child and it's claustrophobic. I'd love to have Evie for the weekend, you know I would. She'll be wanting sleepovers before long, and she won't like it if her mother doesn't let her go anywhere.'

'That's a long way off. Evie's only four. And you know nothing about Anna's business, as I've told you over and over.'

Seb gets up and goes into the kitchen, where he paces up and down. This conversation with Marion is a familiar one and never goes anywhere. His mother is in her sixties, and since the death of his father last year, she has become set in her ways. She's told him more than once how liberating it is knowing what she does and doesn't want to do and having the confidence to say no. On the subject of child-rearing, she can be overbearing, though. Besides, he understands Anna's reluctance to let Evie spend the night away from their house. Routine has been an important tool in bringing her up, and there's plenty of time for that when she's older.

'I've got to go, Mum. I'll speak to Anna, but don't be surprised if she doesn't want to upset Evie's routine.'

'I'd have thought the two of you would welcome a chance to spend some time alone together. You could get away for the weekend, like normal couples do. I still can't believe you took the child on honeymoon with you.'

'Normal couples? Honestly, Mum. And please don't ring me at work if it's not urgent,' he adds. 'I'm going now, bye.' Once Marion gets started on the honeymoon, she'll never get off the line.

For the rest of the afternoon he manages to concentrate on his work, but at around five o'clock he keeps an eye out for Jo leaving work. It's not long before he sees her cross the square, and he waits until he sees her disappear from sight before he switches off his computer and tidies his desk.

Anna texts him on the way home, asking him to pick up some painkillers. Her toothache hasn't gone. Pulling into their drive, his thoughts turn back to their conversation last night. Away from the house, and Anna, he wonders if they are overre-acting – the police are not going to get involved over a couple of weird phone calls and a mix-up in school admin. Perhaps a weekend away would do them good, a change of scene.

'I'm home,' he calls as he hangs his coat up in the hall and goes up to the bedroom to get changed into jeans and T-shirt. When he goes downstairs, Anna is reading at the kitchen table and Evie is drawing. He gives her the painkillers. 'Is it bad?'

She pulls a face. 'It's bearable. I'm hoping it will go away. I don't particularly want to go to the dentist.'

'I'd make an appointment if I were you; you might have to wait ages. I was thinking –why don't we book a weekend away somewhere? Mum could look after Evie ... Don't look at me like that. If you'd rather Evie came with us, then we'll do that. I just thought it might do us good.'

'To go on our own, you mean?'

He nods.

'It would be nice to get away for a couple of days. We could forget about the phone calls if nothing else.' Her expression darkens and she fiddles with the bottom of her skirt. 'But because of what happened at school, I'd rather Evie came with us, just until I know she's safe. I will let her stay at Marion's, but not at the moment. I need time to get used to the idea. You know me and my routines. You don't mind, do you?'

'Not at all.' He clears his throat. 'Have you thought any more about what we talked about last night?'

'The police, you mean?'

He nods. 'The client at work, I checked it out. I don't think it's anything to do with the business. I'm not sure going to the police will solve anything. They'd probably tell us to keep a record of the phone calls, and the school would have notified them if they thought it was necessary. I'm assuming there were no calls today?'

'No,' she says, 'nothing unusual has happened.'

'Shall we give it a few more days, be extra vigilant? But I really don't think we need to worry.' If it happens again, he will have to confront Jo, but he really doesn't want to have anything to do with her. He can't believe she would do this. 'And don't worry about Mum. She means well. She's only been like this since Dad died.'

'I know. We could invite her over more, but she always finds fault with me.' Anna sighs.

'Unlike everybody else, who thinks you're wonderful. As long as you know she's there if you ever need her.'

'Why don't you ask her to the school fete? That would be helpful, as I'll be busy on the stall. She can help keep an eye on Evie. You haven't forgotten, have you?'

'Of course not. And that's a great idea.' He kisses her on the cheek. 'She'd like that.'

The phone rings just as they're getting ready for bed. Seb and Anna look at one another.

'I'll get it,' he says, running downstairs, needing to experience one of these calls for himself. He picks up the phone without speaking. He waits, concentrates, hears faint breathing at the other end.

'Who are you? What do you want?'

'I want her,' a harsh voice says, followed by the click of the receiver.

Seb's feet are cold against the floorboard as he stands trans-fixed. The small part of him that thought this was a joke has evaporated. He's no longer looking forward to sleep; he knows he won't get much tonight.

CHAPTER TWELVE

ANNA

Something is tapping Anna on the arm, and she sits up, instantly awake.

'Mummy, it's cake day, wake up. Daddy, wake up.' Seb stirs beside her and groans. Evie clambers onto the bed and on top of Anna, who pulls her into a hug and inhales the peachy smell of her skin.

'What day is it?' Seb asks, rubbing his eyes.

'Saturday, silly Daddy. It's cake day.'

'How do you know the cakes are still there? I was very hungry last night.'

Evie opens her mouth wide. 'Daddy, did you eat the cakes?'

'Maybe.' He rubs his stomach. 'My tummy is very full.'

'Oh, Seb.' Anna rolls her eyes as Evie climbs off the bed and rushes downstairs.

Seb yawns. 'That's given me five more minutes' peace. I barely slept last night.'

'You're still worried, aren't you?'

He rubs his eyes and pulls himself up to a sitting position. 'I can't help going over in my mind what might have happened if the school hadn't been so astute. If this woman had collected

Evie, what then? What was she planning to do? Is she acting alone? I'm driving myself crazy with all these questions.' His eyes are red with fatigue.

'Don't,' Anna says. 'I can't bear thinking about it. We have to find out who it is.'

'I keep hoping it's just some chancer. Picked a child at random.'

'They knew her name.'

'There are so many ways of finding out a child's name,' Seb says. 'I'm clutching at straws, aren't I?'

'Yes, but it's understandable.' Anna sighs.

'Why don't you leave her with Mum this morning? She could bring her along later. I'm worried about you going to the school fair. I wish you didn't have to go.'

'You know I can't get out of it. If I could, believe me I would. I'll watch her like a hawk. The other mums will all be there too.'

'Are you going to tell them?'

'I'm not sure. Somehow telling them makes it more real.'

'Maybe I should cancel this squash game and be there the whole time.'

'No. Honestly, it will be fine. You're only going to miss a couple of hours, and it's just the people setting up who'll be around for that time. Once the fete opens, I'll make sure she stays on the stall with me until you get there. It'll give her something to look forward to.'

'OK. If you're sure.'

'Mummy.' Evie comes back into the bedroom. 'Daddy's pretending. He hasn't eaten the cakes.'

'Of course he hasn't, he's just being silly as usual. Let's get breakfast sorted.' Anna throws the duvet off. 'We're leaving at ten, Seb, so you'll need to be ready to take us.'

'A shower will wake me up.'

Everything goes smoothly and Seb drops Anna and Evie off

promptly at ten. The fete doesn't start until one, so there is plenty of time for Anna to set up her stall. Kate and Gemma arrive together ten minutes later, and Anna organises them into their roles. Evie rushes off to play with her friends.

'Don't go where I can't see you,' Anna says. 'Make sure you stay in the middle of the field, OK?'

The stalls are arranged around the edges of the school field to form a smaller square. Some toys and plastic structures have been set out as a makeshift play area in the middle. Evie and her friends hurtle across the field and jump onto the large inflatable seats, shrieking and laughing. Daniel dawdles behind them, carrying a book.

Kate unveils some gorgeous-looking cupcakes, with chocolate butter icing and bits of Flake scattered over the top, packed in a white cardboard box.

'You didn't make those,' Gemma says.

'Of course I didn't. I haven't even got time to feed myself, let alone make cakes. Good old Sabrina made them for me.' Sabrina's cake business has flourished since the other mums found out about her amazing skills. 'I've heard she's applying for *Bake Off* this year.'

'Wouldn't that be exciting,' Kate says. 'We could go to the party at the end. Imagine if she got a Hollywood handshake.'

'Please don't tell me you like him,' Gemma says. 'He gives me the creeps.'

'I wouldn't say no.'

'Honestly, you two,' Anna says.

A steady stream of parents have been dropping off cakes, and Kate has been putting them out on plates. 'We need to make sure we keep plenty back. I've no idea how quickly they'll sell.'

Anna chooses the ones to display and cuts them into slices. 'Mrs Thomas has promised me the coffee van will be parked nearby, and the premises manager should be dropping off some tables and chairs so people can sit and eat and drink.'

'It sounds lovely,' Gemma says, 'and the weather is perfect.' She glances at Kate. 'It's unusual to see you without Benjamin. Is Michael looking after him?'

'Don't be ridiculous. My mother offered to have him.'

'No need to rush home then,' says Gemma. 'We could maybe get a drink afterwards.'

'If we've got any energy left,' Anna says. 'Let's see how the day goes. Besides, I've got Evie.' Across the field, her daughter is jumping up and down on the grass. 'She's going to be exhausted at this rate.'

'Seb's coming to look after her, though, isn't he?'

'Yes, he'll be here around one, that's the plan.'

Anna keeps half an eye on Evie as they finish setting up. Once they're done, the three of them go to the coffee van and sit at one of the round tables. The children come running over and join them, clamouring for cold drinks. Kate produces cartons of juice and Anna some cupcakes she has made especially for them.

'When is Daddy coming?' Evie asks, chocolate all around her face. 'He said he was going to show me how to hook a duck. And buy me candyfloss.'

'Candyfloss?' Gemma says. 'I'm not sure you'll find that here. Or ducks.'

Anna wipes Evie's face. 'I think Daddy is remembering his own childhood trips to the funfair. Gemma's right, I doubt you'll get those here.'

Evie pouts. 'I want some. In my storybook they eat candyfloss and it looks like a pink cloud.'

'Yes, it does. I promise you'll get to try it one day, but not today. There will be an ice cream van, though.'

'Ice cream! Can I have one now?' Gemma's daughter Sam asks.

'No, you're eating a cake.'

'Honestly, I don't know where they get their appetites from,' Kate says.

'Sam gets hers from her dad,' Gemma says. 'Have you seen his belly lately?'

'Is Daddy coming?' Sam asks.

'No, Daddy's busy, but when the other daddies get here, we're going to take it in turns to take you around.'

'Can we go back and play in the middle now?'

Gemma nods.

Anna checks her watch. 'Not you, Evie.'

'Please, Mummy.'

'No, I want you to wait till Daddy gets here.'

Evie looks crestfallen and Gemma exchanges a glance with Kate. Anna pretends not to notice. She doesn't care what anyone thinks. *They* don't have to worry about weird phone calls and loitering cars.

People are starting to trickle in. A group of youngsters are carting musical instruments and equipment into the makeshift performance area, and parents are returning to their stalls. The three women gather up their empty cups and plates and stick them in the recycling bag before heading back to the stall. Anna tries to hold Evie's hand, but she pulls away.

'Don't be difficult, darling.'

'But it's not fair, the others have gone over there.' She looks longingly at Sam, who is running after a ball. Anna wishes she didn't have to be so harsh. 'Why do I have to stay with you? You're horrible.'

'If you want to take her over, I don't mind holding the fort,' Gemma says.

'No, she can't always get her own way. Look, Daniel's here, you can play with him.'

The look Evie gives her is pure contempt. They all know

Daniel doesn't play with anyone. He'll sit reading his book at any opportunity. 'I wish Granny was here.'

Anna stops herself from snapping.

'Help Mummy uncover the cakes,' she says, but Evie sits on the floor and refuses to participate.

'Oh dear.' Kate looks sympathetic.

'She'll get over it,' Anna says.

'To be honest, it makes a refreshing change. It's normally my kids who are difficult. Let me know if I can do anything.'

Customers start arriving and pop music blares distortedly from the speakers dotted around as the fete is officially opened. Mrs Thomas makes a speech into a crackly megaphone. She's wearing an enormous hat. 'Do you reckon she thinks this is Ladies' Day at Ascot?' Gemma says.

'Look, Evie,' says Anna. 'It's Teddy and his mum, come to buy some cakes. Do you want to help them choose and then count the money with me?'

Evie jumps to her feet, her bad mood quickly forgotten. She encourages Teddy to choose the cupcakes, because they are 'the best delicious'. Anna looks around the field for any sign of Seb. A queue has formed at the coffee van, and the tables set out to the front of it are almost full. Their cake stall is popular, and she's relieved she kept Evie with her, as it would have been impossible to keep an eye on her otherwise. She is soon having to put more cakes out on the stall. The lemon poppy seed loaf is particularly popular.

'We're going to need more change,' Kate says. 'I didn't bring enough. I'll go and see if I can get some from another stall.'

'Try the book stall, it isn't very busy yet,' Gemma says. 'Which is good, because I saw a few paperbacks I was interested in. Sam could do with some new books too.'

'Seb should be here soon,' Anna says. 'I don't know where he's got to. Let me check my phone. Ah, there's a message. Traffic, he says, he's almost here. Daddy's on his way, Evie.'

Ten minutes later, Seb appears, his forehead perspiring.

'I'm so sorry,' he says. 'Traffic in town is a nightmare. There's a broken-down car in the road leading up to here. Are you having fun?' he asks Evie.

Evie can't speak fast enough as she tells him about her morning and all the different stalls she wants to visit. Anna takes a moment to step away from the stall and drink some water. It's a sunny day and she hasn't stopped since the fete opened. As she looks around the field, enjoying the warm sun on her face, her eyes alight on a familiar slim figure standing in the coffee queue, shoulder-length dark hair and a petrol-blue summer jacket. The jacket is distinctive and stylish. She's seen it before and her pulse starts racing as she remembers where. Automatically she checks that Evie is still with Seb.

The queue shifts and the woman disappears from her sightline.

'Seb,' she says, but he is counting out change with Evie and doesn't hear her. A woman with a loud voice is telling several people around her how she can't decide between carrot cake and the lemon poppy seed loaf, and how her husband prefers lemons but she doesn't like the way poppy seeds stick in her teeth. 'Seb,' hisses Anna. She taps him on the arm.

'Fifty pence,' he says. 'Give the lady her change.' Evie hands the money to an old lady, whose faces crinkles into a smile.

'Thank you so much. Isn't she delightful?'

'We think so,' Seb says, looking proud, ruffling Evie's hair.

'Seb.'

'What?'

'Over there, look. It's the woman I told you about who was hanging around the house.'

'Where?'

'There, in the queue behind the really tall man – she's wearing a blue jacket. Evie, come here, darling.'

'I sold six cakes, Mummy. Daddy said I was very good at doing shops and counting out the money.'

'I'm sure you were.'

Seb looks at the woman and turns back quickly. 'Evie,' he says, 'stay here with Mummy.'

'But Daddy, you promised ...'

Seb pushes her gently towards Anna and disappears into the crowd. It happens so quickly, Anna barely has time to register what he is doing. Evie's lip is trembling.

'Daddy promised he'd take me to look around. I wanted to show him the toys and we were going to find the ducks.'

'I think there's a problem with Daddy's car, darling. He has to sort out the parking. I'll take you, I just need to make sure it's OK with Kate and Gemma. Daddy is very naughty, and you're not the only one who's cross with him.' She scans the crowd but can see no sign of Seb. What is he playing at? 'Ten minutes, I promise. Wait with Mummy, there's a good girl.'

She looks again at the coffee queue. The tall man is almost at the front and his broad back obscures her view. The woman in blue is nowhere to be seen.

'Excuse me.' A man is waving a ten-pound note at her. 'Can I buy that amazing-looking chocolate cake before anyone else spots it?'

Anna glances at Kate, who is in conversation with another customer; Gemma still hasn't returned from her wander around the stalls. Reluctantly she turns her attention to the man, whose bonhomie is turning to impatience. *It's a summer fete, for God's sake*, she thinks. *Chill out, can't you.* 'Yes, of course,' she says. 'That one is ten pounds for the whole cake.' He looks surprised. 'It's for a good cause.'

'Of course.' He hands over the note, no longer quite so jolly.

Evie tugs at Anna's shirt.

'Can we go yet, Mummy?'

'Let me check with Kate.'

Before speaking to Kate, though, she phones Seb. He doesn't pick up.

Where are you??? she texts.

Kate doesn't mind at all, although she's surprised. 'I thought Seb was taking her round.'

'You and me both. I've no idea where he went. I'm furious. Evie was upset, and it's good for them to spend time together. I hate leaving you on your own, but ...'

'Don't worry. I can manage, and anyway, Gemma should be back soon.'

'Do you want me to wait until she gets here?'

'No, you go.'

A familiar voice cuts into their conversation.

'Hello, Anna. Hello, Evie.'

Marion is standing at the stall, a big smile on her face, her red-tinted hair puffed up and hairsprayed to resist any breeze.

'Grandma,' Evie says, rushing around to throw herself at her. 'Will you take me round the fair, please? I want to show you everything. Daddy was going to, but he has to look after his car.'

'Looks like your problem is solved,' Kate says, raising an eyebrow.

'Hello, Marion. Your timing is perfect actually.' Anna explains that Seb disappeared without explanation.

'How odd,' Marion says. 'I'll keep an eye out for him. Come on then, little one, let's go Daddy hunting.'

'I'm not little, Grandma, I'm big and I'm good at finding Daddy. He's rubbish at hiding seek.'

'Evie, be good for Grandma. Don't let her out of your sight, will you, Marion.'

Marion isn't the kind of person to roll her eyes, but irritation flitters across her face. 'Of course I won't.' She takes Evie's hand and Evie skips along beside her, chattering. 'I'll get her some lunch, give you a break. You obviously need it. Hopefully Seb will have turned up by the time we return.'

'Don't look so worried,' Kate says as Marion and Evie are swallowed up by the crowd. She can't help scanning the field for the distinctive blue jacket, but she can't see any sign of it. She'd rather have kept Evie with her, but Marion will look after her; she has to trust other people. She squeezes her hands tight so that her fingernails dig into her palms.

The music that has been playing through the speakers suddenly stops, and people drift over towards the middle of the field, where the band are getting ready to play. The sound of a drum roll competes with the chatter from the crowd. A couple who were eyeing up the cakes lose interest as the soulful sound of a saxophone fills the air.

'That's good timing; at last we can have a bit of a break,' Anna says. 'Gemma just texted me: she'll be back with some sandwiches for us in about fifteen minutes. You get the chairs out and I'll fetch some more coffees.'

'We're lucky to have you,' Kate says. 'Thanks so much for organising us, and sorting out that business with the school entrance. I never notice things like that. You worry a lot about Evie, don't you?'

'I can't help it. I find it so hard to trust other people with her. Like Marion just now. She thinks I'm way too strict.'

'It's difficult to get the right balance, especially now I have Benjamin. He takes up so much of my attention, it's hard to keep an eye on Daniel at the same time. He wandered off in the shop the other day and a lady brought him back. I hadn't even noticed. Talk about a terrible mum. I felt awful.'

Anna can imagine. While Kate is talking, she watches over her shoulder for the blue-jacketed woman. Contacting the school was so brazen, and she can't decide whether to tell Kate about it or not. Gemma is a terrible gossip, and she doesn't want the other mothers to know. A flash of blue catches her eye and she cranes her neck to see better. The woman is at the edge of the crowd that has gathered around the band. They are playing cover versions of popular songs, and children are dancing in front of them. Once again she has her back turned. She reaches up to lift her hair from her shoulders, and a jolt passes through Anna. The move is familiar, and she wishes she could see the woman's face to be sure.

Kate is looking in the direction of Anna's gaze. 'What is it? Have you spotted Seb?'

'Yes, I thought so, but it's not him.'

Suddenly the woman seems to vanish into the crowd. Anna catches sight of Marion's bouffant hair. Her mother-in-law's head turns to one side, then the other, fast, as if watching a tennis ball track back and forth a court. Anna's pulse races. Where is Evie?

She is about to hare across to Marion, convinced the woman has snatched her daughter from under her nose, when Evie pops into view, laughing, and Marion ruffles her curls. Anna's legs feel unsteady and she sits down on a chair behind the stall. A flash of blue, and the woman is in front of the book stall. Anna pulls her chair out of sight, heart thumping. It's possible the woman doesn't know who Evie is. Under no circumstances must she see them together.

CHAPTER THIRTEEN

SEB

Seb forces himself to switch off the part of his brain that knows Anna is mad at him for rushing off. If the woman is Jo, he can't risk her speaking to Anna. Today was supposed to be a family day, and she has ruined it. He was looking forward to spending time with Evie, and he's confused and upset her by dashing away. Anna has confirmed that this is the woman who she's seen hanging around the house – so if she is Jo, as he's pretty sure she is, it has to be her who is behind the calls. To turn up here, where she has no business, is downright brazen, especially after that stunt at the school. He can't report her as a suspicious person hanging around children, because it's a public event – even though the public are largely friends and families – and she isn't doing anything wrong by coming here. His chest tightens. She knows exactly what she is doing.

The woman in the queue was wearing a distinctive blue jacket, and he is sure it is exactly the one he helped her into on more than one occasion. The memory makes him feel hot and uncomfortable. Knowing Jo, she will be deliberately trying to stand out – the unusual metallic colour draws the eye – and he scans the crowd looking for her, trying to work out the best strategy. He has to speak to her, warn her off, make her leave. He doesn't believe she's a threat to his daughter, but he understands why Anna would think she is. Evie is his wife's world. She would never say aloud that she prefers her daughter to him, but he can sense it. It's natural, and although he genuinely feels that he is Evie's dad, at times he has to remind himself that he missed those crucial early years when Evie was bonding with her mother. Of course Anna will put her daughter first, and he wouldn't want it any other way.

He positions himself to the side of a large tent where a physiotherapist is offering trial massages. For a moment he imagines how good it would feel to relax on a couch and let someone pummel the tension from his muscles. He is obscured by the tent flap; it is a good vantage point from which to check out the crowd. Maybe it's better if he doesn't speak to Jo. He could follow her, see what she's up to. If only he could tell Anna what he's doing. She will think he has let her down when they agreed they'd watch Evie together.

A text arrives from her. *Where are you???*

Then another. *WTF???*

He wipes the sweat from his forehead. His shirt is clammy on his back, rendering the hurried shower after his game of squash a waste of time. He spots a flash of blue, but it's a man in a sweatshirt. When you want to see blue, it's everywhere, and he rules out summer dresses, hats, T-shirts and more sweatshirts. His phone rings and he knows it's Anna. He switches it to silent, but the vibration against his leg compounds the guilt. How will he be able to explain himself to his understandably furious wife? He takes a large gulp of air.

'Are you all right, mate?' An older man lights a cigarette and blows a cloud of smoke away from him. 'You can get a drink in there, it's dead cheap. I'm on my second. Told the wife I needed a piss. There's not much of a queue, if you fancy one. No offence, but you look a bit hot.'

'I am. I'm driving, though. Better not, but thanks for the heads-up.'

Seb turns his attention back to the crowd, to see his daughter standing in front of the ice cream van holding a woman's hand. For a split second he's about to charge over there, then he recognises his mother's jacket and her familiar bouffant hairstyle. At least Evie will be enjoying herself and not missing out thanks to him. His relief is swiftly followed by a burst of anxiety. Not far behind them stands Jo, and her attention is fixed on his daughter.

Seb marches up to her and grabs her arm.

'Hey,' she says. 'Oh, it's you.' She shakes her arm free and scowls. 'You're hurting me.'

'What do you think you're doing here?'

'It's a free country. I'm watching this band. They're pretty good, aren't they?'

'Come over here, we need to talk.'

He moves back towards the tent, wanting to put distance between himself and his daughter. He doesn't want to draw attention to Evie in case Jo has no interest in her and is solely interested in upsetting his wife.

'Have you been phoning my house?' He's not normally this blunt, but he needs to know. He's listened to the message over and over, but the caller was muffling the sound of their voice. He can't definitively rule her out.

'What? No, of course not.' Her eyes narrow. She looks indignant, and has no problem meeting his stare. 'Do you really think I would stoop so low?'

He sighs. 'No, I don't, not really, but I had to make sure. Somebody has been threatening us, leaving vicious messages on our answering machine. I didn't want to go to the police before checking with you.'

'That's so considerate.' Her eyes flash. 'Sparing my feelings, are you? That didn't stop you before.' A stricken expression crosses her face, and she looks down at her shoes as she makes patterns on the ground with her foot. 'I can't believe you think I would do something like that.'

Seb relaxes his shoulders. She's telling the truth. He didn't want to believe she could be behind this.

'You're genuinely worried, aren't you? I thought you'd been looking a bit rough lately.'

His interest is piqued. Has she been watching him after all? Is he being naïve in believing her?

She continues. 'Stupidly, I thought it might be because you were missing me, you regretted splitting up with me. We were good together, you can't deny that.'

Heat rises to his face, and he wishes he didn't still find her attractive. 'None of this has been easy for me,' he says. 'I don't want your sympathy, but I'm not callous. I met you at a low point in my marriage. I was weak, and I regret my behaviour.' He rubs his face. 'It isn't just the phone calls to the house. Somebody called the school and asked to collect Evie. Thankfully the school checked with Anna, but it's hit us both hard. I couldn't think of any reason why anyone would do this to us, and—'

'And you thought of me. Christ, Seb, do you really think I would threaten a child?' She kicks the ground.

'Anna has seen a woman hanging around our house. The description fits you.'

'You don't know me at all if you think I would behave like that. Being dumped was bad enough. Does your wife know about me?'

'No.'

'Bit dangerous then, isn't it, talking to me here? What if she sees us and asks who I am?'

He looks around. 'She won't.'

'And if I *was* the caller, what would you tell her? A bunch of lies about me, I bet. That I'm a bunny boiler, a stalker. Was that your plan?'

'No, of course not.'

'Stop lying, it's written all over your face. What if I go and tell her now how much you enjoyed shagging me? I bet she'd be interested to know about that sexy lingerie you bought me, and how much more you loved removing it.'

'Stop it! Keep your voice down.' He glances at the people nearby, but nobody is paying attention to them. 'I made a mistake. I thought we'd dealt with all this, put it behind us.'

'You're the one who approached me.'

'Can you blame me? How do I know you're telling the truth when you turn up at my daughter's school fair? What are you doing here? I thought you didn't even like kids.'

'You're unbelievable. I knew this would happen if you saw me here. Not that it's any of your business, but my godson is in the band. The Cats. He's the one playing the drums.'

Seb looks across to the makeshift stage. The drummer is in the back right corner.

'He could be anyone.'

She shrugs. 'I don't care whether you believe me or not. I know I'm telling the truth. He's Nick Godfrey, the son of one of my old school friends. His little brother goes to this school. What are you doing following me around anyway? Shouldn't you be with the wife you're so devoted to that you shagged me on the side?' The music has stopped and her voice carries.

Seb risks a glance across at his mother, but she is bending over Evie, fiddling with the buttons on her jacket, completely unaware of what is going on around her.

Jo looks away from him, but he sees the tears in her eyes. 'Did I really mean so little to you?'

'I ...'

'Save it. I don't know what I saw in you. I'm glad we bumped into each other today. It's made me see you in a new light. Nick, over here!'

The drummer is making his way down from the stage, and

he looks in their direction and waves. Seb turns his back on Jo, his face burning. How has he got this so wrong?

Seb walks quickly through the school gates. He needs to get away from Jo. He retreats to a pub in the town centre and takes his pint into the back yard, where only hardy smokers usually bother to sit. A lone man nods at him as he sits down and takes out his phone. Anna has tried to call him twice after several increasingly frustrated texts. Another text appears.

OK, I give up. You'd better have a good explanation.

And what if he was dead in a ditch? During the confrontation with Jo, he wished he was. He didn't expect her to have a reasonable explanation for being at the school fete, and now he doubts she is stalking him. Which brings him back to the question: who is behind the calls, and why? Not having a clue is potentially worse. And how is he going to explain his absence to Anna? He rubs his face and groans, making the man across the yard look up from his newspaper. Should he bite the bullet and confess all? He drains his pint and goes in to get another.

Pubs are slightly tainted for Seb now, since the run of illicit meetings he had with Jo. Once he'd crossed the line into an affair, they'd gone to her flat, but their relationship never went beyond that. He goes over their conversation at the fair. He wants to be able to believe her, but after everything she's told him about her past, he isn't sure. Jo is smart, street-wise, and knows what she wants. She grew up in Kent, the only child of addict parents, and ended up going into care when she was fifteen. Like Anna, she is fiercely independent, having had to look out for herself since she was young. She lost her way for a while, hinting at having to grow up fast in order to survive, but at sixteen she got a part-time job at a hairdresser's, and that was where she developed her dream to own her own salon. She moved to London to train, eventually ending up in Ludlow.

What worries him is how tough she is, how she gets what she wants, mostly without help. She has one relative, her aunt Jacky, but she hardly ever sees her. She tried to persuade Seb to go and stay at a holiday flat she owns, somewhere in Wales; it was the thought of going away for a weekend, actively cheating and having to lie to Anna in such a way that brought him to his senses, made him put a stop to seeing her.

He saw another side to her when he finished with her. Her face shut down and she threatened to tell his wife everything. Every time he walked past the salon, she'd watch him, a sneer on her face. She called his phone every night. He changed his number. That stopped the calls. Where once he admired her fearlessness, it terrifies him now. Has she been biding her time, lulling him into a false sense of security, waiting to pounce? How far will she go to get what she wants?

Over his second pint, he runs through the story he'll tell Anna. She'll know he was lying about the client, but he'll tell her he didn't want to worry her unnecessarily, and that he thought the calls were coming from a woman at work who had a crush on him. He saw her at the fete, which was why he rushed off and confronted her, but it was all a big mistake and he believes she's telling the truth. Anna has nothing to worry about and they'll get through this together. Yes, that's what he'll say. Above all, he mustn't give away his fears about Jo's stability.

Just thinking about it propels him to down a whisky before he leaves. He's feeling light-headed when he leaves the pub and heads home. Either Anna will drive back or he'll pick up his car later. Coming straight over here from squash, he forgot to have lunch. The beer swirls around his stomach and he wishes he could wake up and start the day again. Come to think of it, he wishes he could rewind to a time before he first saw Jo in the coffee shop and she set her sights on him. He stumbles over the kerb and hopes he isn't heading for a far bigger fall.

CHAPTER FOURTEEN

ANNA

Anna goes through the rest of the day in a daze. Gemma returns with sandwiches and drinks, and shortly afterwards, Marion and Evie arrive back at the stall, Evie bubbling over with tales of her time with Grandma. Anna tells her mother-in-law that Seb wasn't feeling well. Marion suggests she takes a break and has a look around the fete. Anna declines, preferring to stay on the stall in case the woman in the blue jacket is still hanging around. She asks Gemma and Kate to serve people while she cuts and arranges the cakes and deals with the rubbish. The woman is nowhere to be seen, however. Could she have imagined her? Seb has completely vanished too, and she sends him another message asking where he is and what he is doing. She gets an immediate reply.

I can explain. I know Evie is safe with Mum. Sorry I had to leave, but you'll soon understand. xx

She jams the phone back into her pocket. She very much doubts it.

Finally the afternoon comes to an end. Anna noticed earlier that Seb had abandoned the car and is loading it up when a familiar figure appears.

'Mrs Gold, Mrs Gold,' Evie says, jumping up and down as her teacher approaches. She looks pretty in a flowery jumpsuit.

'Hello, Evie, have you had fun today?'

'Yes. I helped Mummy make lots of money. Do you want to buy a cake?'

'All the cakes have gone, I'm afraid,' Anna says.

Mrs Gold laughs. 'No cake for me anyway, I've just eaten a very tasty veggie burger. I'm glad I saw you, Mrs Forrester. I wanted to ask whether you managed to speak to your cousin, explain our procedures to her?'

Kate has appeared as Mrs Gold is talking, and Anna is aware of her listening to the conversation.

'Yes, I did,' Anna says, lowering her voice. 'It was all a misunderstanding, as I thought, nothing to worry about. But thanks for asking.'

'It's my job.' Mrs Gold smiles. 'Hasn't the fete been a success?' She claps her hands. Evie copies her, and they all laugh. 'I presume you know the funds are going to help the school set up a proper library.'

Anna nods. 'It's a great idea. Evie loves books, don't you, poppet?'

'I know she does,' Mrs Gold says. 'Enjoy the rest of the weekend.'

'What was all that about school procedures?' Kate asks as the teacher goes off towards her car. 'Something about your cousin? I didn't think you had any family apart from Marion.'

'What makes you think that? My cousin rang me out of the blue; I hardly ever see her. Evie must have mentioned it to Mrs Gold.'

Kate is blushing. 'Seb talked about it once, how you didn't have any family.'

'Seb? When?'

'I don't know. At a party, I think it was, maybe New Year, over at Gemma's. It's not a big deal.'

'No, of course it isn't.' *So why is she blushing?*

'Are we ready yet?' Marion asks, bringing the last of the stuff over from the stall.

'We are. See you on Monday, Kate.'

Kate waves them off as they pull out of the car park. Evie has insisted that Marion sit with her in the back, and Anna drives slowly, reluctant to face the inevitable confrontation with Seb. Marion can't be there when that happens. Her conversation with Kate is running through her head. Kate seems to be more pally with Seb than she realised. It wasn't her voice on the phone messages. It couldn't be. Kate is her friend, isn't she?

Evie is chattering away to Marion, who looks relaxed and content. Anna watches them in the rear-view mirror.

'Marion, how would you feel about having Evie at your house tonight?'

'A sleepover? Really, Mummy?' Evie drums her feet against the car seat in delight. 'Please say yes, Grandma.'

'That would be wonderful, thank you, Anna.' Marion's eyes meet Anna's in the mirror. In that instant, Anna feels an affinity with her mother-in-law, a feeling she has never experienced before. She loves their little girl too. 'Do we need to stop off at your house to get Evie a change of clothes or anything?'

'No need, she'll be OK with what she's wearing. Her spare PE kit is in the boot – I keep it in there as Seb always forgets it; you can use that if she needs clean clothes.'

'Excellent. I've got a spare toothbrush she can use. We're going to have a lovely time, aren't we, Evie?'

It's better for Evie to be out of the house so that she doesn't overhear Anna's conversation with Seb. On no account must she let that happen.

Seb is in the kitchen when Anna lets herself into the house. Every muscle in her body aches. A day of physical activity and getting up early has exhausted her. Never mind the emotional trauma. She drops her bag onto the floor and sits at the kitchen table, running her hands through her hair, which needs a wash. *She* needs a wash. A good long soak in the bath with a restorative oil to soothe her aching limbs. What she doesn't need is a confrontation.

'Where's Evie?'

'Your mum's got her for the night. I thought we could do with some time to talk.'

'Mum? Gosh. That's unexpected. You look knackered.'

'Is it any surprise? I've been working hard all day while you were off gallivanting who knows where, leaving me on my own to cope with keeping Evie safe. And worrying about you on top of that. How could you? I never thought I'd say this, but I'm so grateful to Marion. If she hadn't turned up, it would have been so much harder. You know how worried I've been. And when I tell you what's on my mind, you run away. Unbelievable. What's going on, Seb?'

Seb turns to look out of the window, away from Anna.

'Is it the phone calls?

'Yes. But I think they are directed at me, not you. That's why I'm acting a bit weird. I'm worried someone is trying to hurt me by scaring you.'

'And you didn't think to tell me? We're supposed to be a team, Seb. Who would do that? Why would they? You're frightening me.'

Seb turns to face her. He looks as though he is about to be sick. Anna feels a rush of nausea too and covers her mouth with her hands.

'You've been cheating on me, haven't you? That's what this is about. How can I have been so stupid?'

The thought has crossed her mind before, when she was hoping and praying that this wasn't about her deepest fears, that her past wasn't flying back towards her ready to knock her down. She imagined that Seb cheating would be better than anything else, better than old ghosts resurfacing. But now, with the reality right in front of her, that thought turns completely on its head. A pain is splitting her chest in two and she's struggling to breathe.

'No, I haven't. But I think I know who is behind this – at least I thought I did, until the fair. That's why I had to leave.'

'You're not making any sense.'

Seb sighs, rubbing his palms on his thighs. 'There's no easy way to say it. I met a woman in the café near work; we used to say hello and we got chatting once when I popped out for a sandwich. She was easy to talk to. After that initial contact, we bumped into each other occasionally, until one time she happened to be in the pub when I was there and we had a drink together; I'm sorry, but if I'd known what was happening, I'd have put a stop to it, honestly – you know how much I love being with you. I didn't see it coming. Stupid, looking back on it now. She's a hairdresser and she's used to chatting to people. I thought she was just being friendly. She read something into it that wasn't there, thought I was interested in her romantically.'

'She must have known you were married.'

He looks at his ring finger. 'Yes, of course. I used to talk about you and Evie to her.'

Evie. The room feels colder. 'What has Evie got to do with this?'

'Nothing. I mean, you know how it is with people you meet casually, like you do at work, water cooler conversations, discussing what we watched on television the night before, that kind of stuff. Our lives, our families. Normal things. I didn't expect to keep seeing her around the place.' He wipes his forehead.

'One evening I'd arranged to meet Jamie after work in the pub. I was a bit early, and she turned up. I couldn't exactly ask her to leave. Jamie was running late, and she ended up making a pass at me. I turned her down, then luckily Jamie arrived and she left. I avoided her after that, but she wouldn't take no for an answer. It was awkward for a while, but then she lost interest and I thought – hoped – she'd met someone else, moved on. That it was only ever an infatuation on her part, and she'd seen sense. But I was wrong. She started following me, appearing in places I least expected her to. She didn't say anything; she was just there, staring, psyching me out. I didn't know what to do. I talked to Jamie about it. He said to confront her, so I did. I went to the pub, knowing she'd turn up, and made it clear to her that there was nothing between us and I was happily married. That I'd never wanted anything more than casual friendship – if you could even call it that.'

'When did this happen?'

'That last conversation was two months ago. I was so relieved, I thought she'd got the message, properly got it this time, hopefully left the area. And then the phone calls started. Phoning the school was the final straw. She was jealous of you, of Evie, of our little family. She used to say how she disliked living on her own. She didn't have any family. She wanted what I had.'

Anna leans against the wall for support, unsure whether to believe him.

'And at the fete?'

'It was her. Her hair's different now, so I wasn't sure at first, when Evie did the drawing. But when you pointed her out, I freaked. I had to get her away from Evie, and you; she had no business being there.'

'Did you speak to her?'

'Yes. I confronted her. She denied sending messages to the house and calling the school. When I asked what possible reason she had to be at the fair, she told me she was there for her godson, who was in the band. And she was; he came over. I had to get out of there, I felt as if my head was about to explode. You must believe me, Anna. She means nothing to me. But it isn't just me, is it? This is the first time you've voluntarily let my mum have Evie. You normally keep her so closeted. I know my behaviour has been wrong, but you're hiding something from me too, I'm convinced you are. Our marriage can't survive if we aren't honest with one another.'

Anna can't look at him. She paces up and down, trying to unscramble the thoughts in her head.

'You're right. We need to talk. I need to have a bath first, though, get these grubby clothes off.'

He takes her hand. 'We'll get through this.'

She nods.

'I'll make us some food. How did the cake sale go?'

The fete seems like hours ago now. 'Really good. We sold everything.'

'That's great news. Go and have your bath, no need to hurry.'

Her legs are heavy as she goes upstairs.

CHAPTER FIFTEEN

ANNA

'

A spicy aroma greets her as she goes downstairs, refreshed in her lounge pants and sweatshirt with its comforting soft lining. After phoning Marion to check in on Evie, she filled the bath with thick bubbles and luxuriated in them. Though she was relieved to hear that Evie was having a lovely time, she couldn't help feeling slightly miffed that her daughter didn't seem to be missing her and could manage perfectly well without her. Marion thinks the world of her granddaughter and Anna has to learn to let go. This is what Seb wants to talk to her about, among other things, and she is debating how she can explain herself to him. Personal disclosure never comes easy to her. Not for her the route of counselling; the idea of baring her soul to a stranger fills her with anxiety. How can you ever be sure you can trust another person? Some things should never be spoken about.

'Vegetable curry all right? I used up everything we had in the fridge. No rice, but we've got pitta breads.'

'Sounds perfect. Anything but cake. I'm so hungry now.'

'Did the bath help?'

She nods. 'Yes, I'm feeling human again.'

The house feels different this evening. Seb has switched the low lighting on in the kitchen diner and closed the blinds.

'It's strange not having Evie here, isn't it?' Her absence feels like a presence.

'It is. Even though she'd normally be in bed at this time.'

Ordinarily they'd eat on their laps in front of the television, chatting over the day's news, both in the world at large and in their own worlds. Tonight Anna feels as if she's on a date, though instead of the excitement and anticipation that goes along with meeting someone new, she's scared of what will be revealed. Up until now, it has felt like they were holding hands, tackling life together, but now it's as if they are about to test their bond. Another woman has entered their world, and Anna can't work out how she feels about it. She wants to know details. Is she prettier, funnier, more intelligent than Anna? Is Seb telling the truth that nothing happened between them? She has to believe him when he says they haven't slept together; she can't imagine she'd get over something like that once it has lodged itself in her mind, let alone be able to carry on. *Let it go, breathe.*

Seb opens a bottle of wine and puts it on the table. They eat in a somewhat awkward silence, Anna hyper aware of the atmosphere, as if part of her body has disappeared. She's heard of amputees experiencing a phantom limb, and imagines it feels something like this. The awareness that Evie has never spent a night away from her before lingers in the air; she can count in single digits the number of times they've had a babysitter in, Anna often finding a reason to cancel at the last minute.

'Thanks for letting Mum take Evie,' Seb says. 'She sent me a text. She's thrilled. What made you change your mind?'

'I realised how happy Evie was to be with her at the fete. You should have seen her when I suggested a sleepover with Grandma. I thought she was going to kick through the car seat with excitement.'

'There'll be no stopping her now. We'll never get to see her.'

'Don't say that,' Anna says. 'I won't let that happen.'

'Don't spoil it,' Seb says. 'It isn't normal to not let her out of your sight. This evening, just the two of us, it feels great, don't you think? We never go out.'

'Is that why you got talking to that woman? Are you sure nothing happened? I'd prefer to know the truth.'

'Anna.' Seb looks at her. 'Don't do this. I told you nothing happened. It was one big misunderstanding that I could have done without.'

'You were always working late. Are you surprised I'm not sure whether to believe you or not?'

He sighs. 'I know, but I've made an effort to get home earlier recently. We've hired some part-time help for the admin side of the business, and that has freed up a lot of time. Jamie is such a workaholic and I let myself be influenced by him. It's a weight off my mind, actually. I know I'm guilty too, for leaving you alone so much. No wonder you rely on Evie. If I'm not around, she's the only company you have. Why don't you ask one of your friends over?'

'They're all so busy at the moment. I feel closest to Kate, but Benjamin doesn't give her a minute's peace, and her husband is a waste of space.'

'Michael? I'm not surprised. He's always in the pub.'

'How would you know?'

Seb rolls his eyes. 'What I mean is, whenever me and Jamie meet up, which is about once a week, Michael is always in there, propping up the bar. Everyone knows him and he talks to whoever comes in.'

Anna takes a sip of her wine. 'Tell me about this woman.'

'Can we not do this? She's irrelevant.'

'Not if she's been threatening us. It's funny how she always has her back to me so I can't see her face. Do I know her?'

He shakes his head. Emphatically. *Too* emphatically?

'Try me. What's her name?'

He finishes his wine and pours them both more.

'You don't need to know her name. Stop asking about her. You're only hurting yourself. I promise you she means nothing to me and she won't be bothering me again.'

'I thought you said she wasn't behind the calls.'

'She said she wasn't.' He makes an exasperated noise. 'By dwelling on her you're making her important, and what's really important is us. I want you to tell me why you're so anxious about security.'

'How do you know she's telling the truth? And so what if her godson happened to be there? It could still have been a pretext for getting close to Evie.'

'This isn't about Evie.'

'How do you know?'

Anna wants to see a photo of this woman, to know her name, age and vital statistics. She wants to scrutinise her social media and look at her house and her lifestyle. She wants to *know* her, who she is. She is frustrated by this conversation, which is spinning in rings like her thoughts.

'I just do.'

'So it's me she's after, me she wants to hurt.'

'No.' Seb slaps his hand down on the table. 'Don't you get it? It's me, it was only ever about me.'

'You sound as if you're proud of that.'

'Don't be ridiculous. But she was infatuated and now she's over it.'

'Why would you believe her? She sounds like a tricksy kind of person. Did you actually speak to her godson?'

'No.'

'What's the name of the band?'

'The Cats, why?' She shrugs. He groans. 'Don't tell me you're going to track him down.'

It's not a bad idea. Anna will do anything to get to the truth.

She wants to speak to this woman herself, make up her own mind whether she's responsible for the calls. She has to confirm that this is about Seb and not her. Otherwise she'll never be able to settle.

While Seb stacks the dishwasher and tidies the kitchen, she checks out the band online, but there is only one mention of them, playing at a pub earlier in the year. They're sixth-formers and it's plausible the woman really was at the fete to see them, but Anna can't quite lose the niggle that she could have guessed Seb would be there too with his daughter.

Later, when she has made her final call of the night to Marion, they open a second bottle of wine and relax on the sofa. Anna takes up most of the space, with her legs across Seb's, and they are mellow again, the earlier topic of conversation exhausted. She wonders what a passer-by looking in would make of them. A tastefully decorated room, dark green sofa picking out the hues of the lighter green paint, expensive lighting, no clutter. A young couple in love, reclining together, close enough not to need words, insides warmed by home-made food, good wine and interesting conversation. She wants this facade to be true, for the fear to be gone that somebody is lurking out of sight, holding on to the corner of the luxury carpet, waiting for the right moment to pull it out from under them.

Seb interrupts her thoughts.

'How do you feel about Evie's first night sleeping elsewhere?'

'Strange,' she says. 'Wrong somehow.'

'But you know she's safe, don't you?'

Anna strokes the soft material of the sofa. 'Yes.'

'Why the hesitation?'

'You know why.'

'No I don't. That's the point. Tell me.'

'She's precious. I'm scared of losing her. Aren't you?'

'Yes, but only in the sense that it's a worst-case scenario that is unlikely to happen. Every parent must feel like that.'

'How do you know it won't happen?'

He thinks. 'I don't for sure. I can't, nobody can. But you just have to believe that there are systems and safeguards in place that mean she is generally safe. If you went around imagining what might happen all the time, life would be impossible.' He takes her hand. 'Is that how it feels for you?'

'Sometimes.'

'Will you tell me why, what happened to you?'

'Nothing happened to me. I'm just an anxious person.'

'Something must have happened to make you so fearful. If it's too painful to—'

'No. There's nothing.' She pulls away from him and places her feet on the floor. 'I don't want to talk about it. You should be pleased about Marion; she's been on at you to take Evie for long enough.'

'Take her. You make it sound like she's been kidnapped.'

'You know what I mean.' She stands up. 'I'm going to bed.'

In the bathroom, Anna looks into the frosted glass of the window, her reflection opaque and insubstantial. She wants more than anything to be able to answer Seb's question. But it's a risk she cannot take, for to tell him would be to lose him, and that can't be allowed to happen.

CHAPTER SIXTEEN

ANNA

Evie returns in high spirits the following day. She's tired out after the fete and the sleepover and falls asleep earlier than usual that night. The following morning Anna is woken by pain. Her toothache is back worse than ever, shooting through her mouth, affecting her ears and her head, and she groans so loudly Seb wakes up.

'What's the matter? Are you having a nightmare?'

'I wish I was.' She clutches her jaw. 'It's my tooth, it's agonising. I can't believe it's flared up again. It hurts so much.'

'I'll get you some painkillers. It's almost time to get up anyway.'

Seb goes downstairs and Anna rubs some toothpaste onto her gum. The dentist hoped she'd got rid of the infected area, but had warned her it might return, and if it did, the tooth would have to be removed. Anna wants rid of it right this minute.

Seb returns with a glass of water and two tablets.

'Here, take these. Poor you.' He puts his arm round her and she leans into his shoulder.

'I'll have to get an emergency appointment,' she says.

'What time do they open?'

'Not sure, I'll check.' She looks on her phone. 'They open for bookings at seven thirty.'

'It's seven fifteen now. I'll get Evie up and ready for school and you stay here and see if you can get an appointment. I can take her to school if necessary.'

'OK.'

Anna gets through straight away and makes an appointment for lunchtime. The painkiller has kicked in and the pain is more bearable, but still enough to make her want to bury her head in a pillow. At least it distracts her from worrying about the conversation she had with Seb last night.

He appears in the doorway.

'Any joy?'

'Yes. The earliest they can see me is half past twelve.'

'Great.'

'If I can survive until then.'

'Evie's eating her breakfast, but she's saying something about a trip to see animals today. Does she need to take anything special?'

'Oh no.' The class outing. How could she have forgotten?

'What is it?'

'I'm supposed to be accompanying the school trip to a wildlife park this afternoon; they always take a couple of parent volunteers to ensure there are enough adults around. I can't let them down.'

'What time are they leaving?'

'Twelve. They're having a picnic first. I've done her food bag, it's in the fridge.'

'I'm sure they can find someone to cover you. If not, it can't be helped. I'll phone them now so they have as much warning as possible.'

'I hate letting them down. Do you think I should change my appointment?'

'No, I don't. Look at you, you're obviously in agony. Why are you even considering it?'

Anna avoids his eyes. She's furious with herself. She always goes on trips that Evie goes on. That way she can make sure her daughter is safe. She doesn't trust other parents who go along – she's seen for herself how they only want to spend time with their own children and don't pay attention to what the others are getting up to. She recalls the conversation with Seb; here she is falling into the same habits again. She has to learn to trust others. But now, with everything that's going on, should she?

'What if they can't replace me? There won't be enough adults.'

'I know what this is about. You're being overprotective again. I've been patient enough with you, but it's getting ridiculous. You had the opportunity when we talked to tell me about any real concerns or reasons you had for worrying that something might happen to Evie, and you didn't come up with anything. I don't want our daughter to be mollycoddled. This has to stop, Anna, it has to stop now.'

Seb goes downstairs and she hears his voice on the phone. He comes back up with Evie.

'Say goodbye to Mummy, she isn't feeling well.'

'Poor Mummy. Will the tooth fairy come if you have your tooth out?'

'I hope so.' Anna kisses her and hugs her hard. 'Promise me you'll be careful today and stay with the teacher and do everything she says.'

Evie nods.

'The school secretary said they have a list of reserve parents for the trip, so you don't have to worry. I'd have stepped in myself if I didn't have to go to work. Let me know how you get on at the dentist. I hope it goes well.'

He kisses her, and he and Evie go downstairs. The front door shuts and Anna listens to the sound of the car driving off down the street and closes her eyes. Four hours to get through until her appointment. Seb was right about her tooth – there's no way she could have gone on the school outing; the pain is too acute. He obviously isn't that concerned about the calls, so she shouldn't be either. She tries to tell herself Evie will be safer with another fully functioning parent, but she isn't convinced. At least the throbbing pain stops her feeling so anxious, as she can think about nothing else.

By two in the afternoon, she is relieved of pain. She goes to the small park opposite the dental surgery and sits on a bench. The school trip was leaving at twelve, so by now they should have arrived at their destination, had their picnic and be wandering around the wildlife park looking at the animals. Evie loves animals and no doubt will come home wanting something more exotic than a cat for a pet. She checks her phone, but there are no messages from school. Seb texted earlier to let her know that Evie had been safely dropped off. He knows she will worry otherwise. He is tolerant of her, but he's right, she must try and stop being so anxious. It's just so easy to imagine all the things that could go wrong: Evie sliding into the water, an animal breaking loose and biting her … Anna's imagination runs wild with ever more outlandish scenarios. She texts Seb to let him know about her tooth and walks home. The bus is due back at school an hour later than normal pickup time, and she's looking forward to hearing all about the trip from Evie.

Back at home, the numbness wearing off, she makes herself a cup of tea and takes it into the garden. It's a warm day, and she sits in the sun and closes her eyes, listening to the sounds of birdsong and the traffic in the background. Children's voices laugh and shout, disturbing the quiet, and the noise of running feet tells her it is 3.30 and soon she will be able to set off to school and collect Evie. She can't wait to see her.

A ringing tone mingles with the sounds of the street, and it takes her a moment to realise it is the house landline. She rushes indoors, just too late to pick up. Immediately her mobile rings, and she see it's an unknown number. She hesitates – what if it's the malicious caller? She was daring to hope that the calls had stopped and they would never hear from this person again. She takes a deep breath and answers.

'Hello, is that Mrs Forrester?' It's a female voice, slightly breathless, as if the person has been running.

'Yes.' She's still wary, unsure who this is.

'Do you know where your daughter is today?'

Anna's heart threatens to burst from her chest. *Stay calm, Anna, stay calm.*

'Who is this?'

'Haven't you worked it out yet?'

'Who are you? What do you want?'

'So many questions. I'm watching Evie now; she's looking at the goats. I'm not sure she likes them very much. She looks frightened. I can't see the teacher anywhere.'

A scream lodges in Anna's throat, but she's unable to speak.

'You really should take better care of her. Anything could happen.'

The phone line goes dead.

CHAPTER SEVENTEEN

ANNA

Anna runs to the kitchen, where the letter about the wildlife park trip is pinned to the noticeboard. She dials the mobile number given to parents. The phone rings. She's jigging up and down on the spot. 'Come on, come on, pick up ... Hello, is that Mrs Gold?'

'It is. Who am I speaking to?'

'Mrs Forrester, Evie's mum. Is Evie there? Is she safe?'

'Of course she is. In fact, she's right here with me. We're getting everyone onto the coach now and should be back at school a little earlier than we said.'

'Oh.' The word comes out as a gasp, and Anna leans against the wall for support. 'Can I speak to her?'

'Of course. Evie, it's your mummy. Come and have a quick word. Will you be there to meet her?'

'Yes.'

'See you back at the school. We hope to get there in around forty minutes' time. Here's Evie.'

'Mummy?'

'Hello, darling.' It's all Anna can do to keep her voice steady. 'Have you had lots of fun?'

'Lots and lots. I saw so many animals I lost count. And guess what, Mummy, just now, a goat nearly bit me. I got away just in time.'

'A goat.' Anna fears her legs will give way.

'I don't like goats any more. My new favourite animal is a tiger. It's like a cat, but bigger. I'm getting on the coach now. Bye, Mummy.'

Anna bites down on her hand to stop herself screaming.

Anna drives as fast as she dares to the school, not caring that she's half an hour early for the coach. She finds a free meter just along from the gate and sits in her car watching the corner, scouring the road for signs of the blue and cream bus. All she can think about is getting hold of Evie and taking her home to safety. Only then will she address what she needs to do. What *they* need to do. This is a decision she will have to make with Seb. The threat is too great now; the caller knows who Evie is. Anna's worst fears are coming true. She grips on to the locked steering wheel to contain her fear.

A flash of blue sweeps past the treetops, and she's out of her car and at the gate. Other parents join her, and she jostles for prime position, doesn't trust anyone until she has her daughter in her arms. Only when she sees Evie being helped down the coach steps does she allow herself to relax.

Evie wants to go to the park after school. Anna is incredulous.

'Haven't you tired yourself out with all that excitement? We're going home. The park can wait until another day.' She can't imagine taking Evie to a park ever again, not until she's got to the bottom of the phone calls, stopped this threat to her family.

The answerphone light isn't flashing, a small relief. The phone conversation feels like a terrifying dream now. Can it really have happened? She has no evidence. She dials 1471, but as before, the caller withheld their number, although the time of the call is confirmed, which proves that it's not something she's fabricated.

She pours Evie some juice. She wants to fire questions like arrows, but holds back, makes herself breathe deeply.

'Tell me about your trip. How many animals did you see?'

'I'll show you my book.' Evie locates her bag and pulls out a booklet provided by the park, following the trail around the site, with activities at various different points. Evie's drawing of a penguin would normally make Anna laugh, but today her smile is drawn on her face for her daughter's benefit.

'Which other animals did you like?'

'The bears, although they were much bigger than my teddies. They are soft and cuddly, though.'

'I don't think anyone would be allowed to cuddle the bears. They may look friendly, but they are very dangerous.'

'Like the goat who tried to bite me. I didn't like him.'

'Was he the last animal you saw?'

Evie nods, swinging her legs under the table. 'There were lots of animals in the shop, but the teacher said we couldn't go in there.'

'Who else was with you when you saw the goats?'

'Hmm. I have to think. India was with me, and she cried when the goat got angry, but Marcus was there too and he thought it was funny.'

'Were any adults with you?'

'Mrs Taylor.'

'Who's she?'

'Vicky's mum. She came instead of you. She's very nice. She shooed the naughty goat away.'

'And were there any other grown-ups there, anyone who wasn't with the school?'

'There was a lady. She was nice too. She kept smiling at me.'

Anna stiffens. 'Remember, you have to be careful with grown-ups you don't know, although I'm sure she was just being friendly. What did she look like?'

'She had pretty hair, quite long and black, like a princess.' Evie laughs. Anna can't bring herself to smile. 'Or the Wicked Witch, she had long black hair too, but this lady didn't have a wicked face. She looked pretty when she was smiling, but when Mrs Gold said we had to go to the bus, she had a cross face. I don't think she liked Mrs Gold.'

'Oh, I'm sure she did.'

'She went away anyway. She wasn't with any children.'

'She probably just likes to visit the animals. Lots of people do.'

'Do you know her, Mummy?'

'No, I don't.' Anna desperately wants her words to be true.

'Can I go and play in the garden now?'

'Yes. I'll come and sit outside with you.'

'Can I finish my colouring? I didn't do the tigers and the snakes, and I want to do lots of colours. Mrs Gold said we could use our imaginations and make them up. My tiger is going to be yellow and blue stripes.'

Anna slides the bifold doors open wide, and Evie takes her colouring pencils and booklet outside and sits down on the blanket Anna lays out on the grass. With the doors folded open, she can see Evie from the kitchen. High fences separate their garden from the neighbours on either side. Her stomach is churning. Was the woman Evie spoke to the same woman who phoned earlier? Mentioning the goat has to be some kind of clue. How terrifying that she got so close to her daughter. Was she planning to snatch her? Did Mrs Gold inadvertently stop her? But Mrs Gold would never have left the children unaccompanied; she's an experienced teacher who must have been on hundreds of trips. Mrs Taylor was with Evie, she remembers.

She puts the kettle on and watches Evie. She's engrossed in her colouring, but senses her mother watching her and looks up.

'Are you coming outside, Mummy?'

'Yes, in a minute. I'm just making myself a cup of tea.' Out of the corner of her eye she spots the washing she did earlier, still damp in the machine. In her haste, she forgot to hang it out. She makes her tea and takes it outside to drink before she puts the washing out. She wants to phone Seb and see if he can come home early. They need to talk.

Seb's phone rings out but he texts her back straight away to tell her he's in a meeting. She sends a text back.

What's the earliest you can get home?

Six.

Come earlier if you can. She adds *I need you here* but then deletes it. No point in making him worry.

Evie is singing to herself quietly as she presses down hard with her pencil, colouring the tiger's ears blue. She pokes her tongue out as she concentrates. Anna sips her tea – she's made camomile, for its supposed calming properties. It isn't having much effect. Seb won't be back for over an hour.

Sounds from the park beyond the end of their garden can be heard in the distance, boys shouting, 'Kick it, Danny!' 'Over here!' and the thud of the ball being kicked. Anna finishes her tea.

'Your colouring is very good,' she says. 'You haven't gone over any of the edges. Mrs Gold will be very pleased with you.'

'It's not homework, but I told her I would finish it and show her tomorrow.'

Anna can't believe children Evie's age are given homework. She takes her cup inside and fetches the washing basket. The peg bag normally hangs on a hook on the wall by the doors, but it isn't there. She looks around the kitchen, opens cupboards and scans the surfaces, before spotting it obscured by a plant. She gathers everything together and goes outside. The wind has picked up and the washing should dry quickly in the breeze.

'Do you want to help me hang the washing out ... Oh.' Evie is no longer on the lawn, her colouring book still open on the blanket, pencils spread out around it.

Anna drops the basket and peg bag, a sense of dread creeping over her. Next door's black cat appears on the lawn and stares at her.

'Evie,' she calls, 'Evie, where are you? Come here now.' She looks back towards the kitchen – she would have seen Evie had she gone inside, although she was intent on finding the pegs.

The garden consists of a medium-size lawn bordered by flower beds on two sides and a small rockery at the end. Behind that are some raspberry bushes, which need cutting back, a tree in the corner, and iron railings between the bushes and the park. In a panic, she runs over to the bushes. Seb plays hide-and-seek with Evie sometimes, but she scratched herself badly once when she tried to hide there.

'Evie! Are you hiding? It isn't funny. You're scaring Mummy, show me where you are.'

She hears nothing apart from more cries from the distant football game. She wades into the raspberries, which are thick with brambles. The thorns catch on her clothes and scratch her arms. She pushes through until she reaches the tree, squeezing to look behind it. She stops dead. One of the railings has been removed from the fence, a space big enough for a child – or even an adult – to get through.

How long has that been missing?

Anna is shaking, and barely notices the thorns that digs into her leg. She scans the park but can see there is nobody on the field in front of her save for the boys playing football a little way off. The playground is on the far side of the park and can't be seen from here. She whirls around and looks at the house. Evie must have gone back inside and Anna didn't notice.

She runs back through the garden, knocking the laundry basket over, and into the house, her panic rising with each room she finds empty. From her bedroom window she looks out over the garden and the park, but she can't see anyone resembling Evie. She sees how the tree obscures the area where the railing is missing. If it were bent out of place, that she could maybe understand, but to take it away has to be a deliberate act. Surely it would need cutting with powerful tools.

Her mobile rings. It's Seb.

'Seb. You have to come home,' she gasps down the phone.

'What's the matter?'

'It's Evie, I can't find her. She was in the garden and now she's not.' Her voice falters on the last word.

'Oh my God, no. Are you sure she isn't hiding?'

Anna's throat is too dry to speak.

'Anna, Anna, are you there? I'm almost home. I was ringing to tell you I'd left the office early. We'll find her, I promise. I'll be with you in five minutes, and if she's not back then, we'll call the police. She can't have gone far. We won't let anything happen to her.'

As soon as Seb ends the call, Anna charges back out into the garden, through to the fence, and gazes out at the expanse of the park. The footballers are high-fiving one another and gathering up their bags. Evie could easily have got over there by now. A child on her own would stand out. She can't bear to think of the alternative. She slips through the gap and runs over to them.

'Have you seen a little girl with brown curly hair? Four years old, nearly five, about this big, on her own or even with someone? Have you seen a child at all? She might have been looking lost.'

The two lads she is speaking to shake their heads. One of them shouts out to the rest of the group, 'Here, guys, listen up, has anyone seen a little girl around here?' Heads shake – but would they really have noticed, pumped up and full of the game they've just enjoyed?

'OK, thanks. I'm over there, the house behind that big tree, just in case you see anything.'

She hares back across the field and squeezes through the gap, catching her shirt and hearing it rip as it snags on a stray branch. She yanks it free and pushes through the bushes. Washing is strewn over the lawn, but she barely notices, running over damp towels as she hurries back indoors and checks the house from top to bottom again, calling her daughter's name repeatedly. Her breath is coming out in short, quick gasps; she hasn't moved so fast in a long time. She can't wait for Seb to arrive; she has to ring the police now. Everyone knows the first few moments after a disappearance are crucial. *Disappearance.* The word makes her want to weep.

A flashing red light catches her eye: the landline answerphone. She didn't hear the phone ring; it must have happened when she was outside. Has a neighbour found Evie? She snatches up the receiver. As she does so, she hears Seb's key in the front door and puts the receiver back.

'I can't find her, Seb,' she says, and bursts into tears.

'Tell me what happened exactly.'

She tells him, words flying out fast, precious seconds passing.

'OK,' he says. 'Have you spoken to the neighbours?'

She shakes her head. 'No.'

'Right. First let's call the police, then I'll go and ask them.'

'There's a message,' she says.

They exchange a look.

'I'd better play it,' he says, 'just in case.'

Anna's throat is so dry she can barely swallow. In the silence before the message plays, she is sure Seb can hear her heartbeat. She holds her breath. A voice rasps out from the machine.

'I've got Evie. If you go to the police, your dirty secret will be revealed to the world, and you don't want that happening, do you? Wait for further instructions. And remember – don't tell the police, or who knows what I might do.'

Seb drops the phone, his face as white as the recently painted walls. Anna's stomach heaves, and she only just makes it to the downstairs bathroom in time.

CHAPTER EIGHTEEN

SEB

The sound of the toilet flushing brings Seb back to the present. Jo hasn't bothered to hide her voice this time. As soon as he heard it, his insides turned to ice. This nightmare scenario can't be happening. Never would he have imagined she would do this – that *anyone* would do this. He bitterly regrets lying to Anna. The truth is bound to come out now, and he risks losing everything.

He hadn't believed in love at first sight until he met Anna. He was captivated by the way she talked, the way she laughed; he couldn't stop thinking about her. He could listen for hours to the gentle lilt of her voice. He found himself daydreaming about her at work, his thoughts constantly turning to her. He adored everything about her, and loving her daughter was merely an extension of that. He was charmed by the baby, who smiled her gummy smile at him, her hair wispy around her face. He was there to see her grow, and rarely qualified his title of father with the word 'step'. Language was irrelevant to him in matters of the heart. He loved her as if she were his own. The idea that anyone would want to harm her made him want to howl with rage.

Thinking back to how he felt about Anna in the early days fills him with shame and disbelief that he let himself be swayed by another woman. Jo didn't mean anything to him. She caught him at a vulnerable moment, and knowing that his weakness and stupidity with another woman has brought harm to his little girl is like a blade slicing his insides. How could he have been so taken in by her?

He recalled a conversation they had late one night, where he realised why she never spoke about her family. She lay in his arms and he stroked her hair as she recalled the dysfunction of living with alcoholic parents: never knowing what state they would be in when she got home from school – or even if they'd *be* home. Making sure she could feed herself was more of a priority than doing well at school; most days she was too exhausted to make an effort to participate in lessons, and doing anything that required concentration at home was impossible. Every night her parents would roll in from the pub accompanied by whoever they'd been talking to that night, and Jo would cower in her room with her dressing table pushed against the door. She didn't trust the men, with their loud voices and the lewd looks they gave her, running their eyes up and down her hand-me-down school uniform. She was very selective about who she dated, and had no desire to bring a child into the world, given the upbringing she'd had.

'What if you meet the right person?' Seb asked. 'That might change the way you feel about everything.' He felt a twinge of guilt saying that, as he couldn't help recalling how his whole outlook on life had changed when he'd fallen in love with Anna. Jo looked into his eyes and kissed him, and the conversation was curtailed; only later did he realise she hadn't answered the question.

It made no sense for her to take Evie. He didn't believe she'd carry through her threat. How could anyone hurt a child? So many questions rained on him like hailstones, each one a blow on his guilt. He'd have to tell Anna what had really happened between them. Fear at what Jo might be capable of made his insides churn.

CHAPTER NINETEEN

ANNA

Anna emerges from the bathroom, eyes and nose pink, the rest of her face deathly white.

'Someone's got my baby. What are we going to do?' She dissolves into tears, and Seb holds her to him, rubbing her back until the sobs subside.

'Have some water,' he says, leading her to the kitchen and guiding her into a seat. His eyes brim with tears.

'What will we do, Seb? She said no police, but we need them, don't we? How else are we going to find her? We should be out looking. The first twenty-four hours are crucial.' She moves to get up, but he pushes her back down with the briefest touch to her shoulder.

'We need a plan.'

'Is it money they want? I've got savings, we can sell the house, anything to get her back—'

'Stop,' Seb says.

She didn't realise she was rocking backwards and forwards on the kitchen stool.

'Let's talk this through logically.' Seb's a great believer in a plan to bring order to his life. There is always a solution to a problem. His rational mind is usually matched by Anna's desire for order, logic. She doesn't want to ring the police, not if they can solve this themselves without endangering her daughter.

'You know how much I love Evie.'

Anna stares at him. He stumbles over his words.

'Th-there's no easy way to say this.'

'What are you talking about?'

'I ...'

'Just tell me.'

He closes his eyes briefly, then looks directly at her.

'I think I know who's got Evie.'

'What? But the dirty secret, I thought ... Tell me, tell me who's got my daughter.' Her voice goes from quiet to practically shouting.

Seb stands up and looks out of the window, facing away from her. His shoulders slump.

'It *is* the woman I told you about, the one who was hassling me.'

'You mean she's the one who's got Evie? Where does she live? We have to go there now.'

'Let me explain. I don't think she would harm her. She's just trying to get my attention.'

He pauses, and Anna looks at him frantically. 'Hurry up and tell me, every minute counts.'

'It was a terrible mistake. She means nothing to me. I was scared of losing you. When the phone calls started, I didn't recognise her voice – she tried to disguise it – but I couldn't think who else it could be. Then when you reported a woman hanging around the house, the description fitted her. That distinctive jacket – almost like she wanted me to know it was her. At the school fete, I was terrified that she might see us together and say something to you. I especially didn't want her to know who Evie was. That's the real reason I took off. I hated abandoning you and letting Evie down; you had every right to be furious with me. But it seems she's determined for you to know what we did.'

'But why would she take Evie? It doesn't make any sense.'

'She knows how much I love her. It's to punish me for breaking up with her. Oh God, this is such a mess and it's all my fault. I'm so sorry, Anna, but I promise we'll get her back.'

Anna feels numb. She files the information about Seb's betrayal away in her mind for closer inspection later, when this nightmare is over. For now, she is one hundred per cent focused on Evie.

'Let's call the police, then.'

'No. I don't think that's a good idea.'

'Why not? You know where this woman lives, don't you?'

He nods. 'But I don't want to alarm her.'

'You're scaring me now. You said she wouldn't hurt Evie.'

'She's a decent person underneath; I just think she's lashing out. She probably saw an opportunity to frighten us, that's all. I want to tread carefully, because she's pretty tough and knows how to take care of herself.'

Anna jumps up. 'I want to listen to the message again.' Seb follows her into the hall. Her hand shakes as she presses the button, chewing on her fingers as she listens.

'I've got Evie. If you go to the police, your dirty secret will be revealed to the world, and you don't want that happening, do you? Wait for further instructions. And remember – don't tell the police, or who knows what I might do.'

'"Wait for further instructions." I can't wait.' Anna's voice is a tone higher than usual. 'I can't stay here and do nothing. We have to look for her. Let me ask the neighbours; we haven't done that yet, and they might have seen something.' She picks up her phone. 'Where are my keys?'

Seb grabs hold of her wrist.

'Anna, there's no point. We know where she is. Let me ring her.'

'Put it on speaker,' Anna says.

He hesitates, then does as she asks. They both hold their breath. It rings for what appears to be ages, before clicking on to voicemail. Seb clears his throat and glances at Anna; she nods in encouragement.

'This is Seb. Ring me as soon as you get this message.'

Anna gesticulates at him not to hang up, but he takes no notice.

'Why didn't you say more? Let me ring her.'

'No, we mustn't antagonise her.'

Anna paces up and down. 'Are you sure it's her?'

Seb nods.

'You said she lived alone?'

'Yes. At least, she used to, when ...' He lets the sentence trail off and looks at the floor.

His phone beeps with a text and they both jump.

'It's her,' he says. He reads aloud. '"Don't contact me. Wait until I'm ready. Evie isn't in danger as long as you do what I say."'

Anna gasps. *Evie isn't in danger.* 'Ask her if she wants money.'

Seb hesitates, then types: *We can pay.*

Seconds later, the woman replies: *I'm warning you ...*

'Seb, don't,' Anna says. 'She says Evie is OK. Should we believe her?'

'Yes. I can't imagine she'd hurt her. She just wants to get back at me, that's what this is about. I'm afraid we're going to have to sit tight.'

Anna feels a rush of relief, followed by terror. 'Please let her be safe.'

'I feel more hopeful now,' Seb says. 'She wouldn't say that if it wasn't true. She'd be avoiding us, or on the run or something. Christ.' He wipes his forehead and removes his suit jacket, loosens his tie. 'I need a drink.'

Anna follows him into the kitchen. Seb pours himself a whisky.

'Is that a good idea?' she asks.

'It calms my nerves. I won't have more than one, don't worry.'

Anna can't imagine a time when she won't worry. Seb offers her a drink, but she sticks to water. She has to have a clear head for Evie. Having her own child took her such a lot of time and effort, she can't lose her now. She looks at Seb, his hair sweaty and his tie hanging loose. He looks broken, and she wants to pummel him for bringing this danger to their door, but she refrains from doing so, squeezing her hands into tight fists.

'Tell me everything you know about her. The slightest detail might be significant in working out what she's up to.'

Seb recounts again how he met Jo in the café, before their accidental meeting at the pub.

'Does she work?' Anna asks.

'She owns the hair salon near where I work. You went there once before she took over. Jo always wanted to be a hairdresser.'

Anna's face turns grey, and she clutches her stomach.

'Oh God,' she says.

'What is it?'

'Did you say Jo?'

He nods.

'What's it short for? Joanne?' She wills it to be Joanne. Joanne will make the fear go away.

'Josephine,' he says.

She groans and rushes towards the bathroom again. As she retches over the toilet, tears pour from her eyes and fear fills her from head to toe.

Call me Josie. Only my parents call me Josephine. The name sends a shiver through her spine. Seb is staring at her as she kneels on the tiled floor.

'Come over here,' he says, guiding her by the elbow to the

sofa. 'Have some water. It's delayed shock. We need to try and keep our heads if we're going to get the better of her.'

'I don't think it will be as easy as that,' Anna says. Now that the time has finally come to reveal the truth about her past, she wants it over with. He's confided his affair; she has a tiny hope that he won't judge her as harshly as she fears. Better to get it over with now, let the poison spill out of her – it's going to ruin their lives anyway, when it all comes out.

'What do you mean?'

'This isn't what you think. It isn't you she's after, but me. I know who Josephine is, and why she's doing this. And I also know why she doesn't want us to contact the police.'

CHAPTER TWENTY

ANNA

2016

Anna hasn't been to Hampstead Heath for ages. Normally she'd be excited to see her oldest friend, but today the cold wind is getting right into her bones, despite her coat. On the Tube, people jostle and push and she wants to scream at them to leave her in peace. Luke is the person she really wants to scream at, but she's done all that and it won't change anything. She slaps her pass on the barrier and sees the back of Susan's red coat in the Tube entrance, chestnut hair shining. She avoids looking left towards the hospital, the ugly building where her heart was ripped from her body and her dreams from her soul.

Susan wraps her in a big hug and holds her. Anna is determined not to cry, and swallows hard to keep the tears at bay.

'How are you doing?'

She shrugs. 'I managed not to clobber anyone on the Tube, so that's a plus. I know I'm taking my anger out on everyone else, but ...' She shrugs again.

'If it helps, having murderous thoughts isn't going to harm anyone. Apart from you, of course. I hate to say it will get easier, but it's a cliché for a reason. Remember what I was like when I split with Jack?'

Anna smiles. 'As if I could forget. I was scared you were going to do something stupid – that's why I turned up at your flat with a suitcase and didn't leave for two weeks.'

They're on the Heath now; the hospital no longer looms over her and the wind whips through the trees and blows through her hair, which she's washed for the first time in a week, her date with Susan forcing her to step back into the land of the living. She styled it, dressed in an outfit she used to wear to work, added colour to her cheeks and made her eyebrows look presentable, and it made her feel slightly better – until she got on the train and saw people wearing wedding rings and couples canoodling. At least she didn't see any babies. She's off work for another week and resolves to use the time to pull herself together. Luke she will get over; it's everything else that is threatening to drag her down.

'And that's why I'm here for you, always.' Susan links her arm through Anna's. 'Let's walk for a while, and then I'll treat you to coffee and cake in my favourite café.'

They set off through a wilder part of the Heath, the trees obscuring the winter sun and their feet rustling through leaves and twigs and discarded rubbish. Anna doesn't get incensed as she normally would, barely noticing the piles of unnecessary plastic; instead her mind is absorbed by the conversation with Susan, a chance to air and examine her jumbled thoughts.

'Have you heard from Luke since he left?'

'No, but I didn't expect to. He made it quite clear we were finished and there was no going back. I don't blame him. Obviously it hurts, but I feel the same – seeing each other is just a reminder of all the heartache we've been through, and the fact that nothing ever came of it. I would have tried again, but it would have ripped me apart if it hadn't worked, and he said he couldn't face it. He cried, Susan, and he so rarely cries. It was heartbreaking. It's hard that something that started out being so wonderful has ended, despite all the hoops we've been through. I know we're not the first to go through it, but that doesn't make it any easier.'

'Have you thought about counselling, or some kind of therapy group?'

Anna shudders. 'I can't bear to go into it all again by talking to someone new. Talking to you is easier. I know we haven't spoken much in the last few years, but we always pick up where we left off.' Confiding in someone who knows you is like slipping into a favourite dressing gown. Although Susan has been living abroad for the past few years and they've not been in regular touch, that hasn't changed their feelings for one another.

Susan knows all about the long road that Anna embarked upon seven years ago. The first year was more about excitement than heartache; despite the disappointment each month when she felt the familiar gripe in her stomach and knew that it hadn't worked, that there would be no baby for them this time, she still had hope. Back then, she blithely assumed that a pregnancy was inevitable, just a matter of weeks to set the process in motion.

After a year, they visited their doctor, who was full of encouragement and positive platitudes but sent them for tests 'just to be sure'. Anna and Luke discussed possible outcomes and reassured each other that neither of them would blame the other if their body proved to be the weak link in the chain. Results showed that Anna had a low chance of being able to have children naturally, but there were things they could do to improve the likelihood of making it happen: diets to be followed and lifestyle changes to be made. But another year passed, and they each became a little more downcast. As three, four years plus went by, Anna began to research adoption, surrogacy, all the while hoping a pregnancy would happen naturally.

Friends and colleagues recounted tales of couples they'd known who had conceived a child after several years of trying –

always positive, these stories, to boost her up and keep her going. She knew what they were trying to do; they meant well. She should have paid more attention to the letters written to the problem pages of magazines, the articles on women who couldn't conceive. She was a positive person, though, and she preferred the articles where treatments were ever better and more possibilities and strategies were available as medicine progressed. She refused to give up.

IVF was embarked on; they both had money put aside for a mortgage, but in the end the child won, and their savings dwindled along with their hopes. Anna became increasingly demanding of Luke. His willingness to stick to the healthy diet she prescribed for him was another casualty of their failure, and he took to hiding the odd night out at the pub with his mates, sucking mints to disguise the alcohol on his breath and getting in after Anna had fallen asleep. A grown man forced to live like a teenager again, trying to outwit his parents. She always noticed, but bit back her criticism as she didn't want this to come between them. She wanted them to survive. They *would* be a family.

They both took the first failed attempt hard; the second was worse, and Luke began to doubt that changing his lifestyle would make any difference. Where once he'd looked forward to the increase in lovemaking required, and they'd thrown themselves into the task, now he avoided 'appointments' and grew to hate the fertility calendar that ruled Anna's life. They sniped and snapped at each other.

'And then the miracle happened,' Anna says. 'At least, we thought it was a miracle at the time. It should have been.' A sob clogs her throat.

'Nature can be so cruel,' Susan says. 'To go through several months and then ...'

Neither of them can say the words aloud. Anna wishes she could have been drugged when she was forced to go through the motions of giving birth when her little girl was no longer alive. Mimi, they named her. Luke stayed at her side, clutching her hand, wanting to share her pain. Fundamentally he was a good man.

They drifted apart in their grief. Months went by as they avoided talking about it. Luke confided his problems to a new female colleague, who understood him and made him smile again and forget everything for a few hours, until he went home. A year later, and he'd moved out.

'To be fair to him,' Anna tells Susan, 'he realised that flirting with someone else wasn't a good sign. He came home and we talked about it, how trying for a baby was destroying us, and how sad we both were. To be honest – and this may sound cruel and I wouldn't say it to anybody else – I know I'll get over *him*. It's never having a child that I'm not sure I'll ever recover from.'

Anna has wanted a house full of children ever since she can remember. Susan is single, which helps – not that she'll necessarily stay that way forever, but for now, Anna can speak freely to her without feeling that she has somehow betrayed her by having her own child, as other friends have. She knows her thought process is irrational, but for now, it's all about self-preservation. She can't get away from babies – even her hairdresser is pregnant.

'Are you definitely over with Luke? No chance that ...?' Susan raises an eyebrow.

'No.' Anna sighs. 'It's for the best. He's dating the woman from his office now.'

'No. Already? What a bastard.'

'It's hardly surprising, is it? Coming home to someone who only ever talked about one thing, my desperation for a child killing any passion we once had in our relationship. Someone new and exciting turns up at work, and they hit it off straight away ... Classic pattern.'

'Where is he living?'

'He's gone back to stay with his parents. We only have two months left on our rental contract, then I'll have to find somewhere cheaper. He's paid his share of the rent and he collected the rest of his stuff last week. I had to arrange to be out when he did that; it was too painful.'

They're deep in the wooded part of the Heath now, and muffled cries can be heard from the open area ahead. Here it's just the, two of them, save for a dog running past, its owner being dragged along behind. Susan follows the incline of the path to emerge into the daylight, the sudden brightness making them both squint.

'It's for the best,' she says. 'It sounds like you're both pretty sure.'

'Yes,' Anna says, although she doesn't feel sure of anything any more. It's been a month already since Luke moved out, but only a day since she made her discovery. Hence the phone call to Susan, this hastily arranged get-together. She hasn't told anyone the latest twist in her story; her stomach ties into a knot every time she thinks about it. She's not even a hundred per cent decided whether she should tell Susan, in case it all falls through again, as she fears it will.

'The café's over that way.' Susan points across the Heath, past the lake and in the vague direction of Highgate. 'Ready for a cuppa?' They link arms, and Anna swallows down the anxiety and steels herself for a difficult conversation. Susan will try and talk her out of her decision, but her mind is firmly made up.

Ten minutes later, she's sitting at a table, watching Susan in the queue, rehearsing the words she's going to say.

'Are you sure you don't want any of this cake?' Susan asks, putting a plate on the table. A thick slice of Victoria sponge sits between them, one fork each, the one on Anna's side pointing at her like an accusation.

'You have it.' She pushes the plate towards Susan. 'Thanks for offering, but my stomach's a bit delicate.'

'It's all the stress,' Susan says, forking a piece of cake into her mouth. 'Mmm. So good.' She licks buttercream from her fingers.

'It's not just stress,' Anna says, stomach churning. *Just say the words aloud.* 'I'm pregnant.'

The piece of cake poised mid-air on Susan's fork wobbles.

'No way. Oh my God, Anna.' She puts her hand over her mouth. 'But that's good, isn't it?'

'Of course it's good. I'm just sad about the timing.'

'Does Luke know?'

'No. And he isn't going to either.'

'But this is what you've both wanted for so long.'

'I'm not sure he does any more. Apart from the small matter of his new girlfriend, he said as much when we had our last heart-to-heart. Said he'd got sucked up into my whirlwind and now he was coming out the other side to discover it wasn't what he wanted after all. Said he wants to travel more before he settles down. His new woman is Australian.'

'I don't remember him ever mentioning travelling. Are you sure you're all right about that?'

'I haven't got the energy to be annoyed with him. The baby is all that matters now.'

Susan puts her fork down. 'Don't you think he has a right to know?'

'You can't tell him.'

'Of course I wouldn't, not without your blessing. I doubt I'll ever see him again anyway. But being a single mother won't be easy.'

'I'll manage. I doubt I'll get that far anyway.'

'What do you mean?'

'The real reason I don't want to tell Luke is because I may not carry this baby to full term. I've had so many miscarriages, and the doctor told me my chances of giving birth were slim. I can't put him through that again. He's suffered enough.'

'Oh Anna, I hope that doesn't happen. It would be too cruel.'

Anna attempts a smile. 'Wouldn't it just. But there's always hope. I'm going to do everything I can to keep myself and my baby healthy, and who knows what will happen. At least this time I only have myself to worry about. And the hospital will be able to support me, as they know my history.'

Susan wipes a tear from her eye.

'Are you crying?' Anna asks.

'I'm just happy for you. I have every faith in you, and I'll get Mum to add you to her prayer list.' Susan's mum has the biggest heart and is the most fervent churchgoer Anna knows. 'She's always had a soft spot for you. I'm sure she'll get her knitting needles out when I tell her the news.'

'Don't tell her yet; I don't want to jinx it. Just say I need some good vibes. Now eat that cake, for goodness' sake, and let's talk about you. What's been happening in your life since we last met?'

CHAPTER TWENTY-ONE

ANNA

2016

Anna leaves the flat and walks. She has no destination in mind; she just lets her feet take her along the road – anywhere to get away from the four walls of her flat, which crowd in on her and make her want to scream. She can't imagine having lived there with another person; it seems barely big enough to contain her, and it certainly doesn't have enough room to hold the grief that spills out from her and leaves poisonous trails. 'You're lucky to be alive,' the doctor said, and she wanted to scream at him. *Lucky* isn't a word she's ever been able to apply to herself. Instead she smashed her fists into the walls over and over until the nurses came and sedated her and she slipped into blissful oblivion.

Later she was seen by a psychiatrist, an angular man in a suit with a clipboard and an irritating manner of rubbing his nose as he waited for her to answer his irrelevant and intrusive questions. He was so far removed from her life that she simply stared at him and waited for the allotted hour to pass. He dismissed her with his signature added to several prescriptions, and she was discharged with a paper bag full of medicine and a belly full of emptiness. She dropped the bag into a bin on the way home. If she took those pills back to her flat, she'd swallow them all, and she wanted to give herself one more chance. To her surprise, buried deep under her despair is a refusal to give up. Surely there must be another way.

This time she shares her experiences with nobody, not even Susan. She's signed off work for a month and lies in her flat for the first two weeks grieving for her baby and accepting that she will never be a mother naturally. She can't go through this again. In the third week, she rouses herself from the bed and sets about rebuilding herself. She drinks tea and eats toast spread with thick peanut butter for protein as she watches television. When she can no longer ingest another programme on doing up her non-existent home, she switches channels and watches a documentary on surrogacy, where young women offer up their wombs to couples unable to conceive a child. The programme is all about couples, and she's unsure whether she would qualify. She wonders about surrogacy. What is to stop her finding someone to carry a child for her? Is it legal? So many questions she has to seek answers to. Adoption might also be a route open to her. Research will occupy her, stop her mind from going into dark places.

This time next week she has to be ready to go back to work, but it's possible now she has her mojo back. She will have a child by some other means, she knows that now, and that's enough to get her on her feet again and stepping back into her life.

She walks past a row of shops and sees a woman in the window. She looks dowdy, depressed, and she's stunned when she realises it's herself. She needs a good haircut and colour if she's to avoid curious questions when she goes back to work next week. She calls her hairdresser to make an appointment.

The receptionist is bright and bubbly and her voice is up and down like a song.

'You're in luck, we're very quiet next week. Let me see when your usual stylist is in. Ah, she's only here on Wednesday and Thursday next week.'

'Friday is best for me.' Anna settles on 3.15 for a cut, colour and blow-dry and breathes a sigh of relief when she hangs up. She wants to avoid her usual stylist, who on her last visit had just found out she was pregnant and was determined not to have the baby. Anna squirmed through the conversation, unable to hide her dismay that this woman had the thing she wanted most in the world yet was determined to throw her chance away. Now she doesn't want to be reminded of her loss. She's feeling better, but not *that* much better. She regrets telling Josie so much about her personal situation; superficial chit-chat is one thing, but she couldn't bear the loss of her baby to be fodder for salon gossip, along with holiday plans and highlights.

By Friday she's been out every day and is fitting into her old life again. Taking one day at a time, one hour at a time gets her through, and a haircut always improves her well-being.

She passes the trendy salon on the corner, where the walls are sheets of glass and the clients can be seen in various states of bleaching and chopping, heads leaning back over bowls, and continues to the smaller salon further along the street, which offers more privacy. As soon as she enters, however, she'd give anything for those glass walls, which would at least have afforded her advance warning that her usual hairdresser is on reception, her baby bump barely fitting into the small space behind the counter. Her hair is vibrant pink, and matches the pink jumper she wears under her work apron.

'Anna,' she says, broad smile on her face, 'it's your lucky day.' That word again. 'I had to switch my hours around at the last minute so that I could go to my antenatal class – bloody baby dictating my schedule as ever – so I can do your hair after all.'

Anna plays out a scenario in her head where she bolts out of the salon, calling to apologise when she gets home, feigning the sudden onset of illness. But already her coat and bag are being taken from her and a black gown is being placed around her neck, as if they know she is in mourning.

'Can I get you a tea or coffee?' Every time Anna comes here it's a different youngster making drinks, sweeping up hair and running errands for the stylists. The smell of hairspray and chemicals tickles her throat, which is still dry from the shock of seeing Josie.

'Just water, thanks,' she says.

'What are we doing for you today?' Josie pulls up a chair. 'You'll have to excuse me sitting down more than usual,' she says, rubbing her stomach. 'I get so tired, and it's hard to stay on my feet for long periods.'

'She should be at home,' the male hairdresser who is cutting long blonde hair into layers at the next station chips in. 'But she won't listen to us, you know what she's like.'

Anna doesn't want to talk about it, but she can feel Josie's bump pressing against her, see it looming at her in the mirror. There is no escape. She pushes discarded clumps of hair around the floor with her feet.

'You decided to keep it then?' she asks once they are over at the wash basin, away from the others. 'Last time I was here, you were talking about not going through with the pregnancy.'

Josie nods. 'I did. But I'm still not sure it's the right decision. The father doesn't want to know, and he left me.'

'That's harsh.'

'He made it clear he didn't want children when we first got together. Told me on our second date. Such a romantic. I never wanted kids either. This wasn't meant to happen. But I kept putting off making the appointment because I thought he'd change his mind and maybe it would be interesting to have a kid, just the one. Now I've left it a bit late. It's a right mess.'

Interesting – the word outrages Anna, as if having a child is some kind of experiment to be abandoned at will if the appeal wanes.

Back in her seat, she focuses on her own face in the mirror, her skin washed out against the black gown, and wonders why she is being punished by not being able to have a child, while Josie, who clearly doesn't want to be pregnant, manages it without even trying. The unseen powers running the world are unfair. This is what prevents her from praying.

'You all right, love?' Josie asks, and Anna sees she is frowning back at herself.

'I've got a headache,' she says, 'so I'm not feeling very talkative.' She asks for a magazine, hoping Josie will take the hint, but Josie keeps up a steady stream of conversation as she cuts Anna's hair, her voice rising to cover the sound of a hairdryer. Images blur into the text as Anna stares at the magazine and tries to zone out from the conversation, whilst nodding her head every now and then as if she's listening. But it's impossible to tune out. Imagine not wanting to be pregnant. Life is so unfair.

'Anyone who tells you being pregnant is great is a liar,' Josie says, combing Anna's fringe over her eyes, forcing her to close them. If only she could close her ears instead. 'Morning sickness is the worst, and it wasn't just mornings for me. Honestly, it's like my body has been invaded by aliens and there's nothing I can do about it. I'm only four months in, and now the sickness has stopped, I can't stop eating. I'm massive already – I'm going to be the size of a house by the time it gets to the birth. I'm already panicking about all the stuff I'm going to have to buy – where is all this extra money going to come from?'

'Can your parents help?'

'You obviously haven't met my parents. Total waste of space they are. No wonder I'm always attracted to useless men. He's proved to be no better than they are. I'm moving out before my due date; I'll set up somewhere on my own. So no, it's just me on my tod.'

'You'll get some kind of child allowance from the government, won't you? Family credit? Something like that.'

Josie nods. 'I need to look into all of that. Honestly, it's such a pain. I can't believe all the hassle this is causing me. If only I'd followed my gut instinct when I first found out about it.'

Anna twists the ties of the voluminous gown around her fingers. Josie is selfish and completely uninterested in the baby. Tears spring into her eyes and she fakes a cough, prompting the junior to rush over with another glass of water. This small act of kindness makes her want to open her mouth and howl. The girl comments on her haircut and Josie explains what she's done, while Anna stares at the thick clumps of her hair on the floor and composes herself.

Josie is blow-drying her hair now, and in no time Anna is at the desk and settling her bill. She shows her disapproval of Josie by leaving the junior assistant a more generous tip. Despite the irritation the selfish woman has aroused in her, however, her head feels lighter and she welcomes the way a good haircut makes her feel. These experiences are part of life, and she must learn to get through them. It makes her more determined to be a better mother when she eventually is one; women like the hairdresser are always going to exist, and she can only lead by example. And who is she to judge, after all? Who knows how the experience will affect her when the time comes?

She steps out of the salon, away from the chemical smells and the noise of chatter and hairdryers and ringing phones, and takes a deep breath of welcome fresh air. The little girl who has started appearing in her mind smiles at her. *Don't give up on me.*

CHAPTER TWENTY-TWO

ANNA

2017

Anna already prefers the new area. Away from Luke, away from her devastating loss, where nobody knows her. In only two days she's discovered walking routes, shops, and cafés, although she's yet to meet any neighbours.

She chooses the park today. It's a decent walk, taking around twenty minutes to get to down the back streets, and the park is a glorious space to explore, with a café where she can sit with a drink and look out over the boating lake. She takes a book and a bottle of iced water with her, as the weather promises to be sunny today.

As she walks, she mulls over the pros and cons of moving. It's been over a year since her split with Luke, and it's been a while since he popped up in her thoughts every day, like a jack-in-the-box with a broken lid, bursting out when she least expected it and setting her thoughts spiralling downwards. Time *is* a healer. It used to annoy her when well-meaning friends came out with such platitudes. *You have no idea*, she'd say, nodding. But going for days without even noticing she isn't having intrusive thoughts, that's the key. She doesn't need a man to prop her up; she's managing OK, at least on that front.

Children are everywhere in the park. Families are taking rowing boats out on the lake, parents queuing patiently with their little ones jumping up and down at their sides, like dogs straining on a leash. In the distance, the playground is busy. No longer the familiar see-saw, swings and roundabout that she remembers as a child, but fun structures with ropes and ledges to clamber on. She didn't realise it was half term, and she was lucky to get a table.

A group of runners pass, chatting loudly. Mothers with babies and dogs stroll by. Perhaps she should get a dog. She seriously considered it for a while – a small companion that would be considerably less demanding than a child – but it always comes back to the need deep in her gut, which hasn't gone away.

After the last failed pregnancy, she channelled the boundless energy that was just waiting to be used into researching her next step. Age is still on her side – she's only in her thirties and she wants to make use of her relative youthfulness. She has so much to give as a mother. She's ruled adoption out; there are too many uncertainties and procedures to go through. Today, here in this spot where the sun is stroking her face and she's immersed in the sounds of the outdoors, the voices of both adults and children, dogs barking and running feet, she feels sure that she is emotionally ready to take on a child. A surrogate is her latest plan. Not through her GP; she wants to have total control. Finding the right person is the challenge, being able to trust them. The plan is in its infancy and gives her something to focus on.

In the distance a woman is approaching along the path, pushing a buggy. She's wearing tight jeans and a red hoodie. The buggy veers towards the grass every so often and she jerks her arm to make it swerve back into position. She's still quite far away, but Anna can see she's holding her phone with one hand, hence the erratic steering.

A flash of irritation spoils her good spirits. When she has a baby, it will have her attention one hundred per cent. She plans to give up work when the child is small, hence her decision to work as a temp. She's had several different administrative roles, accruing favourable references along the way, and her current placement suits her perfectly, plus she's been saving money with her virtually non-existent social life. Instead she spends her evenings doing embroidery – she's good at it and finds it therapeutic. When the time comes, she'll be able to step away for as long as she needs.

The woman is closer now; she has stopped on the path and is studying her phone. The way she looks and moves is familiar – she reminds Anna of her old hairdresser, only without her flair. She shudders at the memory.

She doesn't use that hairdressing salon any longer. Even if she hadn't moved out of the area, she would never have gone back. In fact, she hasn't bothered with any hairdresser for a while, growing her hair out of its former layered style, preferring to pull it back into a ponytail. It's neat enough for the office, and she's letting the highlights grow out.

After that last appointment, she rushed home and buried her face in her pillow, howling at the injustice of it all. She often wonders whether she did something terrible in a former life to be treated so unfairly in this one. Once she'd calmed down, though, she gained a bit of perspective. The hairdresser, Josie, was entitled to her thoughts and decisions, and who knew what kind of background she'd had. She'd hinted at a dysfunctional family, and her own life was a struggle too. Anna recognised that she'd overreacted, but her decision not to go back to that salon seemed justified for her own emotional protection.

However, she hadn't bargained on the chance meeting she had with Josie a few months later. She was returning home from the supermarket on the bus, seated at the back, the only passenger, her bags placed on the seat behind her, when she spotted the other woman getting on. She thought about jumping off, but the bus was already moving, pulling out into the traffic. Josie swayed and grabbed a pole to steady herself. Her bump was enormous; she had to be almost due.

Don't look up.

Josie looked straight over, giving her a weary smile.

'Anna,' she said. Anna was surprised she'd remembered her name. She must see hundreds of clients, and Anna hadn't exactly been talkative last time. 'Fancy seeing you here. Not being funny, but you look as if you could do with a haircut.' She looked at Anna's stringy hair, which needed a good wash. It was at the time when she was missing Luke and letting herself go with the misery of being single and childless.

Anna shrugged. 'I'm a bit broke, to be honest.'

Josie heaved herself into the seat across the aisle, manoeuvring her impressive bump into position, leaning back against the window so she was facing Anna. Anna squeezed into the corner of her own seat, wishing she could disappear. She couldn't take her eyes away from Josie's stomach, feeling compelled to ask the inevitable 'When's it due?'

'Three weeks,' Josie said, 'and it feels like three months. Each day is hell. My back and legs are killing me, and it's costing me a fortune in clothes as I never seem to stop growing. I can't wait to have my body back. I bet it's going to take forever to shift all this revolting weight.'

'But it will be worth it in the end.' Anna imagined other people must have said the same thing to this selfish woman who appeared to have no filter on her mouth.

Josie grunted. 'Will it, though? I never wanted a kid in the first place. They say history repeats itself, don't they? My mum didn't want me; she tried to get rid of me and cocked that up like she does everything else in her life.'

Anna gripped the arm of the seat. She wouldn't put it past Josie to announce that she'd tried to do the same, and she couldn't bear to think about it.

'This is your chance to do motherhood in a different way,' she said. She still had three stops to go, but she rang the bell, anxious to escape.

'Are you getting off so soon? That's a shame, we haven't had time for a proper catch-up.'

Anna stood up, hanging on to the rail as the bus lurched around a corner. Josie held her stomach and made a groaning noise. 'Wish I was getting off too, but I can hardly walk at the moment. My ankles are enormous. Don't ever get pregnant, it's the pits.'

Anna gripped the rail harder to stop herself from striking out. *How dare she.*

'Look after yourself,' she forced herself to say, 'and good luck with everything.'

'Yeah. Cheers, mate.'

She moved down the bus towards the exit.

'Come and get your hair cut when I'm back,' Josie called. 'I'm going back to work as soon as I can. No way am I getting stuck at home for anyone.'

The woman is pushing the buggy again now, and as she approaches the café, Anna realises that it *is* Josie. She can't believe her eyes. This isn't Josie's area, and Anna never expected to see her again. The terrible things she said about being pregnant were bad enough, but the ingratitude she is displaying now she is a mother is astounding. Anna hoped that when Josie had the baby, she'd fall in love with it and realise what nonsense she'd been spouting about not wanting it. She knows she will fall in love with her own child the minute she sets eyes on it.

She grips the wooden table for support and cries out as a splinter drives into her skin. She tries to pull it out, the skin angry and red. All the grief and pain from her pregnancy is welling up inside her.

She puts on her sunglasses and turns away so that only her profile is visible. Now that she can see Josie up close, she is shocked at the change in her. The pink hair has grown out, and is long and greasy. Her sweatshirt is faded and drab, and her trainers are muddy. Gone is the confident woman who took pride in her appearance. She's still talking on the phone. 'I'm taking the brat to the playground,' she says.

Brat digs into Anna, hurting more than the splinter, and she wants to shove Josie in the chest. *You have a baby!* She can't resist a peek as the buggy passes by, so close she could reach out and touch the bundle under the blanket. The baby's face is barely visible, and Anna thinks the child might be too hot. If Josie isn't caring for herself, how on earth can she look after her baby properly?

As Josie passes, her back to Anna now, Anna picks up her bag and follows, drawn by a desire to see the baby close up, check that it is all right. It could be a girl or a boy, impossible to tell. She doesn't mind whether her own baby is a boy or a girl, or wants to express how they see themselves in a different way.

She hangs back, not wanting Josie to see her. Children's voices fill the air as Josie walks past the disused public toilet block and round the corner into an open field. Anna hovers behind the toilets, obscured from view. On the far side of the field, two little girls are running in circles, squealing with laughter. A man chases them, and a woman stands watching them, a pile of bags at her feet.

Josie's phone rings, and when she answers, she looks across the field and waves. 'I see you,' she says. The woman waves back. Josie attempts to push the buggy over the grass, which is muddy and patchy. The wheels dig into the ground and the buggy almost tips over. Josie looks at her friend again, then back to the path, glances around the empty field. Afterwards, Anna feels a twinge of guilt, because Josie did at least check there was nobody hanging around; she wasn't completely reckless.

She heaves the buggy back onto the path, not noticing the furry penguin that falls onto the grass, and puts the brakes on. Then she glances around once more.

'Don't move,' she says to the baby, as if it can climb out of the pushchair and follow her, then she runs across the field, calling her friend. 'Terri, Terri, wait up.'

As soon as Josie leaves, the baby starts to grizzle. Josie has reached Terri now. She points back to the buggy and Terri looks over, then they start talking, turning away. Anna is rooted to the spot. How can someone abandon a baby like that? Anyone could grab the child and there is not a soul around to see. The baby is properly crying now, and Anna's fury and indignation at Josie being such an ungrateful mother who clearly never wanted this child spills out of her. She picks up the penguin and approaches the buggy.

The surprise at seeing a new face peering in makes the baby stop crying for a moment, the tiny mouth open in an O shape, big eyes staring. So perfect. Anna's heart melts. Nothing else matters.

'You're OK now,' she says, jiggling the buggy to calm the child, holding up the penguin. 'She'll be back soon.' She looks across to Josie, who is having an animated conversation with her friend. They both have their backs to her. She looks around again to see if anyone else shares her concerns, but this end of the field is empty. Can this really be happening? She feels for her phone and takes a photograph of the abandoned buggy, the group of oblivious adults in the distance.

The baby makes a noise and holds out a hand to grab Anna's finger. She decides it's a little girl: she's dressed in pink, and Josie is exactly the sort of woman who would conform to stereotypes. Josie herself wears a lot of pink. The tiny fingers grip hers and the baby's skin is cold. She looks to Josie again; she's not even pretending to keep an eye on her child. She doesn't deserve to have her. This little girl could do so much better.

Her fury propels her. She releases the brake with her foot and the buggy jerks forward. A bag full of baby stuff weighs it down, and it's heavier than it looks. She stares across at Josie once more to give her a chance to stop her, then she pushes the buggy out of sight around the closed toilet block and along the path into the woods.

CHAPTER TWENTY-THREE

ANNA

2017

Anna holds her breath as she pushes the buggy along the bumpy track, stopping only to remove the bag from underneath and hoist it onto her back. The baby fixes her with her gaze, and Anna drinks in her features. She must be two months old, she calculates, her mind working fast, running over what is happening, not quite believing what she has done. Josie clearly didn't want this baby, and Anna has been waiting for what feels like her whole life. She knew she would know when the time was right; this wouldn't have happened if it wasn't meant to be. Anna is a great believer in fate. She likes to believe that a greater power is guiding her life, steering her to make the right choices.

She has to stop herself from looking behind her, convinced she is being followed, her heart in her mouth as she anticipates the firm hand on her shoulder, the shattering of her dreams. But it doesn't come. On her doorstep she allows herself a casual glance behind her, up and down the street, but she sees no person, no car, no camera. She breathes out and tries to control her jittery hand as she pushes the key into the lock.

She eases the buggy over the front doorstep and into the hallway. It just about fits. She puts the brake on, then removes the bag and takes it into the living room, talking to the baby the whole time. 'I'm not leaving you, darling, I'm still here.' She dumps the bag on the sofa and rushes back to the hall, not wanting to take her eyes off the child for a minute. She won't be one of those mothers. She leans over the buggy and peels back the cover.

She is transfixed. The little girl is wearing a pink Babygro with flowers all over, and she pummels her legs up and down, making the pram bounce. Her fingers with the tiniest pink nails are spread out and her arms stretch towards Anna. Anna's breath catches in her throat. She's perfect.

'Look at you, beautiful.'

The baby watches her with serious eyes, kicking her feet. Anna recognises those eyes as belonging to the little girl she can sometimes picture in her mind. Wisps of brown hair cover her head, and she has a tiny mole under her left eye. This was meant to be. She lifts the warm bundle with the utmost care, as if she is a delicate china ornament, and cradles her to her chest. She smells of talc mixed with baby sick, and she makes little snuffling noises into Anna's shoulder. For those few moments Anna's thoughts stop racing and her head is completely clear as she holds her child for the first time.

'Hello, Evie. I've been waiting for you. I've been preparing for your arrival.' She takes her into the tiny box room, where everything she has bought over the last few years for her baby is packed up and labelled. Cans of pale yellow paint are piled under the window. 'Your carrycot is in that big box there, but we don't need it yet. For now we'll have to improvise. We won't be staying here. I'm taking you out of this dirty city; we'll go somewhere green and clean, where you can breathe fresh air and we can afford to live somewhere nicer. You'll be sleeping with me for the moment, and you'll always smell fresh and clean. I won't leave you alone, don't you worry. Good mothers never abandon their children.'

As evening falls, she closes the curtains against the darkening sky. Evie sleeps in the little bed she has made up in a drawer from the dressing table. Anna goes through the bag from the buggy. Everything she imagines a baby might need is in it, even down to a bottle of powdered milk, and for the first time, she wavers. Has she got this all wrong? Is Josie a good mother? Is she taking this child away from someone who cares? But in the side pocket she finds a note. The name Jacky Redish is written on the envelope in capitals, but has been crossed through and the name Josephine scrawled instead.

> I know it's been tough for you lately, but lots of mothers will have had thoughts about not wanting their babies, wanting to give them away like you've been telling me. Don't be so hard on yourself. I know it's tough for you at your age, when all your friends are going out clubbing – you're bound to feel as if you are missing out. Plenty of time for that later! You'll soon learn to love her. This bag has everything you need to make it easier for you. Every mother needs one. I've tried to think of everything, but some things you'll need to replenish quite soon. Don't forget what I told you. Please don't give up. She needs you. This is what I wish my mother had given me, God bless her soul.
>
> Love, Aunt Jacky

The envelope is crumpled and tea-stained. It helps Anna believe that she *is* doing the right thing for Evie. As she guessed, Josie never wanted the baby. The child must sense it and this can't be the best start for her. *She doesn't want her.* A crime, in Anna's eyes. Fear grips her at this thought: she is the one who has committed a crime, but for the right reasons.

She wonders what name the baby had before. It's for the best she doesn't know. She switches on the television, and Evie jerks in her sleep at the sudden noise. Anna lowers the volume, undecided whether she can face the news. She's scanned her phone and social media, but nothing has come up yet about a missing baby. Her heart has been beating like a drum from the moment she took hold of the buggy. She takes a herbal supplement to calm her down. It has no effect.

The ten o'clock headlines come on. There's been a gang shooting in a northern town, the government are defending a controversial new housing bill, but nothing about a disappearing child. The local news headlines are announced next: rubbish piling up on the streets again, a special report on policing in the capital ... She sits through the whole programme just in case. She has to be prepared.

She switches to the news channel to watch the headlines scrolling endlessly across the bottom. BREAKING NEWS: CHILD ... The screen freezes, the buffering circle appears and Anna's heart pulses harder. She hugs a cushion to her chest. The picture returns and BREAKING NEWS: CHILD POVERTY REACHES NEW HEIGHTS scrolls past. She switches off the television set, then pulls down all her blinds and checks that the door is locked. Her phone doesn't ring and nobody knocks at the door.

Evie wakes up and starts to cry. Anna lifts her out from under the covers. Her body is warm and her nappy needs changing. She carries her through to the nursery and lays her on the plastic mat. Despite reading up on how to change a nappy, her hands shake a little, as she's anxious to get it exactly right. Having no younger siblings, she's no experience of learning from her own mother, but she's careful to be gentle when she touches the baby's soft skin. Changing the nappy comes surprisingly easily to her, and using the mat for the first time gives her satisfaction. Luke used to say it was tempting fate, buying all these things in advance, and later he'd say it was futile and pointless; now she can see he was being cruel, knowing her weak point and pressing on it.

She's too wired to sleep, and every now and then a huge panic engulfs her. What on earth has she done? What if Josie is missing her child and desperately worried? Even if she wanted to, she can't possibly undo what she has done; returning the baby is not an option. She's crossed a line and nobody would understand. Not only that, but she's not sure she would survive the loss, not again. Giving her back voluntarily ... No, Evie needs her.

She lies on her side watching the baby, who barely moves. At first she constantly holds her hand up to Evie's mouth to check she is breathing, but when Evie curls her hand around her finger, she leaves it there, calmed by the tiny twitching movements the baby makes as she sleeps. Has Anna harmed the child by taking her from her mother? Has Evie already bonded with Josie? She sits up in bed, clutching her head. What she has done is terribly wrong, criminal.

In desperation she replays every conversation she has ever had with Josie, and satisfies herself that she cannot recall a single positive comment about being a mother. Josie never wanted the child, and seeing her in the park just confirmed that the baby was an inconvenience to her, a nuisance to be tolerated. Anna has to believe she has done the right thing.

She doesn't sleep, and by the end of the night she has come to terms with what she has done. She will let fate decide. If the police come for her, she will willingly accept her punishment. The street outside is silent; the only sound is an occasional snuffling from the makeshift cot, which melts Anna's heart. She is sad for Josie, that she was unable to love her own child. Anna will make up for this, and deep down she is sure Josie will thank her for it.

. . .

The hammering on the door doesn't come the next morning either, and by the end of the week Anna is sleeping better, only waking when Evie needs her. With every touch, every bath, every cry, every feed, she watches and learns; her hands stop shaking and her heart rate calms down. She gives notice on the flat, and starts to hunt online for a new place to rent. On Saturday morning she hears a vehicle pulling up outside and she knows it is happening, the police are here, but when she drags herself over to look out of the window, she sees a removal van. Two doors down, the neighbours are out in their front garden, surrounded by boxes. Anna goes back online, continues her search.

She finds a property far away in Shropshire, an area she has always wanted to visit. It's a tiny two-bedroom flat, one of two properties above a draper's shop in Ludlow, a small town with a castle. She has the first-floor flat; the second floor is currently empty.

She's only been there a couple of weeks when she hears a commotion on the stairs. She peeps through the spyhole, dreading the heavy tread of a police officer, but a young woman with a huge rucksack on her back and carrying a suitcase takes the stairs up to the top floor. The rest of the day is full of the commotion of the new tenant moving in. That evening, a loud rapping at the door makes Anna jump. She peers through the spyhole to see her new neighbour. She's tall and athletic, with a lovely smile that lights up her face.

'Hey, I'm Tess. Sorry about all the noise today, I've just moved in upstairs, though I'm sure you worked that out your-self. I'm starting at the college in Shrewsbury next week.'

'Hi, I'm Anna. I only moved in recently myself.'

'Are you on your own too?'

'It's just me and my baby daughter.'

'That's so cute. I love babies. Look, I promise I'm going to be a good neighbour. I won't play loud music or anything young people are supposed to do. And if you need any help at all, I have twin five-year-old brothers, so I'm pretty good with kids.'

'Thanks. That's kind of you to offer.' Anna can't imagine ever leaving her baby with anyone else, but it's good to know the offer is there, and she warms to Tess immediately. 'I hope Evie doesn't disturb you too much. She's a good sleeper, and these walls seem pretty solid. The road isn't too noisy at night. I like living here so far.'

'I'll invite you up for a cuppa when I'm more settled.'

'That would be lovely.'

Anna doesn't go out much to begin with, organising her shopping online. Every day she watches the television news and follows the London news stories on her tablet. Still no word of a missing baby. Every day she expects a hammering on the door, a police car screeching to a halt outside, but nothing. Evie settles into a routine and doesn't appear disturbed in the slightest. She rewards Anna with gummy smiles, and Anna understands why she needed to be a mother, the maternal love she has always dreamed of flowing through her veins.

Tess invites her upstairs, and over the next few months they become good friends. Anna confides in her about Luke, telling her how he changed his mind so suddenly about being a father and she moved here to start again. Slowly the stillbirth dissolves from her memory, and Evie becomes the child she was carrying. She stops watching the news and starts planning her future. She learns how to deal with the jolt of fear that can strike at any moment, to sit with it and let it pass, remind herself how loved and cared for Evie is. The lack of news must mean Josie didn't want the child. She wishes she knew for sure, but clearly this is impossible, so she has to accept what her gut is telling her.

'You're such a good mother,' Tess says. 'It comes so naturally to you. I hope I'll know what to do when the time comes.'

'Oh, you will. It's terrifying at first, but instinct kicks in.'

Anna basks in the praise and her confidence grows. She

deserves this life. She takes Evie for long walks and explores the local countryside.

One day a few months later she has a specialist hospital appointment back in London, and after much deliberation she decides to go. The bus takes her past the salon. She's upstairs, Evie asleep in her sling, and she cradles the child's head as the bus stops at the traffic lights. Standing on the corner smoking a cigarette is Josie, immediately recognisable on account of her pink hair. Not the beaten-down Josie Anna last saw on that fateful day, but the bubbly Josie of old. She's chatting with a fellow hairdresser, and the smile becomes a laugh – a proper throw-back-your-head belly laugh. The shard of anxiety that has never quite left Anna melts away, and she laughs too.

CHAPTER TWENTY-FOUR

ANNA

The knock at the door never comes, and Anna stops looking over her shoulder. Her needs are frugal, and she buys clothes for herself and household items from charity shops and pound shops. One time when she is out looking for summer dresses for Evie, she discovers an old sewing machine, selling at a bargain price. At school she uncovered a talent for needlework during her design and technology lessons, and the teacher encouraged her to keep it up when she left. She fully intended to, but life took over and she became interested in other pursuits.

At another shop she finds a beautiful piece of flowery material, which she turns into a pretty dress for Evie and a headscarf for herself. The process of sewing occupies her overactive mind, and she amasses material from charity shops and offcuts from department stores. Soon she is making all their clothes. Tess requests a dress from her and refuses to accept a freebie, offering to babysit in return, but Anna doesn't go out in the evening. She says they'll do it some other time; it's safer that way. Evie doesn't go to nursery, but she will have to go to school in a couple of years' time. Anna thought she might miss living in the city, but she loves it here, far from the pollution and noise, away from anyone who could possibly know her.

With Tess's encouragement, she works hard at making clothes and is amazed at how demand grows. She takes online courses, teaching herself how to create and market her own brand. Soon she is taking commissions and earning enough money to keep the two of them and save a little for their eventual move to a house with a garden.

Evie adores her mother and grows into a happy little girl. People stop Anna in the street and tell her how delightful she is.

After two years, Tess's course finishes and she moves abroad. Anna worries she'll be lonely without her, but it is only a week or so later that she meets Seb in the park.

She never expected to meet such an attractive man. He's a web designer, tall, sporty, with a winning smile. His blonde hair flops across his forehead and Anna feels flustered, wishing she wasn't wearing her old faded dungarees and a scrap of material tied around her head to keep her hair out of her eyes. But the mutual attraction is instantaneous, and within a month she can't imagine life without him. Their relationship develops quickly, but not once does it feel wrong. Anna prides herself on her instincts for people, and has a lightning antenna where her daughter is concerned, but Seb gives her no reason for concern. He loves Evie as much as he loves Anna herself. They find a house with a lovely garden, and Seb sets up his own website design practice. Anna's future is thriving, and she discards the past like an unwanted garment.

She has everything she has ever wanted.

CHAPTER TWENTY-FIVE

JOSIE

2017

Josie scrubs the kitchen table, trying to get rid of the milk the baby has spat all over the wood. The baby cries in the next room. *Rosie.* Rosie is the name she was forced to put on the birth certificate when she was barely able to hold a pen without dropping it, let alone decide on something so important. Giving her a name made it real. She cast her eye over the desk in the registrar's office and alighted upon red roses in a vase. The registrar was an unprepossessing middle-aged woman in a cheap navy suit, but even she had a ring on her finger. Josie tried to ignore Valentine's Day this year – all she got in the post was another bill and a load of junk mail.

'Baby's name?' The registrar tapped her pen on the form. A petal dropped from the roses onto the desk in front of her. 'Rosie,' Josie said. In her mind she calls her *the baby*, because it's more honest. She doesn't deserve this child and she wishes she could have done what the baby's father did – legged it as soon as he got a whiff of the pregnancy. The baby isn't a tiny newborn any more – she's growing at an alarming rate.

When you've spent your childhood being shunted around from parent to care home to foster home, and then repeat, when you've changed schools so many times you know there's no point bothering to make friends, when you don't even know what your accent is because you've lived all over the country, it's hard to have a sense of who you are, let alone care for another person. Hairdressing has saved her: it's the one thing she is good at and has kept her going since she left the care system to fend for herself. But she needs to work full time to get the money and the experience to open her own salon one day. And having a child does not fit into that.

The plan all along was adoption, but she kept putting off making a decision, delaying and delaying, and then the baby came and she still had no plans in place. She tried to explain to the nurses that she wasn't capable of looking after the child, but they wiped her forehead and told her she was still delirious from the medication she'd been given to make the birth manageable. They gave her leaflets and explained what would happen next, and said that if she was still feeling low she must be sure to tell the health visitor at her first appointment. But this was unlikely, they said, because by then she'd be full of love for her baby, who was beautiful and the image of her mother, and what was she going to call her? All Josie could see was a pink wrinkled object with lots of demands she couldn't possibly meet. She was discharged from the hospital with the baby in her arms and terror in her soul. A name would mean there was no going back, and that made her blood run cold.

The wailing gets louder. Josie has fed her – despite what her auntie says, she cannot breastfeed – changed her and given her a toy to play with. Why is she crying? She heaves herself up and goes into the other room as if she's entering a torture chamber. The baby's face is scrunched up, tomato red, and she's about to do that thing where she stops breathing, limbs rigid in the air, terrifying the life out of Josie. She picks her up as carefully as she can. She would never hurt the child, but she is baffled by her. What should she do, how did she let this happen?

She tried to involve the father, but his sister said he'd gone abroad. When she holds the baby, she tries to feel motherly, she wills her body to respond to what she knows is her own flesh and blood, but her heart remains frozen, her emotions numb. She watched a soap opera once where a young mother wheeled her newborn baby to the nearest hospital and left her outside with everything she needed. Viewers wrote angry letters, tweeted their opinion of this character, vitriol or sympathy depending on their sensibilities, but Josie thought it a sensible thing to do. Let someone who cared and could give her a better life have the child.

She's always been determined never to have a family and repeat the mistakes her own mother made. She can't cope with this situation. Her life is falling apart and her energy has been sapped, replaced by a terrible lethargy. She's going to lose everything – her independence, her career – all because of one terrible mistake. Well, two, if you count not getting her act together in time to stop this happening. She sighs out loud and puts the baby into her buggy. A walk should calm her down, surely.

She takes the back streets, not wanting to pass the bars and restaurants she can no longer go to, forced to save her money and spend every night at home as if she were middle-aged already. A breeze blows her hair from her neck, cooling her down, and she pushes the buggy forward at a brisk pace, willing the baby to stop crying. After several minutes, she does, and as Josie walks her pulse returns to normal.

Her phone rings and she controls the buggy with one hand as she ferrets with the other in her pocket. It's her friend Lisa.

'Hey,' she says, switching on hairdresser Josie, full of life and customer service. 'No, I'm in the park, I've been walking for ages, me and the little one out for a walk. Nursery, no, of course not. She's way too young.'

If only. Josie keeps a calendar on her wall and has counted down the days until she can get her child into the local nursery. If she had the money, she'd pay someone to look after her now, but the cost is astronomical, even for just a few hours a day. This is where grandparents come in handy. Aunt Jacky means well, but she's holding down two jobs as it is. Josie has logged on to her savings account to check her balance, done some calculations, but she cannot use that money, she mustn't; owning her own salon has been her dream ever since she can remember, and she won't give that up for anyone.

'Come over later?' she says. Lisa lives a few streets away, still with her parents, also saving money; all she wants is her own place to rent.

'That sounds great. We can get a takeaway and I'll bring a bottle. How's the little one?'

'She's asleep; she likes me pushing her.' It's about the only thing she does like that Josie does. If she hadn't given birth herself, she'd swear this child was nothing to do with her.

Last time Lisa came over, they ordered pizza and opened a second bottle of wine, and for a few hours she completely forgot about the kid. The music was loud, and Lisa was on top form, making her howl with laughter. Then the next-door neighbour banged on the door.

'Can't you hear the baby? She's been crying for ages. What kind of mother are you?' Josie was mortified. The neighbour was right; she wasn't fit to be a mother, but she couldn't see a way out.

'Come round at seven,' she says.

She follows the path along past the café, not wanting to stop now that Rosie is asleep, although a coffee would help her stay awake. As she heads towards the playground, her phone vibrates again. She's switched the sound off so that it doesn't wake the baby; she can't risk setting her off again. She pushes the buggy round the corner, past the old public toilet block.

'Josie, it's Terri.' Her friend's voice is loud in her ear. 'Look to your right, I can see you.'

Josie looks across the field and sees Terri waving frantically. Her twin girls are running around with a man; he must be her new partner, Dennis.

'I see you.'

'Come over here. We've got to get off in a minute, pick up Simon from his football club, but I haven't seen you for ages and I've got that tenner I borrowed off you. Look who's here, Den, it's Josie.'

The little group are right across the field, and there's no path. She pushes the buggy onto the grass and the wheels dig into the ground. The earth squelches underneath her. The wheel is stuck. She pulls the buggy backwards, looking around her. There is nobody else in sight, and it will only take a minute to run across and speak to Terri; she could do with the money for the takeaway. She's always shooting her gob off, suggesting takeaways, regretting it later when she's hunting for loose coins in her pockets. She puts the brake on the buggy, checks around her once more.

'Don't move,' she says to the baby, calling Terri's name as she turns and runs across the field to her friend. She looks back at the buggy when she reaches her. She'd never have got across the field with it.

She's with Terri barely five minutes. They exchange a few words, and she gets the tenner. She turns to run back across the field, then stops short. The buggy is no longer there. Did she put the brakes on? She pictures it rolling down towards the pond, and runs. She races over the grass, slipping and breaking her fall with her right arm, landing awkwardly on her hand. The buggy still isn't there when she gets up, her jeans covered in mud, her heart in her throat. She runs around the toilet block, which is deserted. The sound of music reaches her ears, and she sees a large gathering across the park and a few people crossing in that direction. That explains the lack of people around her. She goes back to where she left the buggy. She feels her back pocket. Her keys and cash card are there, her phone in the other one. She runs up and down the path, looking everywhere, but there is no sign of the buggy. She scans in all directions, but the baby has gone.

The baby has gone.

Josie's heart skips a beat.

She's alone, for the first time in weeks, since she left the hospital after giving birth.

Alone. An icy fear grips her and she scans the area again, but there is no sign of a runaway pram, no sign that a baby was ever here. Her whole body is shaking.

She's alone.

She's forgotten how that feels.

It feels good.

She feels light-headed, scared, excited at her own thoughts. Forbidden thoughts.

Her baby bag is underneath the buggy, the one her aunt sent her when she saw how inadequately prepared Josie was. It contains everything a person with a baby could possibly need.

'Are you all right, love?' An older woman appears in front of her. 'Have you lost something?'

'I've lost my ... my friend. Have you seen anyone around here in the last few minutes?' She can't bring herself to mention the baby.

'No,' the woman says. 'Most people are over at the talent show. I only saw one other person besides you, a woman pushing a buggy.'

'That might be her. What colour was the buggy?'

'Navy blue.'

'That's them, which way did they go?'

'That way, along the path towards the street. Are you sure you're all right?'

But Josie doesn't stay long enough to reply; she runs in the direction of the buggy, of *her* navy-blue buggy, she is sure. She reaches the park gates, but there is no sign of the buggy. She stands in the street getting her breath back, a stitch digging into her ribs. She hasn't run for ages, and her chest is tight. Tight with fear, and exhilaration.

The lady saw a *woman* pushing a pushchair. A woman wouldn't hurt a child. Josie herself would never have hurt the baby; that's what made her feel so trapped. A man would have been different; she would have worried, would have called the police. She knows the gender bias is wrong, but some men do not act as they should.

The police. She doesn't want to call the police. That would make it real. She doesn't like the police, not after the way they treated her mum, who impressed on her that they must be treated with suspicion.

Someone she knows must have taken the child. That will be what has happened. She'll go home, wait for a phone call. She'll wait a while, and if the call doesn't come, she'll take action then.

The phone doesn't ring.

More time passes.

Josie doesn't like to bother the police.

At 7 p.m., the doorbell rings. She always knew Rosie would come back; it was too easy this way. Nobody need know what a terrible person she is, what shameful thoughts she had, how relieved she felt that the baby had gone, if only for a little while. Was she such a bad person for wanting a few hours' respite?

Lisa stands on the doorstep, raises a carrier bag to show her she's brought alcohol.

Lisa. Of course. She'd forgotten she'd invited her.

'Where's Rosie?' Lisa asks. 'Can I see her?'

Afterwards, Josie will tell herself she hesitated.

'Didn't I mention? She's gone to her aunt's for the night.'

But there is no hesitation. The words slip out, surprise her. And so the lies begin.

It is as easy as that.

CHAPTER TWENTY-SIX

JOSIE

Josie can't believe her business has done well enough to allow her to open a second salon. Winning a national prize has catapulted her career and she's spent months considering where to place her next branch. Finding the perfect site for her new salon hasn't been easy; rental prices in cities are so expensive and she's reconsidering her options. She spends her weekends driving around the country looking at possible venues.

Sometimes at night Josie thinks about her daughter, wonders who she is now and what she is like, hoping she is loved. The knock on the door that she expected every minute of every day for the first few months never came. She waited a year, then another. Afterwards, when she decided for her own sanity that she must lead her life as if it had never happened, she realised she'd been holding her breath. Initially she wondered, entertained countless scenarios of what had become of her child, the worst of which was that she was being held captive somewhere, and by not alerting the authorities, Josie had sentenced her to a living death. Some nights she woke up shaking, bathed in sweat. But these incidents were rare. Eventually she settled on the only option that wouldn't give her nightmares: someone who'd wanted her had found her. She was happy and well looked after. Deep down in her gut, she believed this had happened, and she was finally able to let go.

Until a couple of years ago, when a television show started up helping relatives find long-lost loved ones, almost every case involving a mother who had given up a child, usually against their will. The thoughts began churning in her mind again. A dark force inside her compelled her to watch the programme, to examine the feelings played out on camera, the years of anguish that separations between parents and children had caused, spreading roots of unhappiness throughout families. She had to believe that her child would never know her mother had abandoned her. She couldn't.

The question burrowed into her subconscious, though, and the dreams began again. If she could only talk to a therapist, she'd ask why this is happening now, when she has reached a place in her life where she finally feels proud of herself. She has her own flat and a successful business, and has done it all on her own, through sheer hard work. The dreams belong to a different person, the young woman she was then. Her childhood of turmoil catapulted her into adult life, and she landed in the world forced to make decisions she wasn't ready for. She was at a crossroads in her life, and she chose the right path. Having a child was out of the question, and she grabbed at the solution. Nobody was hurt.

Or were they?

In the dreams, this thought underpins the reel of horror that creates pictures and scenarios in her mind, the starring character always a little girl who is the image of Josie herself when she was a child. Curly brown hair, wide blue eyes, the distinctive mole under her eye stretched as her mouth opens in a scream. This morning, after a dream that wakes her in the early hours, she gets up at five, wraps herself in a blanket and sits out on her balcony, watching the night transform into morning. As the dark skies become clearer, so does the thought that has eluded her, teasing her, hiding just out of sight like the fox that slips through the trees in the half-light, leaving the watcher unsure of what they have seen – indeed, whether they have seen anything at all. For the first time in her life, she is in a place where she could look after her daughter, *if* she were to find her.

Obviously that is impossible. Real life isn't like the television show, a machine that relies on a team of professional research experts and financial backing to dig out these people who have been lost for so long. Sure, she could poke around a little, but with no clues to go on, it would be a complete waste of time. Plus, how could she explain losing her child? She is a strong woman, and she must find a way of stopping the dreams, enabling her to work for the life she has striven for. Only one aspect of her plan eludes her: a partner. It's not a deal breaker – she's content as she is – but having someone to support her would help keep her mind off the past and focused on the future, where it belongs.

The street lights are off now, and the sky is awakening. She unfurls the blanket from around her shoulders and steps into her flat.

It happens when she least expects it. Her aunt Jacky is back in touch, and Josie has taken her up on her open offer to stay at her holiday flat in a seaside town in North Wales. It's a duplex flat with a balcony looking out towards the sea. Just the break she needs. She drives back on a Monday, and decides to stop for lunch in Ludlow, a place Aunt Jacky recommended she visit and where a hair salon is up for sale. As she leaves the motorway and approaches Ludlow, she's forced into an abrupt stop. Rounding a bend faster than she should, she brakes hard as ahead she sees a woman step out into the road, hand raised to stop the traffic. A daisy chain of small children make their way in front of her, two at a time, hand in hand. They look to be aged around five, and are all wearing high-vis vests. Josie notices how well behaved they are as they line up on the pavement.

The little girl closest to her car turns and stares at her, and Josie jerks as if she's been struck by lightning. The child is the image of her at that age. Brown curly hair to her shoulders, delicate features, and a tiny mole under her left eye. Her expression is serious, and she appears not to blink. Josie's been told she blinks less than other people; being able to out-stare an opponent was a useful tool when she was being hassled in the care home or the school playground, and a teacher told her once that she mustn't stare so as it frightened the other children. She runs her hands through her own hair, straighter and naturally darker now, reaching her shoulders, then grips the steering wheel so hard her knuckles turn white.

The girl turns her head and the children move away, following the teacher down the road. They're wearing a uniform of blue sweatshirts and blue trousers or skirts. Josie sees *Greenside School* emblazoned on the bag one of them is carrying. A horn beeps loudly behind her, and she shakes herself out of her daze and drives on.

In her flat, she chucks her keys and bag onto the sofa and rummages in the sideboard for the box of old photographs she keeps there. The contents are pitiful; she didn't have doting parents taking reams of photos and sticking them in albums to show off proudly or hand out to visiting relatives and friends. There is one photo of her from her childhood, a school portrait taken when she was around seven, in a small cardboard frame. She found it at the bottom of her mother's underwear drawer when she was living with her for the last time, and shoved it in her bag when she had to pack up and leave.

Her hand shakes as she holds the photograph up to the light

and stares at it, studying her features. Heart-shaped face, brown hair falling in a tumble of waves, a smattering of freckles across her nose. Her blue eyes command attention, wide open, framed by dark lashes, the expression too solemn for such a young girl. She was expecting to dismiss the likeness of the little girl in the street as fanciful thinking, but as she conjures up the memory from this afternoon, the child's solemn stare, she is more sure than ever. Could this be her baby? Could it really be her? The desire to find out incentivises her and a new plan begins to take shape.

After the sighting of the child in Ludlow, there's only one possible solution – a small Shropshire town wasn't exactly what she had in mind but a different kind of challenge has been presented to her now, and the new salon will be the perfect camouflage. She engages an estate agent to rent out her London property for six months, and rents a small flat in Ludlow. She finds the venue for her new salon on one of the main streets in town, and already in use as a hairdresser's, it is perfectly placed on the street of cafés and boutique shops. The current owner is moving to the country and anxious for a quick sale. Josie gets a good deal on a lot of the fixtures and fittings, and she embarks on a total refurbishment to get the salon up to the standard she requires. She retains a few of the staff on a temporary basis, hoping to keep them on if the salon is a success. She'll train up a good manager so that when she goes back to London she can leave the salon in a capable pair of hands. When she's not in the salon her thoughts are occupied by one thing only – finding that little girl again.

Greenside School isn't far from the crossing where she spotted the children, and the next afternoon she walks through town and waits in a small park situated across the road. She arrives way before three o'clock, as she's unsure what time the school day ends. She buys a coffee from a stand in the park and wanders up and down, killing time until she sees parents beginning to arrive. Cars pull up nearby, engines running. At 3.15, the doors burst open and a stream of children dart across the playground to the waiting crowd. Cars begin to move, blocking her view, and she curses as she cranes her neck to see through the gaps. Parents and children leave, and when there are only a few left behind, she admits defeat and leaves the park.

She's back the next time she's off, once again in the park, knowing what to expect this time. She's wondering how many times she will have to do this before she admits defeat when she spots her, the little girl from the other day, running towards a woman with long blonde hair, arms outstretched and holding a piece of paper with splotches of colour on it. The woman takes the painting and hugs the child, then takes her hand and leads her off down the road.

Josie follows, hanging back, letting a couple of people get between them but keeping her eyes fixed on her target. Being tall gives her an advantage, but it's frustrating because she can't see the woman's face. She wants her to turn around, to get a look at her, but at the same time she doesn't want to be seen herself. The child skips along the pavement, chattering all the way, tempting Josie to get closer so that she can hear her voice, but she keeps her distance, crossing the road when the woman lets go of the child and she runs ahead along the pavement and stops in front of a house. The mother is close behind, opening the gate, and they disappear down the path and around the back.

The house looks large, set back from the road, the front garden well maintained. Josie wants to be able to turn away and leave the child to the life she has, which on the surface looks to be a good one. But she thinks about the way the little girl skipped along, right foot kicking out at an angle, about the hair, the build and the feeling in her gut, and she is convinced this is

Rosie. She *knows* this is Rosie; why else would she have uprooted her life to move down here? Josie believes in fate – Aunt Jacky's invitation was what set off this particular chain of events, and led to this incredible sighting of her daughter. Of course it was meant to be; it would never have happened otherwise.

On the walk home, she tells herself to leave it. Even if she is right – and she knows that is a big flashing neon *if* – it can only lead to heartache and will bring the life she has constructed for herself tumbling down.

Next morning, though, she's outside the house before seven. She's wearing a black hoodie, leggings and a baseball cap, and holding a bottle of water, to make it look as if she's running. She tries to run a little of the way to make herself out of breath, which is pointless as she has no idea how long she'll have to wait, and her unused muscles scream with indignation.

Fifteen minutes later, the front door opens and a man emerges, carrying a school bag. He unlocks his car and puts his bag in the boot, then goes back to the house, returning with the girl running behind him. Once she is strapped into a car seat, he walks across to open the gate. Josie begins jogging, crossing the street to get a closer look. As the car cruises past her, the little girl watches her from the back window with those big solemn eyes.

Josie stops running as soon as the car is out of sight and doubles over, clutching her sides, breath wheezing out of her, shocked by both the sudden exertion and what she has just seen. Her stomach heaves and she thinks she's going to be sick. She is even more convinced now that this is Rosie, being driven by a good-looking man who presumably she sees as her father.

Josie has an idea.

CHAPTER TWENTY-SEVEN

JOSIE

SIX MONTHS AGO

Josie goes back to the school on her next free afternoon, in her car this time. She's now convinced this child is her daughter, and the handsome husband falls right into her plan. But it's Anna Delaware who turns up to collect the girl, and Josie sits open-mouthed at the wheel, unable to believe what she is seeing. She didn't know Anna that well, but now she thinks about it, she remembers bumping into her on the bus, barely able to walk with her swollen belly. She sits at the wheel, stupefied. That this woman from her past is here, of all places, is so incredible. She was right about fate. *She* stole her child. Anna Delaware, an insignificant client from her London salon? Imagine if she hadn't decided to stop in Ludlow that day – and that was also because of Aunt Jacky. Josie can't stop shaking her head in disbelief.

Was she planning this all along? She wishes she could recall more of their conversations in the salon, but she's had so many clients, it's impossible to remember details. Knowing that it was Anna who took her child from under her nose has made this personal, though, and she's even more determined now to see her punished.

It's Anna who collects the little girl every subsequent time Josie goes back to the school after that first bombshell moment. Josie hides her hair under a baseball cap and watches her from the car. Seeing the woman hug and handle her daughter gives rise to unexpected feelings in her. Anna is a criminal who brazenly snatched a child from the street, and she deserves to be punished. Contacting the police is out of the question, though, as Josie didn't alert the authorities in the first place. She might end up in nearly as much trouble as Anna. Looking back, she feels sorry for her younger self. Making bad choices and not being able to deal with the aftermath, suffering from extreme anxiety with nobody to confide in, she took what appeared to be the easy option when the opportunity presented itself. Even now, she can recall the relief she felt as the unwanted responsibility of motherhood was lifted from her.

But she's no longer as young, and her life is different now. She's a responsible adult with her own home and a career. Why shouldn't she have her daughter back?

She takes her time. This has to be done right. Over the next few months, she builds up the foundations of her plan. She instructs her stylist, Chloe, to give her a new look, and emerges with a neat black bob. She adds a pair of funky glasses with clear lenses. Even she doesn't recognise the character looking back at her from the mirror. Pleased with her new appearance, she swings into action.

The husband becomes her target. She follows him to work and watches him go into a building on the high street. On the plaque outside she discovers that he works at Forrester Web Designs. The offices must be on one of the upper floors. It doesn't take much hanging around for her to establish that he visits a particular coffee shop frequently, and she makes a point of hanging out there too. After a few weeks they know one another to say hello to. All she has to do is engineer an 'accidental' encounter with him, away from his office.

The significant encounter happens easily. She's about to finish work one evening when she sees him leaving his building, walking fast, with a determined look on his face, towards the pub where he and others from his office go on a regular basis. She watches through the window as he goes to the bar and buys a pint of beer, exchanging a few words with the barman. He leaves his drink on the bar and heads off to the bathroom. Before she can talk herself out of it, she's inside ordering a drink. By the time Sebastian returns, she's at a table by the window, a gin and tonic in front of her. It takes him a while to spot her, but once he does, she makes sure he won't forget her.

Several weeks of flirtation follow, made all the more thrilling by the illicit nature of their relationship. As she gets to know him better, she loves the way he talks about his stepdaughter as if she were his own. Fantasies began weaving themselves in her mind. What if he were to learn the truth? Surely they could make it work for them? It's not impossible.

She works hard to seduce him. Most of their meetings take place at the same pub, but surely it's only a matter of time before he gives in to his obvious lust for her? Finally it happens. He comes back to her flat and they spend a passionate few hours together before he scurries off just before midnight.

She continues seeing him for several months.

The weekend away in a country hotel is meant to be special. She booked it a while in advance, told him to keep the date free as it's her birthday. It isn't, but these minor details aren't important and can be sorted at a later date. The hotel has an award-winning restaurant, which she knows he'll love. He wanted to be a chef when he was younger, but his life took a different direction. They arrive separately – unnecessary, she thinks, but she indulges him as he's paranoid about his wife finding out.

She gets to the room early, smiling to herself when she sees how luxurious it is: a four-poster bed, a huge walk-in shower with gorgeous toiletries, and two fluffy white dressing gowns hanging in the wardrobe. She changes into the cocktail dress she bought specially, spending way more than she could afford, and orders a bottle of champagne to be brought up when Mr Forrester arrives. She signed in as 'Josephine Forrester', unable to resist the thrill it gave her to use his name. While she waits on the softest leather sofa she's ever sat on, she has to remind herself what this is all about and what her end goal is. Falling in love and discovering that he is a fabulous lover were unexpected benefits, but she mustn't lose sight of what she wants – what she is, after all, entitled to. The excitement of anticipation fizzing in her stomach, she contemplates telling him everything, allowing herself to imagine how it would be if he were overjoyed at her news. But the downside is still too much of a threat: judge him wrongly and she could lose everything.

She knows something is up when he's late. He's normally a stickler for timekeeping. He once explained to her that his parents were extremely disorganised, and one summer when he was ten they managed to miss the plane to their holiday on a Greek island. They couldn't afford replacement tickets, and the family spent a miserable weekend in a caravan instead, the only accommodation they could find at such short notice. It rained all week, his parents argued, and he'd rather have been back at school with his friends. He'd never been late for anything again once he was able to run his life on his own terms.

He looks terrible when he finally arrives, and her stomach fills with dread. He could easily have sent her a text and avoided the trip to the hotel, but he says he owes it to her to tell her in person. He loves her and desires her, he continues, but he loves his wife more. That is the crux of it. In her hour of need, he's realised how scared he is of losing her. If she were to find out he was having an affair, she'd be devastated, and he can't face the thought of it.

'What about my devastation?' Josie yells at him.

'I'm sorry,' he repeats over and over, and she sees that he is. His emotion is genuine; he is a man torn in two.

'It's easier if we don't contact one another, for a while at least,' he says. 'I know I've behaved terribly; you don't know how awful this makes me feel, but I can't risk losing my wife and daughter.'

She's not yours! The words tantalise her tongue, but she can't say them aloud; that would risk losing him forever. This is her trump card, and it has to be played at the right moment.

She's not hers either. That will be the knife digging in, twisting. *She's mine.* And those are the words that will kill.

She gets used to seeing him passing the salon, always scuttling, head down lest, heaven forbid, he catch her eye. Does he really think looks can kill? That would be too easy. After some time has passed, she is glad it ended the way it did, because falling for him made everything so much harder. His rejection has enabled her to move on. His cowardly dumping of her means that soon her tears are tears of anger rather than heartbreak. He has fuelled her determination, and she is able to pick up the phone and start with the threats as has always been her intention. But now there are two people to punish instead of one.

When Seb confronts her at the fair, she can see his fear. Fear that she is going to be difficult, that she will pursue him again, try and pick up where they left off. When he accuses her of being behind the phone calls, she successfully swats his concerns away as if they are an irritating fly. Fooling him with that random drummer is a genius bit of luck. Everything is set up now; it is time to move on to the final stage of her plan.

It is time to claim back her daughter.

CHAPTER TWENTY-EIGHT

EVIE

My tiger has wiggly stripes of blue and yellow. He looks like a flag I saw on the classroom wall when we did about countries. The blue bits are hard to colour in and I went over the line two times but Mummy says it's good.

The tiger I saw today had a grumpy face like Mrs Cotton's cat. That's why I wanted to stroke him, to make him smile, but the nice lady said that was wrong. Grown-ups are funny. She said the sign said not to touch the animals, but I can't read all the words yet. I can read some and I know all my letters. Mrs Cotton's cat likes being touched even with his grumpy face. Mummy says all faces are nice, but sometimes Mummy is wrong. Like she was wrong about the nice lady. She had black hair and Mummy has long blonde hair. Most daddies have short hair except for Alistair Brown's dad, who wears a bun. Mummy says it doesn't matter how daddies wear their hair.

The colouring is for my teacher, Mrs Gold. Mrs Gold is my best teacher. I like Mrs Thomas but sometimes she has a scary face when she gets cross. I don't like it when people get cross. My best friend Daniella said her daddy is always cross with her mummy and sometimes he hits her. That bit is a secret. I don't tell anyone my secrets. I wouldn't like it if my daddy did that. My daddy is a kind man like the kind lady.

Mummy goes inside to get the washing. She's going to hang it up on the line and the wind will blow it dry. I won't try and help her because I can't reach so high and the washing fell down last time.

A wasp is buzzing near my head and I get up. I don't like wasps. I can see Mummy's back is in the kitchen, but Mummy doesn't like wasps either. Big boys are playing in the park behind the fence. Mummy and Daddy say I mustn't go in the park on my own. I mustn't go anywhere on my own. When I'm big I will go in the park and on the swings all by myself.

Somebody is talking and I make myself be still so I can hear.

Evie, Evie.

Somebody is calling my name. The somebody is behind the tree. I like hiding games. Daddy plays the best hiding seek, but he hasn't played it with me for the longest time. He's always busy working.

Evie, Evie. Over here, Evie.

I'm very good at hiding seek. The tree is big and the best place to hide. Behind the tree is a hole in the fence, and behind the hole and the fence is a park. The somebody is wearing a green dress and she has black hair. She looks like the Sleeping Beauty lady. She's playing hiding seek and is hiding behind the tree. The Sleeping Beauty is a princess. The Wicked Witch has black hair too, but she is a bad lady.

I look at the house where Mummy is inside. Mummy tells me not to say bad things about people even if I don't like them like Holly Denver. Holly Denver is mean and says rude words when Mrs Gold can't hear.

I look again. The nice lady from the animal park is hiding behind the tree. I can see her and I run and surprise her.

'Catched you!'

'Shh,' she says. 'It's a secret game. You're such a clever girl. Now we have to hide together.'

I think about Mummy.

'But Mummy—'

'Shh, Mummy is coming to look for us. This is Mummy's game.'

'Mummy doesn't like hiding seek, but Daddy does.'

'Today she does. And look who wants to hide with us.' She puts her hand into her bag and pulls out a furry tiger. It's the toy tiger I wanted from the shop window in the animal park shop, but Mrs Thomas said we mustn't go in because of the coach and the clock and all the mummies and daddies waiting at school for us to come home.

Tiger is orange and black and smiles at me. I go to the lady. It is dark and cold behind the tree because the sun is hidden. I can't see the house from here. I can't see Mummy. It's a good hiding place.

This lady is Sleeping Beauty because she is good. She gives me the tiger and he's soft and I cuddle him. The lady takes my hand.

'I know a better hiding place,' she says. 'Come on, Rosie, we have to be quick.'

The lady says I'm rosy because the sunshine is making me pink. Daddy goes all pink when the sun is hot. Mummy makes us put horrible smelly cream on to stop the sun burning us.

The lady walks very fast and I try to go fast too. I can see another tree to hide behind but the lady pulls me past it. Tiger is soft in one hand but the lady's hand isn't soft like Mummy's is. It's scratchy. My tummy feels wobbly.

'After this we can get an ice cream,' the lady says. I like ice cream lots and lots. The lady *is* nice.

Mummy would think she was nice if she met her. I know she would.

CHAPTER TWENTY-NINE

SEB

Anna stands in the doorway, arms hanging down, leaning against the door frame to hold her up. Seb feels his energy drain away, the reality of what she has told him like a thump to the chest.

'Sit down,' he says. He can see she's in shock, but he makes no move to help her. The words coming out of her are poison, and he can't touch her, not now. Not until he understands what she is saying.

She sits on the sofa, not looking at him.

'This can't possibly be true, but it is, I see it in you. You stole a baby.' He shakes his head. 'Did you steal a baby, is that what you're telling me?'

She nods, still not looking at him.

He shakes his head again and walks across the room, then back. He doesn't know what to do. He is hot; his face is burning.

'How could you?' His voice is different, stuffed full of tears. 'You stole a baby, you took someone else's child and passed her off as your own, and you've been doing it for years.' He paces faster. 'You're a criminal, you should be locked up. You stole a baby, for fuck's sake, Anna, how could you?'

She flinches and swipes the tears from her face. He never swears at her. He stops pacing.

'You took a baby, who is no longer a baby, she's Evie, a little girl I've watched grow and develop and ...' His voice catches in his throat. 'I love her. She's my stepdaughter, my daughter.'

He's shouting, bursting with pent-up emotion from his confession about his affair. With her revelation it is too much to contain, and he smashes his right fist into the wall. Pain shoots up his arm and he cradles his hand to his chest. Now he is crying too. 'I love that little girl so much, and she'll be taken away from us, she *has* been taken away from us, by a woman who must be crazy with grief.' He slumps onto the sofa. 'What have you done?'

'I'm sorry,' she whispers, 'I'm so sorry.'

'What good is that?'

His energy has gone, smashed into the wall with his fist. All he can see is Evie, and Jo; he pictures her face screwed up with fury when he finished with her. What is she capable of? What will she do to Evie?

'Your hand,' Anna says, 'it's bleeding.'

He stares at her. 'We have to find her.'

She nods, gets to her feet, returns with a tea towel. She goes to wrap it round his hand and he snatches it from her. 'Don't touch me.' She flinches, steps back, sadness on her face.

'What are you going to do?'

He presses the tea towel to his hand, his skin stinging. The pain helps. He needs to think. His energy returns, fuelled by anger. She's staring at him and he wants to push her into the wall. He would never hurt a woman. He has to get out. He jumps to his feet and runs into the hall.

'Where are you going?' She comes after him. 'Let me explain.'

'Leave me alone.'

He grabs his car keys and slams the front door behind him.

Anna's cry rings in his ears. No doubt she wants to explain herself, to make him understand, but it won't excuse what she has done, even though she only ever wanted the best for the baby.

His phone vibrates as soon as he's in the car but he leaves it in his pocket. He has to find Evie. He revs the engine and chucks the bloodstained tea towel onto the passenger seat. He drives too fast into Ludlow, swearing at any traffic that gets in his way. He's sweating. A map slides to the floor as he takes a corner too fast, a plastic bottle rolls around the floor and he forces himself to slow down. He has to get to Jo's in one piece; he has to find Evie. He can't think about Anna right now, focuses on Jo. *What is she capable of?*

He parks outside her flat, glancing up at her window as he slams the car door. The last time he came here she stood naked at the window as he drove away; it was this brazenness that jolted him to his senses, and he knew then what his next move had to be. His phone vibrates with another message. He can't deal with Anna right now. He leaves the phone in the car and forgets to lock the door.

He rings the doorbell, hammers on the black door. He stands back and looks up at Jo's window. The blinds are drawn. What is she doing in there? He rings a different bell, hears footsteps. A man opens the door, peers round the frame, his face wary.

'Can I help you?'

'I'm looking for Jo. The upstairs flat. Can you let me in?' He steps forward but refrains from pushing the door open and charging up the stairs to where Evie might be. The man makes no move to let him in.

'Jo moved out. Took all her stuff and disappeared a week ago. She's selling up, so I heard.'

'Can I go up?'

The man frowns. 'Have you got a key?'

'No.'

'Then there's no point. She's not here and I won't let you break the door down.'

Seb comes to his senses. 'No, of course not, sorry. Do you have any idea where she's gone?'

'No. Like I said, she just took off. Didn't even say goodbye. I'm surprised, we got on OK. I hope you find her.'

'Yeah, thanks.'

Seb sits in the car, deflated. His stomach churns and he feels sick. Where has she gone, and what has she done with Evie? Was this premeditated? His hand throbs. His phone rings and he grabs it; it might be her.

'Where are you?' Anna says. 'I've been going out of my mind.'

'I'm looking for Evie. I haven't found her.'

She's silent for a moment. 'We have to call the police.'

'No, wait, don't do anything, I'm coming back.'

His eyes rest on the bloody tea towel, and a tremor overtakes his body.

CHAPTER THIRTY

ANNA

Anna watches the car disappear too fast down the street. Her guts have been ripped out from her. Seb's revelation that he'd been unfaithful winded her, but telling him the secret she's guarded for so long knocked that into the shade. What has she done? He reacted so badly; he'll be on his way to the police now. Will she ever see Evie again?

Evie. Oh God, please let her be safe. She runs inside and calls Seb. The phone rings out. She tries again, no response. She texts him. Repeats.

Please don't go to the police. We'll never see Evie again. Help me find her.

I love you.

Where are you? I'm sorry. We must stick together.

Help me find Evie I'm begging you.

She stares at the screen, which stays blank, then hurls her mobile onto the sofa. This isn't helping get Evie back. Should she go to the police before Seb does? She sinks to the floor. She can never go to the police; she has to find Evie herself.

Her daughter's face looms in her mind, and she looks up through tear-misted eyes and sees her own reflection in the glass of the window. A pathetic heap, snivelling on the floor. That person isn't going to do what is needed. After what she has gone through to get Evie, she will never stop fighting for her. Yes, she is in the wrong, but she loves that little girl fiercely and will never let her be harmed. She may well be guilty in the eyes of the law, but Josie didn't try and find her daughter – she can't have done, because Anna would have seen it in the news. She didn't want her, and she told Anna as much, moaning while she cut her hair like the selfish individual she was.

Anna jumps to her feet and retrieves her phone from the sofa. Still no word from Seb. He doesn't need to tell her how much he loves Evie; he's shown her that every day since he first met her. He's hurting, and she understands. They need to be strong for one another, to outwit Josie.

She phones him, and to her relief he answers, tells her he's coming back.

While she waits, she goes online, googles Josephine Redish but finds nothing. Periodically over the years she's looked up the name with her heart in her throat, feeling compelled to search just in case she has missed anything, but nothing baby-related has ever come up. Now the search brings up a news article about the success of Josie's Ludlow salon, and Anna's heart thumps as she clicks on a photograph, sees a picture of her as she is now, this woman who seduced her husband. She barely looks any different from how Anna remembers her, her hair still pink, though no longer the brazen pink of old – more tasteful lilac streaks as she moves with the times. Anna looks into her eyes, desperate for some kind of clue. *What have you done with my daughter?*

She hears the front door opening, and stiffens. What if it's a trick and Seb has called the police, and now they are here to arrest her? She thinks she might pass out, but it's just Seb who stands in the doorway, staring at her. She has never seen him look so awful. His hair is sweaty and his skin has a greenish tinge as if he has just been sick. Maybe he has. She hates that she has done this to him.

'Come and sit down.'

He obeys her, a shadow of the man who stormed out barely an hour ago.

'Where did you go?'

'I went to her flat.'

Anna daren't breathe.

'She wasn't there. A neighbour said she moved out last week. Unexpectedly.'

She feels herself deflate. 'I appreciate you going. I know this is hard for you.'

He shrugs. 'It doesn't matter. Finding Evie is what matters.'

She takes his hand, nods, choked up. She bites her lip to stop herself from crying, can't stop nodding. 'Let's concentrate on that. Can we agree to put our feelings aside, focus on finding her? We need to stay strong, make a plan.'

'Yes. Pool all the information we have about Jo, try to out-psych her. Most importantly, we have to do what she says.'

Relief floods through Anna. Together they can do this.

'Why doesn't she want to go to the police?' Seb asks.

'Because she didn't report her baby missing.'

'What? Tell me again what happened, why you did it.'

'I'm not making excuses for myself, what I did was wrong, but my intentions were good. I wanted what was best for that baby. I'd been driven mad with grief, losing my partner in the process. I don't expect you to fully understand, but it's like how I imagine an addiction must feel, a craving inside you, gnawing away at your soul, where you want something so much and no matter what you do, no matter how much money you spend or how hard you try, the thing you want – like that first high – is never attainable. You think you have it, only for it to slip through your fingers like a handful of sand.

'Josie was my hairdresser at the time. I saw her regularly; it was during the time when I was trying to get pregnant. She wasn't like a friend or anything, I didn't confide in her, but we chatted. And she used to talk openly about how she didn't particularly like children and couldn't see herself ever having any. That's why I stopped confiding in her about my own situation, because I didn't expect her to be sympathetic, to understand. When Luke left and I was at my lowest point, getting my hair cut wasn't something I bothered with. Eating enough to survive was a drag, let alone worrying about my appearance. When I began to feel better, and took myself in hand, I made an appointment. I deliberately chose a day when Josie wouldn't be there, but she had changed her shifts around so she was there after all. She complained about it, how she hadn't intended to get pregnant and had then left it too late to have an abortion ...' Anna swallows hard, overcome with emotion, recalling the anguish she felt sitting in that salon with the smell of peroxide poisoning the air. 'I felt so cheated; life was so unfair.' She looks up at Seb, tears brimming in her eyes. 'Hideous self-pity, I know. I just want you to understand why I did what I did.'

He nods, his face set. 'Just tell me.'

She focuses on her breathing before continuing, telling him how she encountered Josie unexpectedly in the park, how she didn't seem to care about the child, abandoning her to go and see a friend, not even bothering to keep the pushchair in her sight.

'I took her baby. I know it was wrong, though I told myself at the time that it was better that I had taken her – anyone could have snatched her and hurt her, whereas making sure she was cared for was my priority. It was a moment of madness, and as soon as I got back to my place the full force of what I had done hit me. I assumed it was only a matter of time before the police came calling. But there was nothing. No missing baby story in the news, no headlines, nothing online or in the local papers. I couldn't understand it. One day, two days, a week went past, and somehow I got away with it. Josie didn't go to the police, don't you see; she didn't want the child. It hampered her lifestyle and threatened her career. Someone had taken her baby and she saw it as the solution to her problems. At least that's what I think must have happened; what other explanation is there? A missing baby would have been all over the news, you know what it's like. Especially a pretty white baby like Evie.

'I never heard or saw from Josie again until the phone calls started. I've always dreaded there would be some kind of payback but hoped I was wrong. Josie must have changed her mind. But how she found us – I have no idea about that. I've always been so careful about stuff I put online, security. It's just incredible that she is here.'

'Christ, what a mess.' Seb gets up and walks over to the window. 'I can't believe any of this. Snatching a child, not wanting a child. It's mind-boggling.'

'You must hate me.'

'I don't know what I think. But for now I'm going to do what we agreed: forget all that, put it aside until we know that Evie is safe. That's the only thing that matters now, that poor little girl. No matter what you've done – that you're a *criminal* ...' His voice falters, his face a mask of anguish. 'Jo worries me. She's never been particularly stable, and we have to make sure she doesn't hurt Evie.'

'We can't go to the police.' Anna's voice is a whisper.

Seb paces up and down, running his hands through his hair. 'I agree – for now, at least. Jo's message indicates she won't hurt Evie as long as we stick to her demands, and she was very clear about not involving the police. I think she still has feelings for me, no matter what she says, so we can play on that, let her believe I'm on her side. We'll need to be very clever, keep one step ahead of her.'

'What makes you think she has feelings for you?'

'When I spoke to her at the school fete, I could just tell. If I can make her believe I feel the same, we could trick her into giving Evie back.'

Anna nods, but a chill creeps down her spine. What if Seb has feelings for Josie that he's keeping from her? How does she know she can trust him, especially now that he knows what she's done? Her body shakes and she folds her arms tight, not wanting him to see that she is falling apart in front of him.

What if he's in on this with Josie, and it's a trick to take Evie and run so the three of them can start a new life together?

CHAPTER THIRTY-ONE

ANNA

'We can't just sit here.' Anna wanders around in a daze, hugging her arms to her chest. She goes back to her laptop and refreshes the screen. 'I was looking Josie up,' she says. 'We need to know everything we can about her.'

'She looks very different there,' Seb says. 'Her hair is longer. She wore it in a bob when I first met her. You saw her too, at the fair.'

'This is older; this is how she looked when I first knew her. Her hair was pink usually, a bit wacky, that's why I didn't recognise her at first. Other than that, I knew it was her. Just didn't want to accept it.'

'Did you find anything useful?'

'Not yet. We need to work out where she's gone. Did she mention anywhere, any friends, family?'

'She hasn't got much of a family. I'm not sure she'd go to them in a crisis.'

'Friends? Think, Seb.' She wants to shake him. His affair has made this worse. So what if Josie was trying to trap him, to get closer to Evie; he should never have got involved with her.

'The first hours when a person goes missing are crucial, everyone knows that.'

A memory fills her mind, those dark moments when she returned to the flat, each minute stretching out, endlessly watching the news, blinds down, lights off, counting down the hours until she could breathe again, knowing with each passing day that she was a little bit closer to getting away with what she had done ...

'We can't just do nothing. I'm going out of my mind here. What about her salon? Would she have taken Evie there?'

She opens the link to the salon, cursing the slow internet connection as the page takes an age to connect. The picture of the familiar shop frontage. There's a list of staff, each with a photo. 'Is she particularly friendly with any of these girls?'

'I don't know,' Seb says. 'She never mentioned any of them.'

'I'll ring the salon. Ask if they've seen her.' She locates her phone and dials the number. 'Shit.' She paces up and down.

'What is it?'

'The usual please hold nonsense, your custom really matters to us, blah blah blah.' She waits impatiently, sighs with relief when the receptionist answers.

'Cutters, good afternoon, this is Julie speaking. How can I help you?'

She switches the phone to speaker.

'Please could you put me through to Jo?'

'I'm afraid she's not in this afternoon. Can I help? Are you a client of hers?'

'Not exactly. I've been trying to get in touch with her but she isn't answering her phone and I'm a bit concerned about her.'

'No, sorry, she's taken a few days off.'

'You don't happen to know where she's staying, do you? Or anywhere she might go. I have some urgent news for her. That's why I need to get hold of her.'

'Hang on a minute,' the receptionist says.

After a moment she returns.

'Nobody else here has heard from her, but we'll get in touch with her next of kin just to make sure. Thanks for flagging this up, but I'm sure there's no need to worry; she's a tough cookie is our Jo.'

'So you don't know anywhere else she might go—'

Seb grabs the phone and ends the call.

'What did you do that for?'

'She'll get suspicious. It's clear they don't know anything.'

Anna glares at him. She wants to yell and shout at him for getting involved with Josie, for hurting her so badly, because submerged under the sharp, ever-present pain that is the loss of her daughter is the smaller knife wound of what he has done. How can they ever come out of this? The spark of hope she felt on ringing the salon is extinguished. She sinks onto the sofa.

'That didn't get us anywhere.'

'Not exactly,' Seb says. 'We know she was telling the truth about taking time off, and presumably she's going back at some point.'

'In theory. She's stolen our child. She might never go back.'

'Somehow I doubt it. Her business is her life, she made that clear. You said as much too – how a child wouldn't have fitted into her career path. To give it up now doesn't make sense. It's not as if she's waited until Evie was a teenager, able to fend for herself.'

'Evie would never let that happen.'

'You don't know that, you can't, not if she knew all the facts.' Seb softens his voice and sits down beside her. 'Whatever feelings we have for Evie, the stark fact is that she is Jo's biological child. You took her illegally. Nothing will change that.'

'Don't say that,' Anna says, trying to hold back the scream that she wants to let rip every time she thinks about how powerless she is right at this moment. Hearing Seb spell out their predicament is like one of those television dramas where credibility is stretched and you have to ignore it if you want to continue watching. Is she the only one who sees that she loves Evie more than anyone else in the world, that she is best placed to care for her?

'You look cold,' Seb says, taking a blanket from the back of the sofa. 'Here, put this around you.' He goes into the kitchen and pours himself another shot of whisky. 'Want one?'

She nods. Anything to numb the pain.

'Let's listen to the message again,' she says when the whisky is warming her insides. Action is what is needed, not sitting around like a character frozen on a stage, lines forgotten, waiting for a cue.

'Are you sure?'

'Yes. Play it.'

'I've got Evie. If you go to the police, your dirty secret will be revealed to the world, and you don't want that happening, do you? Wait for further instructions. And remember – don't tell the police, or who knows what I might do.'

'What I don't understand,' Anna says after a moment, filling the space left by the harsh voice, 'is why she would do this now. What's changed, what's made her want Evie now?'

'Yeah, me too. Could it be chance; she just happened to see you somewhere? You recognised her, despite her change in appearance. Most people look fundamentally the same, just older. Or has she known all along?'

'No, she can't have.' The thought is out there, though. What if she has? Out of the corner of her eye, Anna sees Evie's favourite red chair, the one she loves so much she often carries it from room to room. Her heart lurches and she blinks away tears. *Focus. Be strong.* She pours herself another shot of whisky – her last; she needs to be prepared for any eventuality. Not that she needs to worry. Her mind is razor sharp where Evie is concerned; she's had to live like that ever since she first touched that buggy, long ago back in London.

'Tell me about her,' she says to Seb. 'What state of mind was she in when you last saw her – before the fair, I mean?' She doesn't want to spell it out, but she hardens her heart for the details. She has to know why they split up, who instigated it, all those little obsessive details that some people need to know to rub salt into the cut and feel the pain, the hurt. But her reason for knowing is to burrow down into how Josie's mind works. 'If we're going to outwit her, we have to be one step ahead.' She thinks of the crime books she likes to read, the criminal profilers who out-think the perpetrators, delve into their psychology to work out the kind of person they are likely to be and what their next move might be. They both know Josie; that must help. For now she has to put aside any notion that Seb may still have feelings for her, could even take her side. He'll want the best for Evie, she knows that, but she can see he's still struggling to get his head round this situation and work out what is right. Law-abiding Seb; she has to make him see that together they offer the best life for Evie.

Seb swills his whisky round in the glass, watching the golden liquid almost slosh over the side. He puts it down.

'She wasn't happy. It was sudden, from her point of view. She ... she'd booked a weekend away ... Sorry ...'

'Just tell me. That doesn't matter any more. All I care about is Evie.'

Seb flinches. 'She'd booked a weekend break at a hotel, but driving over there I knew I couldn't go through with it. It was as if I'd woken up suddenly, escaped from a horrible dream. I'd just left you and Evie, who I adore – believe me – and I'll admit, I was a little scared by Jo. She was getting demanding, and the hotel was a step too far. We hadn't even agreed to it; she sprung it on me. I told her as soon as I got there that it was over, and left. Told her that I loved you and Evie, that it was a terrible mistake and it was best we didn't see one another again. She didn't take it well. We had words – it wasn't nice.'

Anna can't believe Seb behaved like that. Does she know him at all? No wonder Josie was hurt; what woman wouldn't be at such behaviour? It helps to be an outsider looking in, to be objective. Does she want to be with a man who can act in such a way?

'So you just left?'

He nods. 'She called me right away, but I didn't pick up, switched my phone off. I sent her a long text apologising for my behaviour, saying she didn't deserve any of it. After that, I avoided the café where we first met, avoided going anywhere I thought she might be.'

'And did she ever talk about wanting children?'

'No, it didn't come up.'

'Are you sure? Think. Anything. Did she *like* children? She certainly didn't when I knew her. And she was gobby, she used to go on about them all the time, what a nuisance they were running around the hairdresser's, that kind of observation. She certainly didn't care what people thought of her.'

'I don't remember.'

'What about places she likes, friends she sees?'

Seb sighs. 'I didn't know her that well. She mentioned an aunt once, that's all, but nothing much about her.'

Anna mulls over his words and thinks about the Josie of old. Quick to react, hot-headed, but after the initial reaction when she hounded him immediately after being dumped, she left him alone.

'How long between you ending it and these calls?'

'A good few months.'

'Exactly?' She drums her fingers on the table.

'About six months.'

'Text her.'

'What?'

'I think you should text her again. She's had time to stew for a bit; she must be anxious, no matter that she thinks she is in the right. She hasn't gone to the police, has she? She knows that not reporting Evie missing back then was wrong. She didn't know she was safe, did she? She could have been kidnapped, tortured, worse. So go on, text her.'

He stares at her.

'What's the worst that could happen?' She closes her eyes. 'Scrap that.' She can't go there. 'She won't hurt her, I'm sure of it.'

'What shall I say?'

Anna takes the phone and types: We need to know you're receiving our messages. *Please let us know that Evie is safe.*

As soon as the phone beeps on sending, her stomach is in knots. What if it's a mistake? What if Josie has lost her mind?

The reply is almost instant, and she grabs Seb's hand.

Await further instructions in the morning.

They stare at one another.

'Evie's OK, she has to be,' Seb says. 'I think she wants something other than Evie. It's me she wants to punish. She's building up to it.' He squeezes her hand. 'We'll get through tonight somehow, and if we don't hear anything in the morning, then it might be at that point we have to tell the police.'

Anna goes into the bedroom and throws herself face down on the bed, buries her face in the pillow, welcoming the inability to see, the pillow muffling sound. Evie has been missing for several hours. There are several more to get through until morning. Every second without her feels like a minute. How will she get through the night not knowing what is happening to her baby? Is she hungry, tired, in pain? Tears spill from her eyes and are soaked up by the pillow.

CHAPTER THIRTY-TWO

JOSIE

The toy tiger was a genius idea, and Rosie clutches it to her chest with one hand as Josie pulls her along with the other. Her tiny hand is trusting in hers, but they have to hurry otherwise Anna will see them. Josie was behind the tree for ages, just watching the little girl, curls falling over her face, the tip of her tongue tickling her top lip as she concentrated. It was like looking at a better version of herself at that age, a child who was well fed and loved and happily colouring in a picture. A child who had never experienced the gnawing hunger Josie endured as a child, the desperate need for a hug. Could she really take Rosie away from all this, from the life she had grown up in? Unexpected guilt overpowered her.

'Evie.' She stopped the unwelcome thoughts by putting her plan into action. 'Evie.' Her voice was a stage whisper, the name carrying in the wind. Rosie hesitated, crayon in the air, looked up. Josie called her again. 'I'm over here.'

Rosie batted at an insect in front of her face and scrambled to her feet, looking back at the house before walking down to the end of the garden. Josie could have stayed watching the girl for hours, transfixed by her likeness, so unexpected yet so welcome. The delicate blemish of the mole that marked her out as special. The girl was hesitant, but with the tiger out of the bag, the long-awaited moment unfolded as they crossed the park, leaving the row of houses behind, the shouts of the boys playing football fading into the distance.

'My legs hurt,' Rosie says now, tugging at Josie's firm grip, dragging her feet as if they're attached to weights.

'We're here now, just a few steps more.' Josie rummages in her pocket for her keys, glancing around the street as she arrives at her block. Once inside, she slows her pace, letting go of Rosie's hand and allowing her to climb the stairs at her own pace.

'I'll get you a nice cold drink now we're here,' she says.

'Is Mummy coming?'

'I think it will be Daddy who's coming, not Mummy. He just wants me to look after you while he's busy, and then we can all be together.' When they reach the flat, she helps Rosie out of her coat and gets out the box of toys she picked up the day before at a local charity shop. 'I'll get you some orange juice, and while you play I'll send Daddy a message to tell him we're here.'

'I'm playing with Tiger,' Rosie says. 'We're going to play hiding seek. Isn't Mummy looking for me?'

'No, Mummy's busy, but Daddy is looking. Daddy will find you.'

Once she's poured some juice for Rosie, she calls the house and leaves her message, relieved that nobody picks up. Both of them must know now who she is. She stands in the doorway watching Rosie playing with Tiger on the floor. She talks to him the whole time, telling him they are hiding and all the other animals are looking for them. Every now and then she looks around her, as if her mother could be hiding somewhere in this unknown flat.

Josie opens her laptop and clicks onto a live travel site to check for roadworks, not wanting anything to disrupt her plan. They'll get away early tomorrow; no point in hanging around. She's pretty convinced Anna won't go to the police, but she will try and find them. Seb knows where she lives, but she's got that under control. She'll use the time at Jacky's flat to decide on their final destination. It can't be somewhere too isolated, as everyone will spot the new arrivals; rather a town far enough away that they can get lost. Scotland, maybe; she's always wanted to go there.

Rosie has stopped chattering and is dozing, head against the edge of the armchair, Tiger in her lap. Josie goes to the bedroom and takes the rucksack she has bought for the journey. It's ugly and cumbersome and she wouldn't normally be seen dead carrying such an unfashionable item, which is exactly what she wants. The wig she plans to wear is a short blonde bob with a fringe – not too blonde, but the fringe changes her appearance, makes her look younger. She has a different pair of glasses too, smart dark frames with clear lenses. Jeans, navy-blue jumper and hiking boots complete her outfit. She's leaving most of her clothes in the flat; she can't take them with her, and all she cares about is getting Rosie safely away. She grabs items from her wardrobe: some changes of underwear and a couple of sweatshirts.

'Josie.' Rosie is calling her.

'Coming.' She puts the file of essential documents she's had prepared for a while into the inside pocket of the rucksack and carries it into the hall. She sticks her laptop in too and goes back to the living room. Rosie is sitting on the floor, rubbing her eyes, widening them when she sees the rucksack.

'Are you going on holiday?'

'Yes. Do you like holidays?'

Rosie nods slowly, as if she's unsure, chewing her finger. 'Where's Mummy? I want my mummy now. Mummy thinks I'm hiding behind the tree and I'm not. Is she coming here?'

'She's not coming here, but we're going to meet her and Daddy tomorrow. While you were asleep, I packed my case and Mummy packed yours and hers. We're going to drive in the car and meet her at our holiday house at the seaside.'

'Seaside? I love seaside. Can Tiger come?'

'Of course he can. Mummy can't wait to meet him.'

'Can I talk to Mummy before we go?'

'No, we don't have time.'

'What about Daddy, can I talk to him?'

'Not now, but you'll see him on holiday. You'd like that, wouldn't you?'

'Yes. Daddy likes playing on the beach. We build sandcastles and he splashes in the sea.'

'Daddy will be joining us shortly.'

'I'm hungry.'

A car door slams down below in the street. The noise makes Josie jump. She crosses to the window, sees her downstairs neighbour Nathan unloading his boot. She's relying on him to fulfil his part of the plan. She scans the street, but nobody else is around. She closes all the blinds. It will be dark within half an hour and she'll keep the lights off and go to bed early, then they will be fresh for the morning. Nathan's music starts up. *Yes.* He's so predictable. Her plan is running like clockwork. Nobody will hear a child crying through that racket.

'I'll make us some tea.'

'I don't like tea, I'm hungry.'

'Tea, dinner, whatever.'

'I'm hungry now.'

'You can have a biscuit while I make something.'

'I like biscuits,' Rosie says. 'Jammy ones are my favourite.'

Josie searches the kitchen cupboards and finds an open packet of chocolate digestives. She gives Rosie the packet.

'All of them?'

'Eat a couple and we'll take the rest with us.'

'Mummy doesn't let me eat biscuits. She tells Granny off if she gives me some. Granny is naughty. Granny gives me secret biscuits, but I mustn't tell Mummy.'

'Eat as many as you want.' Josie likes the sound of Granny. Seb's mother, she presumes. He's mentioned that she lives nearby. She sounds more like the kind of woman who would want to indulge her granddaughter, disapproving of her daughter-in-law's whims. Seb told her Anna was strict – she's bound to be one of those fussy mothers who thinks her child is allergic to everything and keeps her closeted from the real world. If Seb does the right thing, she hopes to meet his mother one day, when everything has settled down. If they dare, that is. Everything they do from now on must be done with care, although if they have to keep to themselves and stay away from people, she'll be quite happy with that. Seb will be used to Rosie and her routines, which will make everything easier. If he could be a stay-at-home dad, that would be the best outcome, enabling Josie to concentrate on her new salon. They won't be able to stay around here. Shame. She loves her flat. A fresh start will be best for all three of them.

She checks her phone. She knows they won't dare contact her, not with the threat of the police hanging over Anna. She'll have to tell Seb what she's capable of, and then what will he do? Josie has been going over the possible scenarios in her mind for weeks. She can't remember what a good night's sleep feels like. Now that her plan is in motion, her body is pulsing with adrenaline.

'There are crumbs,' Rosie says.

'Never mind.'

'But I don't—'

'Why don't you watch television? Sit there.' Josie pushes the child down onto the floor and switches the television on. She flicks through some channels. 'Here we are, cartoons, sit and watch that. And don't disturb me while I make us some food.'

Rosie stares at her with solemn eyes, her lips pushing into a pout.

'Don't look so sad. We're having fun, aren't we? I bet you can't wait to go on holiday.'

'No. Not fun. Don't want to go on holiday. I want Mummy.'

Josie grits her teeth. 'Mummy's coming tomorrow, I told you. Now sit quietly and watch the television – look, there are little pigs jumping up and down, you'll like that. And be a good girl and don't mention Mummy again, OK? Or Daddy.'

Rosie's eyes brim with tears. She sticks her thumb into her mouth and looks at the screen. Josie goes into the kitchen and takes a beer from the fridge. She drinks sitting at the table. The beer helps her relax. Rosie hugs the tiger toy and watches the screen; Josie is relieved that she's settled. She'd better not play up overnight. Nerves steadied, she finds a can of baked beans and puts some bread under the grill.

'Tea's ready,' she calls.

Rosie hesitates at the kitchen door as if she's walking the plank. She sits at the table and Josie puts a plate of beans on toast in front of her, then opens the fridge.

'Do you want ketchup?'

Rosie's lips tremble. 'I don't like beans.'

Josie slams the fridge door. 'Yes you do, just try them.'

'I don't like beans.'

For fuck's sake.

'Fine. If you don't like beans, just eat the toast then. Here, I'll scrape them off.' She takes the plate, forcing herself not to snatch it, and scrapes the beans into the bin. 'This is a waste of good food, you know.'

'Mummy doesn't give me beans.'

'Mummy isn't here. And what did I tell you about not mentioning her?'

Rosie starts to grizzle and pushes the plate away, then yells, making Josie jump.

'I want Mummy. Don't want that.' She shoves the plate and it slides across the table. 'I don't want to be here I want to go home. I want Daddy.' She is crying now and kicking her feet under the table.

'Shh, shh, you don't have to eat the toast. I'm sorry I upset you. Mummy told me you don't like beans and I forgot. I'll throw those horrible beans away, they're all gone.' Josie can hear herself talking in a silly voice and can't believe this surreal drama is happening. She removes the plate and gives Rosie some kitchen roll. 'Here, wipe your eyes, don't cry. You're just tired after the exciting day we've had at the zoo. Remember the animals? What fun it was? And Tiger here, he doesn't want you to cry. Give him a cuddle.'

Rosie looks unsure, but she takes the toy and hugs it to her chest.

'Tell you what,' Josie says, 'forget the nasty baked beans. Do you like hot chocolate?'

Rosie nods slowly.

'Why don't you get ready for bed – I've left some pyjamas in your room – and I'll make you a hot chocolate. And if you promise not to tell, you can have some more biscuits. Would you like that?'

Rosie nods.

'Good girl.' She ruffles her hair. 'Off you pop, and I'll come in when the drinks are ready.'

'Yes.' Rosie hesitates.

'It's just down there.' Josie points and Rosie heads towards the bedroom.

When Josie goes in a few minutes later with a cup of hot chocolate, Rosie is sitting in bed talking to the tiger. She looks sweet in the pyjamas, and Josie thinks maybe it's worth it after all. When Seb joins them, he can take over all the boring routines while she concentrates on her business. She can't be doing with all that drama every day. She hands Rosie the hot chocolate, to which she's added a teeny drop of Night Nurse.

'I'm going to bed now too so we can get lots of sleep, and before you know it, it will be morning and we'll be off on our journey. Isn't that exciting?' She daren't mention Mummy in case she sets the child off again. Josie is her mummy now, and she'd better get used to it.

'Can I leave the light on?'

'Of course you can. I'll put this little lamp on here and I won't close the door properly, OK?' The room is at the back of the property and the blackout blinds are drawn; no danger of the light being seen from the street.

Rosie's eyes are already drooping as she drinks the not very hot chocolate, and Josie slides the cup out from her hands as she falls asleep.

Josie decides she might as well go to bed herself, and once she's checked that everything is ready for the morning, she pulls on a long T-shirt. She's brushing her teeth when a loud knock at the door makes her drop the toothbrush.

Shit. She stands still. A shuffling noise, as if somebody is out on the stairs. She switches her phone torch on and tiptoes to the front door. The police would make a lot more noise than this. Nathan texted to say that everything had gone to plan – he'd been quite willing to help when she'd told him she needed to get rid of an unwanted admirer. He'd made it quite clear she was his type; a little flirting was all it took. Seb wouldn't come back, would he? Nerves grip her and her heart hammers against her chest. She stands by the door, listening. If only she had a spyhole. When she gets out of this predicament, she and Seb will have a gorgeous home together: security camera, the works.

'Jo, are you there?'

Recognising Nathan's voice, she collapses with relief against the door. She listens for any sound that Rosie has awoken, but all is quiet. She leaves the chain on and opens the door. Nathan is holding a bottle of wine, and her heart sinks. He's made an effort with his hair, which is smoothed into place for once, and smells of aftershave.

'Mission accomplished,' he says.

'Yeah, thanks, I got your text.'

'I reckon he swallowed what I said. I told him you left a week ago.' He waves the bottle at her. 'Aren't you going to let me in? Thought we might celebrate.' He comes closer. 'I was hoping we could pick up where we left off the other night.'

'No,' she says. 'I mean, yes, it was great, but not tonight, OK? I'm knackered. I was getting ready for bed when you knocked. I've got an early start tomorrow.'

'Me too, but so what. Why not live a little?'

'Look, we'll do this, for sure, just not tonight. But thanks for doing me that favour. I owe you one. I'll ring you.'

She closes the door before he can protest any more. Did he really think she was interested in him? He's done what she asked for and she deletes the messages and his number. Nothing more from Seb, which she takes to be a good sign.

She checks on Rosie before she goes to bed. The child is lying under the duvet looking angelic. She watches her chest go up and down; she's not making a sound.

As she gets into bed, the thud of music comes from downstairs. Nathan's having his party by himself. Making a point, knowing him, but she's still glad of the noise. Lucky she can sleep through anything. Her phone buzzes.

Please let us know that Evie is safe.

She is not called Evie. His wife is behind this message, she can tell. She can't deal with these reminders of her and taps out an answer.

Await further instructions in the morning.

She's just dropping off to sleep when a noise wakes her. She sits up, puzzled, wondering what it can be. Too close to be a cat. A wailing sound. A thumping noise. *Rosie.* She hurtles out of bed, frantic to stop her, no idea what time it is. Why isn't the kid asleep?

Rosie is out of bed, her face red and scrunched up, and she lets out a roar that cuts right through Josie.

'Shh, shh, quiet, quiet, stop crying, I'm here.'

Thank God the music downstairs is still thrumming, not as loud as before but loud enough. Nathan will be crashed out, stoned, no doubt, wallowing in rejection. Rosie continues to cry.

'I'm here, I'm here, are you having a bad dream?'

She nods.

'Come here.' Josie tries to hug her, but she wriggles away.

'No, no, want Mummy. Mummy.'

'Stop it,' Josie whispers loudly. 'Mummy's asleep. We can't wake her now. The sooner you go back to sleep, the sooner you'll get to see her.' Rosie sucks her thumb, tears clinging to her long eyelashes. 'Come on, let's get you back into bed.'

She coaxes the little girl back under the duvet and tucks her up with Tiger. 'I'll stay here with you, just try and get some sleep.'

'Too noisy,' Rosie says.

'It's the bad man downstairs. Try and ignore it.' Under normal circumstances she'd have been down there hammering on the door, threatening to chuck his music system out of the window, but for now she'll put up with anything as long as they get through the night and away from here as early as possible. She endured an evening of heavy metal when she went down with a bottle of wine to butter him up and involve him in her plan. Just the thought of his filthy flat makes her shudder.

Rosie lies on her side with her thumb in her mouth, face still red from her tantrum, far from the way Josie imagined their reconciliation, the two of them cuddling up together, making up for lost time. She breathes a sigh of relief when the child drops off again. Her head is beginning to ache and she goes back to her own bed, desperate for some sleep, wishing she'd decided to leave this evening. The sooner this is over the better.

CHAPTER THIRTY-THREE

SEB

Anna goes into the bedroom and he lets her be. He hasn't the headspace to think about what she has told him. What started as an ordinary day has descended into something he could never have imagined happening. His thoughts and emotions are waiting in the wings until it is their time to go under the spotlight. Nothing matters until Evie is safe. Evie – the poor little girl. Who knows what her name really is, who the poor child is. Yet Anna is right: she is safe and happy, living in a stable loving home. A home that no longer exists, he realises, their little family shattered by Anna's revelations. It can never be the same. Anna won't be able to come out of this without consequences. His affair is a trivial misdemeanour by comparison, but he doesn't feel any less guilty.

The whisky has taken the edge from his nerves and he rereads Jo's text. She holds the power now. He picks up his glass, changes his mind. He pushes open the bedroom door. Anna is sitting on the bed, mascara tears written on her face.

'I'm going for a drive round the area.'

'What for?'

'See if I can spot her, you never know. Check the park behind the house, just in case. If the police were involved, they'd be hunting for her no matter what. I need to get out. I won't be long. I'll do anything it takes, Anna. We have to find her.'

He drives through town, past the pub where they used to meet, then takes the route towards Jo's flat. Her street is away from the busier part of town and the only car on the road is his. Most houses are in darkness, but lights lure him from halfway down the street and he speeds up. It's Jo, she's back, Evie is safe. But as he draws parallel with her block, he sees it's the ground-floor flat that has its lights on, and he can hear music playing. He hovers outside, the bubble of hope burst. The upstairs flat is in darkness.

He drives back home, windows open, letting cold air blow on his face. He wants to be awake and alert. His mind churns, going over conversations he had with Jo, trying to recall every detail she ever told him. Instead of turning in to their road, he parks round the corner, close to the park gates. The park is closed, but he walks round the circumference until he reaches their back garden and the offending railing that has been cut out. Would Jo have been capable of doing that? Once again it hits him how little he really knows about her; he has no idea whether she is one of those women who are adept at DIY, relish an IKEA flatpack, or whether her capabilities only extend to changing a fuse. Has she involved someone else?

Their house is lit up from the inside, curtains closed. Is Anna still weeping in the bedroom, or is she back at the laptop desperately searching for Jo? He should be with her. He wishes he could run across the lawn and into the house through the back, but it would terrify Anna, and anyway they will need the car close by, so he heads back to the road. He turns his mind again to the gap in the railings. Something is niggling him, something Jo told him that he can't quite grasp. He recalls that last assignation in the hotel, how he ruined her plans, and he knows the nugget of information is there, if only he can retrieve it.

CHAPTER THIRTY-FOUR

ANNA

It might be at that point we have to tell the police.

Anna's blood freezes whenever she thinks of Seb's words. Once the police are involved, her life is over. Evie will be taken from her and she will go to prison. And so she should. But if there's any chance she can keep her daughter, she will grab it with both hands. And if there's any chance of her hanging on to Seb too, then she has to play this right.

Seb is talking to her; he's going out, and she lets him, dazed from her heightened emotion. She should be out with him, not sitting here waiting. She runs into the living room and holds back the curtain, looks out into the street. Most people are in bed. Is Evie in bed? Is she awake, hungry, hurt? Anna's job for the past five years has been putting Evie's needs before her own, and now she is powerless, useless; she has failed her. She should have moved to an isolated rural area, stayed in the house with her, just the two of them, instead of sending her to nursery, to school, trying, daring to live a normal life after what she did. She collapses to the floor and sobs. 'Please look after her, don't hurt her. I'll do anything.'

It's midnight. Six hours until morning. Does that count as

morning? What does Josie consider morning? Will she make them wait until midday; or worse, change her mind, or disappear? Will Seb really ring the police? He could re-evaluate, turn on her at any moment. Anna wants to scream. He isn't back. Doubts creep in with the street light through the chink in the curtains. Is he really looking for Evie? He says he doesn't know much about Josie. Is he telling the truth? She calls him.

'I haven't found her. I'm coming back now,' he says. 'Sit tight, I'm almost there.'

Anna stands outside the house and waits until she hears the car engine, sees his headlamps light up the drive. She doesn't care if the neighbours see her, a madwoman pacing the lawn, hair wild and eyes smeared black, when she should be asleep, a responsible mother looking after her child.

Not her child.

Not really.

Seb puts his arm round her and steers her inside.

'We should try and get some rest.'

He is soon snoring gently and she lies next to him seething. How can he possibly sleep? She manages a couple of hours and eventually opens her eyes to light outside. She lets him slumber for a while, scrolls through her phone. No messages. Although she doesn't like to, she casts her mind back to those hours when she first had Evie. She pictures the scene in her flat, blinds down, lowering Evie onto the mat that had been in her bag ...

She sits up, wide awake, alert. The bag, the letter in the bag, who was it from? She screws up her face and tries to recall the envelope, the handwriting, but it's a blank. So successfully has she wiped those memories that reminded her of what she had done, she's unable to dredge the name back. She lies back down. It will come, it has to.

Seb shows no sign of waking up. How can he sleep? What if – a cold hand squeezes her heart – what if he knows what's really going on? She grips the edge of the mattress. Until she's sure, she'll keep the memory of the letter to herself. She looks at his face, his unshaven chin, so unaccustomed, wishing she could get inside his head and read his thoughts. She can't stand him sleeping any longer and shakes him awake.

'Check your phone. Has she sent anything?'

He is instantly awake, sitting up and frowning at the screen.

'Nothing. Did you get any sleep?'

'A few hours.' Her eyes feel gritty, half open. A headache creeps across her forehead. Seb has dark circles under his eyes. Maybe he didn't sleep as well as she thought. Maybe she's wrong.

His shoulders slump. 'I can't stand this much longer. I drove past her flat again last night, just to be sure. Still no sign of her, she's definitely gone.'

'We need to find her.'

'Maybe we should call the police. That's what they're there for. They have the resources. We have nothing.'

'You know why I don't want to do that. I'll lose her forever then – and if we anger Josie, who knows what she might do.'

'It's madness not to involve the police. If anything goes wrong, we'll have to contact them, and they'll want to know why we didn't do it earlier. It will go against us.'

'Please. Just a few more hours. If we don't make any progress soon, we'll go to them.'

He sighs. 'I hope we won't regret this. Let's get some breakfast and make a plan.'

'I can't stomach any food.'

'We need to stay strong. Try a bit of toast at least.'

Evie is fussy about her breakfast. She uses the same bowl every day, the one with the kittens on that Marion bought her, and she likes Weetabix with exactly the right amount of milk. If it gets too soggy, she won't finish it. Will she have any breakfast at all? Anxiety creeps through Anna's veins as she worries about her daughter, but there's no point letting her mind wander down tunnels leading to a dank cellar where her daughter is being held against her will. She must stay positive. She's alive, she knows she is; she would feel it in her bones if she were dead.

She continues her online search. Josie's Facebook page isn't restricted with privacy settings, and she tries to find out who she hangs out with, where she goes, but she's barely used it for the last six months.

She sighs. 'She stopped posting ages ago for some reason.'

Seb puts toast on a plate and sits down with her, pours them both some coffee.

'What if we try the salon again? Ask if she's got any close friends?' Anna says.

'No, it's not a good idea. They won't tell us anything and it might raise their suspicions. The police would be able to trace the call.' He bites into a piece of toast.

'What about old friends? Someone from her past. She must have talked about other people, surely? Is there anywhere she mentioned, a town she wanted to visit, a place she liked to go on holiday—'

Seb coughs when she says this, splutters, almost choking, trying to speak. 'That's it,' he cries, dropping the toast on his plate. 'Her aunt! It's been bugging me since last night, and now you've reminded me. Her aunt has a holiday place and she was trying to get me to go there.'

'Where is it?' Anna feels the adrenaline rush of hope.

'It's in Wales, but' – the glimmer of excitement dissolves – 'I have no idea where.'

'Think, think. You have to remember. She must have told you something.'

He rubs his forehead, as if trying to massage a memory to life. 'I'm trying, but I'm not sure she ever told me much about the place.'

'What's the aunt's name?'

He thinks for a moment. 'Jacky! That's it, Jacky.'

'Jacky.' Anna repeats the name. That was the name on the envelope. 'Talk me through the conversation.' She sees the hesitation on his face. 'Don't worry about sparing me the details – we're way beyond that. I'll do anything to find Evie. Nothing else matters now.'

'After we'd met a few times, she wanted us to spend a night together. I wasn't comfortable, I kept fobbing her off, changing the subject. But she wouldn't let it drop. I know, I'm a hypocrite, I was already cheating, but going away somewhere felt like a step too far, an unforgivable betrayal. And the risks of being seen were too high. I used the expense as an excuse, which is when she brought up her aunt's place. Said she could go there any time and it was in another part of the country so we wouldn't see anyone we knew.'

'Did she describe it at all?'

'Small, with a view of the sea. She used to go there occasionally when she needed to get away from London; said it needed doing up but had the basics. That's all she said about the place. The aunt is her dad's sister. Jo mentioned her being the only one in her family she could stand. Said she was a bit of a loner, independent, with strong opinions. Didn't judge her.'

'That means she'll have the same surname, as long as she hasn't married and changed her name. Jacky Redish.'

Anna goes back to the laptop and pulls up a map of Wales, zooms in on the coastline, rubs her eyes. She could be anywhere.

Anna searches for a Jacky Redish in Jo's Facebook friends. The profile photograph is of a beach scene. Her pulse picks up. She opens the page.

Jacky is one of those users who leaves months between posts. Most of the pictures are of her dog, a Yorkshire terrier with a cute face. The dog running along the shoreline, the dog near a beach hut, the dog outside a block of flats, location pinned – Borth, Wales.

'I've got it, Seb, I think I've got it.' She puts her hand over her mouth.

Seb clicks on Jacky's friends, types in *Redish*. Clicks on a Josephine Mary Redish.

There, grinning at the camera, pink hair piled on her head, just as Anna remembers, is Josie.

CHAPTER THIRTY-FIVE

JOSIE

She must have slept, because the alarm screeches into her consciousness and she's instantly awake. *Rosie.* She rubs her eyes, which feel sticky, and recalls last night, the thudding, the grizzling, the trauma. She can't wait to get going.

She dresses quietly, listening for Nathan heading off to work. As soon as he's gone, she'll get Rosie up and they'll leave. While she waits she types out the email to Seb and presses send. Next she unpacks the new pay-as-you-go phone she's bought and flushes her old SIM down the toilet. She hugs the phone to her chest and hopes everything continues to go her way. It has to.

Nathan clatters around in the hall, and for once his inability to be quiet doesn't annoy her. Just before six, he wobbles off on his bike, his cord jacket flapping in the wind. She watches him until he turns out of sight, then lets out a sigh of relief. Did he seriously think she was interested in him?

'Up you get, Rosie.'

Rosie sits up, looking confused. 'Are we on holiday?'

'Not yet.'

'Is Mummy here?'

'No, but the sooner we get off, the sooner we'll be with her. We can have a quick breakfast before we go.'

Rosie sticks her bottom lip out. 'Not toast.'

'No, cereal, is that what you like? I've got lots, so you can choose.'

'Mummy gives me nice breakfast.'

'I'll do my best. Shall I help you get dressed?'

'No. I do it by myself.'

Josie wishes she could smoke. As soon as they get to Borth, she'll be able to relax. She avoids thinking about the journey, and the hours she'll be alone with the child. Is she doing the right thing?

She sets out the variety pack of cereals on the table, along with the milk carton. She makes herself a strong coffee. Rosie is chattering in the corridor, taking her time. Josie goes to hurry her up, finds her sitting on the floor with the toy tiger.

'Come on, darling,' she says, smiling through gritted teeth. 'We really must get going.'

Rosie pushes herself up from the floor. In the kitchen, she sits at the table, needing a cushion to reach it, frowning at the plain white bowl in front of her.

'Mummy gives me a kitten bowl.'

What? Is she a cat now? Josie will never understand children, though she'll have to learn to.

'Yes, well that's all I've got. On holiday there will be nice bowls.'

Rosie lines up the small cereal boxes in front of her and studies them one by one.

'Hurry up and choose, there's a good girl.' The silly child-friendly voice coming from her mouth again.

After what feels like an age, she chooses Coco Pops. Josie doubts saintly Anna gives her that sugary delight. She rips the packet open and pours milk on it.

'Too much.' Rosie's voice is close to a whine – Josie can't

abide whining. She pours the excess milk down the sink and puts the spoon in the bowl.

'You've got five minutes. Eat up while I get our stuff ready to put in the car.'

'Is it Daddy's car?'

Stop mentioning Mummy and Daddy! She counts to ten, controlling her breath.

By some miracle, they are ready to go by seven. Rosie has eaten her breakfast and Josie gives her a carton of juice to drink in the car.

'Right, we have to be very quiet when we go out, because people are still asleep. I'm going to bring the car round to the back. I want you to sit here like the good girl you are, and I'll come and get you. You'd better use the toilet before we go.'

'Don't want to.'

Give me strength.

'You have to. You'll soon be yelling when you need a wee on the motorway. I don't want you wetting my seats, so no arguing. We might not be able to use the toilet for ages, and you'll thank me then.'

'Tiger is coming.'

'Whatever,' Josie mutters under her breath, dragging Rosie by the arm to the bathroom. She recoils at the thought of having to wipe her bum. She's only just had her nails done. 'You can manage by yourself, can't you?'

'I'm a big girl.'

'Of course you are. Good girl. Wait in the hall when you've finished, and I'll be back before you know it. And then we must be very quiet, like a mouse, got it?'

The alley running behind the block is empty, as she knew it would be, and she bustles Rosie into the back seat as quickly as she can. No cameras or prying eyes at windows here – she hopes. Rosie clambers into the back seat. She looks too big for the car seat Josie found at the charity shop, but it will have to do. She hasn't said a word since Josie collected her from the back door. Hopefully she'll fall asleep and be quiet for the journey. Josie is not in the mood for conversation. She slams the car door and types her destination into the satnav app on her phone. The journey will take a while. Hopefully Seb will agree to her plan, and only then will she tell him where she's heading.

'Will we be there soon?' Rosie asks.

'No,' Josie says, switching the radio on.

'Tight,' Rosie says.

Josie's seat belt cuts into her side as she swivels around to look. Rosie tugs at her own belt.

'It's meant to be, to keep you safe.'

Rosie kicks her feet at the seat in front.

'Stop that.' Josie turns up the radio.

She texts Seb before she lets up the handbrake, butterflies flitting round her stomach as soon as she presses send. The wife will no doubt be hassling him for news of Rosie, so most likely she'll have read the email she sent too. That's up to him. It would be better if she doesn't see it, easier for them to make a clean break. She shoots over a speed bump, jolts into the air, swearing as all the crap on the dashboard drops to the floor. Rosie shrieks.

'Again, again.'

As if this is a bloody fairground ride.

Rosie perks up after that, chattering to the toy tiger, and Josie wishes she'd shut up. She isn't used to children and their constant presence, their demands. For a second she experiences the sensation of how she felt back when she was pregnant: this presence inside her that she was constantly aware of, the moves and the kicks, the insistent pressing on her bladder, reminding her that she had created another person and it wasn't going away, was threatening to ruin her future. The baby she didn't want that had miraculously been taken away. She knew she was doing the right thing back then because she didn't have the mental or material resources to cope with the demands of a child. But is she doing the right thing now?

She reminds herself this is what she wants. Her life has led her to this point and it's the only way she can get Seb to admit to his true desires and follow them. Follow her.

CHAPTER THIRTY-SIX

SEB

It doesn't take long, once they've found the Facebook account for Jacky Redish, to locate the whereabouts of her holiday home. In another of her photos she's posing outside a small block of flats, the name signposted above the door: Langton Villas. It's an attractive block with a landscaped garden to the front. Jacky herself is in her fifties, cropped grey hair and a wiry body. No resemblance to Josie whatsoever, but they're both confident they have the right person. The caption reads: *My holiday pad near Borth!*

They pack a bag and are ready to go within half an hour. As they leave the house, Seb picks up a recently delivered parcel from the hall table.

'What are you doing?' Anna says. 'That's a book I've ordered.'

'It might come in handy to get into the building. If anyone asks, I can say I'm a delivery man.'

His ability to make such quick decisions both impresses and alarms her. What else is he capable of? They hurry to the car and he goes to the driver's seat.

'I'll drive. You should try and get some sleep.'

With good traffic they should be there by early afternoon. They haven't discussed what they'll do once they get there – plenty of time for that later in the journey. They'll have to stop for a coffee fix at some point.

Anna's asleep by the time they get onto the motorway, head resting against the window. She needs it. His phone is in a holder on the dashboard, and he almost swerves when a text message pops up – from Jo.

Check your email for further instructions. You'll regret it if you don't.

He glances over at Anna, but she's still asleep. He carries on for a bit until there's an inevitable traffic hold-up, and slows to a crawl before opening his mailbox. Sure enough, there's one from Jo marked *Urgent*.

If you're wondering why I've taken 'Evie', I suggest you ask your wife. Have you ever seen your stepdaughter's birth certificate? When Anna tells you the truth about who Evie is, you'll see why I've taken her and that I've done nothing wrong. Rosie – her name is Rosie – is fine; she'll be happy with me and you don't need to worry about her. When she's old enough, I'll tell her the truth about what happened to her. Hopefully she won't even remember the woman who brought her up under false pretences for the first few years of her life. She's only four. I can't remember anything from when I was so little. Probably a good thing considering my upbringing.

I expect you're wondering whether our whole relationship was a sham. You have to believe me when I say that I love you, Seb. I didn't mean for anything serious to happen, but as soon as I met you, something clicked and I knew you were the right person for me. I've never had that before, which is why I'm offering you a choice.

Stay with Anna, who won't get over this, and nor should she. I won't go to the police. No longer having Evie will be punishment enough. She'll pay for this every day that passes without her. She'll never be happy. You'd miss Evie too, wouldn't you? I've seen the way you are with her. Exactly the sort of father I want for my child. That's why I'm asking you to come with me and Rosie; that way she can be with her rightful parents. You're the closest thing to a dad she's ever known. We'll be a happy little family, and maybe we'll have more children. I'm finally ready for that, and it's what I want. I hope you want it too.

I'm leaving town and taking Rosie with me. If you choose to stay with Anna, you'll never find us, I'll make sure of that.

What will it be, Seb? Stay with Anna, or start a new life with Rosie and me? The choice is yours. Give me an answer within twenty-four hours.

CHAPTER THIRTY-SEVEN

JOSIE

Aunt Jacky is in Spain. She met a woman on her last holiday who invited her over for the summer. Josie asked her once if she'd ever wanted children, and Aunt Jacky laughed. 'No chance,' she said. 'I've always wanted to travel the world, and I can't do that lugging a kid about.' She could have done if she really wanted to, but Josie couldn't imagine it; Jacky didn't stand still long enough. She was always out and about, involved with local politics and her allotment, to name but a couple of her interests – she certainly wasn't the mothering type. Josie wonders if she's inherited some of those genes.

She glances in her mirror at Rosie on the back seat. She's fast asleep, head lolling back, cheeks two rosy patches on her pale skin, drool on her mouth. She'll have to get used to the bodily functions side of things now she's got her daughter back. She wonders what dreams are going on in that funny little head of hers, hair fluffed up like a gosling, just like her own used to be. She grips the steering wheel. She can do this, she can. Ever since she glimpsed Rosie in that school crocodile in the street, saw the little mole below her eye and had the feeling of looking in a mirror, she's wanted her back. A wrench in her gut that she's never felt before. She acted on that instinct, focused all her passion on the search without spending much time preparing herself for the reality of looking after a child.

If it wasn't for Seb, and the way they hit it off, she might not have gone through with her plan, but his relationship with Rosie was the final piece of the jigsaw – the part that was missing all those years ago when she was alone with the baby. Babies are better off with two parents instead of one – if the one is an inadequate one like her. She did the right thing. She wouldn't have suited the baby years; she was a nervous wreck then, always scared of doing the wrong thing and hating the clipping of her wings. She didn't show it, of course – Lisa always said what a fantastic mum she was. She often wonders whether Lisa missed her, or was just pissed off that she upped and disappeared without a word. Obviously they couldn't have stayed friends; she knew too much.

A yell from the back seat and she nearly loses control of the car, the driver in the next lane looking across at her as he speeds past. She slows down; mustn't draw attention to herself.

'What's the matter?'

'Tiger, he's on the floor and I can't reach him.' Rosie is snivelling, snot running down her chin.

'I can't get him while I'm driving. You'll have to wait.'

'No, want Tiger, want Tiger now.' She kicks the seat with her rigid little legs.

'Stop!' Josie is shouting while trying to stay in control of the car. She isn't a great fan of motorways at the best of times. 'I can't get it, all right, not when I'm driving, so shut up.'

Rosie is properly wailing now, sobbing and snorting, and Josie wants to scream along with her, get into the outside lane and see how fast she can go, feel the tension ebbing away. Her knuckles are white as she stops herself from doing anything crazy. Instead she holds her breath and counts to ten.

'We'll stop in a minute,' she says. 'As soon as we can.' She scans the horizon for signs of services, or an exit, until at last a sign flashes up: *Services 10 miles*.

Those ten miles with a child screaming in the back of her car are the longest of Josie's life. 'I want Tiger' has changed to 'I want Mummy'. She turns the radio up loud and tries not to look at the screwed-up red face accusing her from the back seat. All on account of a bloody tiger.

Finally the services appear and she turns the radio off, trying to say the right thing to calm Rosie down. She must be knackered. Josie's head is ringing and the first thing she's going to do when they get to Aunt Jacky's is to have a giant drink of whatever she can lay her hands on.

Rosie goes limp and quiet the minute Tiger is placed back on her lap. Josie's breathing sounds as if she's run a fast 10K, and she's been gripping the steering wheel so hard she has a crick in her neck. She locks the car and buys some food when she pays for her petrol, plus a takeaway coffee and a hot chocolate for Rosie. Anything to keep her quiet, anything.

When they get to the flat, Rosie runs around checking each room on the first floor of the duplex.

'Where's Mummy?'

'She's not here yet, darling, something has come up. But Daddy should be here soon.' Josie keeps checking her phone, but he hasn't replied to her email yet. He must have read it by now.

Rosie has that look on her face that indicates tears are imminent.

'Why don't you come and play through here. I've got you some toys. Look.'

Rosie follows her into the room and spies a cat out on the balcony.

'Cat!' She squeals and runs across the room, and the cat leaps out of sight. Rosie presses her nose against the glass.

'What can you see?' Josie asks, joining her.

'No cat.'

'Forget the cat. It's the sea, look.' She points, and Rosie stands on tiptoes.

'Let me show you,' Josie says, lifting her up. Rosie squirms, drumming her feet against Josie's legs.

'No, get down. I want Mummy.'

Josie lets her drop to the floor. She doesn't understand kids. The sea was exciting to her as a child.

'Ouch.'

'That didn't hurt. You're a strong girl, I can tell.' Her own leg throbs where Rosie kicked her.

Rosie sticks her thumb in her mouth, looking as if she's about to cry, until she spots an old tennis ball lying on the floor. She rolls it along, then chases after it, back and forth, Tiger hanging from her hand. Josie has noticed how quickly her moods change; she can disappear into a world of her own and play happily by herself, as if to distract her from anything unwelcome. But it's only a matter of time before she asks for Mummy again. How long will it take her to realise that Josie is her mother? It was stupid to say Anna was coming on holiday with them, but it was the easy option at the time.

She watches Rosie playing for a while, marvelling at her physical presence. After so long, she isn't going to give up that easily. Just as Rosie is a strong kid, she can be a strong mother, and she won't be beaten. No matter what the child throws at her.

CHAPTER THIRTY-EIGHT

ANNA

Seb shakes her awake. Anna starts, disorientated, unsure where she is. In the car, parked on a street, unfamiliar. A street light shines onto the car bonnet. She remembers, and part of her dies.

'Are we here?' She pulls herself up to a sitting position, struggling to breathe in the stuffy car. She winds down the window. The air is different. Seaside air. Outside, the sky is grey.

'Yes.'

'Has she texted yet?'

'No.'

Anna closes her eyes. She wasn't properly asleep when his phone displayed the text, and she read the words *check your email*. She feigned sleep until the traffic jam, then watched him read something on his phone, glancing at her as he did so. Then he typed something himself.

Her racing mind prevented her from sleeping. What if he really *was* in league with Josie? After that she dared not open her eyes, and next thing she knew Seb was waking her.

'Are you sure she hasn't been in touch?'

'No, I told you already.'

'Where is the flat?'

'It's round the corner from here. I'll go and check it out, see if I can locate it, what the access looks like, then we'll make a plan. We can't just go storming in there.'

'You should have woken me; we could have worked it out on the way.'

'You needed the rest. We have to have our wits about us. This has to go right.'

'What if she sees you?'

'I'll be careful. She won't be expecting to see me. I'll be quick.' He closes the door softly behind him.

He's left his phone. Anna stares after him, convinced he'll turn round and come back for it, but he doesn't, and she snatches it from the holder, opens his email, fingers fumbling, eyes flickering up and down, keeping a watch for him coming back.

I'm leaving town and taking Rosie with me ...

'Evie. Her name is Evie.' Anna says the words aloud and kicks the front of the footwell. Why hasn't he said anything to her? She replaces the phone.

She can't bear to believe he isn't going to tell her about the email. That he wants to go away with Josie, raise Evie with her. Not telling her must mean ... She shakes the thought away, not wanting it to be true. She'd only just awoken; as soon as he gets back he'll tell her. She opens the window further and composes herself. What if he doesn't come back? He's without his phone, and anything could happen ... He rounds the corner and her heart is racing. Maybe he's trying to protect her.

He's back in the car and she daren't speak.

'I've found the flat. There's an entryphone so we should be able to get someone to buzz us in. We're in the right place – Flat D is marked J. Redish, I didn't go right up to the front door, but it's a four-storey block. It's impossible to tell whether she's at the front or the back.' He removes his phone from the holder.

'Make sure she hasn't been in touch.'

He looks at the phone and she grips the sides of her seat. She forgot to check whether he replied to Josie – she must keep one step ahead of him.

'Nothing.'

'She said she would. Why hasn't she? What does that mean?'

'It's hard to say where her mind is at right now. Clearly she's not thinking straight.'

He isn't going to tell her about the email.

This, then, is her nightmare made flesh. She knows the truth and it's worse than she could ever imagine. Josie wants her daughter back. After all this time Anna has dared to believe that that was in the past, she has gone beyond the time when Josie would turn up to accost her with the truth. Only last week she was baking cakes without a care in the world. Now she has lost her daughter, and as if that isn't bad enough, Josie wants her to pay for what she did. That she can understand – in the eyes of the law, she deserves to be punished for her crime, abducting a child – but Jo will go one step further. She won't be reporting her to the police, but she will be taking her husband from her too. Anna wants to believe that Seb is on her side, willing to overlook for the moment the fact that he had an affair and she hadn't a clue. But he has read the email and there can only be one reason for not telling her about it. He is a man capable of deceit after all.

Her movements from this point forward are crucial. Nobody can be trusted.

Nobody will take Evie away from her.

'I can move the car a bit closer,' Seb says, turning the ignition key. He drives round a bend, passes a small block of flats on the right, set slightly back from the road. 'That's Langton Villas.' He unfastens his seat belt. 'You stay in the car and I'll check out what's going on.'

'But—'

'This is delicate, Anna – we have to be so careful. I promise I'll be back. I just want to get an idea of the layout inside first.'

Anna chews on her lip as she leans out of the window and watches Seb walk up the path, holding the parcel in front of him, pretending to check the address. It seems unnecessary now it's dark. There's no way she's letting him go in there alone. She undoes her seat belt and gets out of the car.

He rings the bell and waits. No answer. He rings again, then steps back, his jaw tightening as he looks up at the windows. He glances around casually, up and down the street, then Anna sees him ring another bell. She runs across the road to the gate at the front of the flats. He rings a second time, and a male voice answers.

'Yeah.'

'Parcel for Flat D.'

'OK, mate.'

The door buzzes and Seb pushes it inwards. As he struggles with the unexpected weight, Anna runs down the path to his side.

'I can't stay out there and watch,' she says, keeping her voice low. 'It's better with two of us. We don't know what to expect from Josie, and Evie will want me.' Her voice catches on her daughter's name. 'I'll stay out of sight.'

The small lobby area comprises a cupboard plus pigeon-holes for mail; no lift, just a staircase. Seb heads up the stairs, Anna close behind. Flat D is at the top of the building. His phone vibrates in his pocket, and he checks the notification. Anna moves close so there's no way he can hide it from her. It's a voicemail from Josie. She tugs at his arm and pulls him down a flight of stairs to the landing below. He retrieves the message, turning the volume down low, holding the phone close to his ear. Anna watches his face intently, leaning in to listen.

'Have you made a decision yet?' Josie asks.

'What does she mean?' Anna hisses. Cold air blows in from an open window.

He shrugs in an exaggerated fashion, pulls her further into the stairwell.

'She must be losing the plot. Having some kind of psychotic episode. I have no idea what she means.'

Anna's stomach contracts. He's really going to do this to her. If she goes into that flat with the two of them, she could be in danger. But she has to if there's the slightest chance that Evie is in there.

'Has she had one before?'

'I don't know. I've told you the little I know about her.'

'You knew her well enough to—'

'Stop. This isn't the time. Evie is what matters here.'

She wants to strike him. How dare he say that to her when her insides feel as if they are being gouged out. But he's right. None of that matters until Evie is safe. She could be just feet away.

'I'm going in,' she says, pushing past him, but he's quick to follow.

'Let me speak to her,' he whispers.

She nods reluctantly; Josie is more likely to let Seb in. She moves to the side so she is out of Josie's sightline should the door open.

Seb raps on the door. Anna is sure Josie will be able to hear her heart thudding. They should have called the police. She doesn't care what happens to her – only Evie's safety matters. She feels for her mobile, makes sure it's in her pocket. But what if they decide to give Evie back to Josie? Her chest is gripped with pain. Is this what a heart attack feels like?

CHAPTER THIRTY-NINE

JOSIE

Josie watches Rosie playing on the floor. Quiet moments like these make her feel more optimistic about the road ahead, the memory of last night's stress and the journey fading a little. She hears a noise in the corridor and goes into the entrance hall, strains to listen. It's a shuffling sound, as if somebody is outside. Why isn't there a spyhole when you need one? She doesn't move.

The doorbell rings and she jumps, pulse racing. Seconds pass; she doesn't move.

Someone bangs on the door.

'Jo, Jo, are you in there?' Seb's voice. Mustn't make a noise. 'Jo.' More banging and the door vibrates. 'It's Seb. I know you're in there. Let me in. We need to talk.'

'You shouldn't have come.' How did he find her? 'I warned you ...'

'I had to come, don't you understand? I got your email.'

'Are you alone?'

'Of course I'm alone. Why do you think I'm here? I'm choosing you, Jo.'

She freezes in position, staring at the dark wooden door.

Then she hears a shuffling sound behind her and turns to see Rosie. She lowers her voice.

'Get back in there! I told you not to move.' She grabs her by the arm and pulls her into the living room. 'Get under the table.'

Rosie's lip wobbles.

Josie clenches her fists. 'We're playing hide and seek. It's our game, remember? Hide under the table and don't come out until I tell you.'

Rosie scuttles underneath the round dining table, hugs her knees to her chest, not making a sound. Josie is momentarily ashamed. She sees fear on the little girl's face. Seb is banging on the door again, and her resolve strengthens. With him she can do this – he can teach her how to be a mother.

'Did you hear me, Jo? I'm choosing you.'

'Are you sure you're alone?'

'Yes. Let me in, Jo, please.'

The door opens with a scraping sound, followed by a few seconds of silence as they look warily at each other. Instead of looking happy to see her, Seb looks tired.

'You'd better come in,' Josie says.

Before he can move, Anna appears from nowhere. As she barrels into Seb and pushes them both into the flat, she stumbles, managing to break her fall with her hands, slamming her left hip against the wall.

'You bloody liar!' Josie screams at Seb as Anna scrambles to her feet, clutching her hip and grimacing with pain. Her skin is sallow and she's no longer the yummy mummy Josie first saw outside the school. She wonders if Seb has told her about them, shown her the email. Why is she here? 'You said you were alone!'

'Where is she? What have you done with her?' Anna's high-pitched voice grates on her nerves.

'Mummy!' The child's voice is unmistakable. Josie risks a glance back at the living room door.

'Don't you dare move, Rosie,' she shouts.

'Evie, her name is Evie.' Anna raises her voice. 'Evie, are you all right, darling?'

'Her name is Rosie,' Josie says, calm now, faced with this hysterical woman.

'She's Evie. You didn't want Rosie. I took her and you didn't care enough to bother to find her.'

'Shut up!' Josie bellows, making them jump. She takes advantage of their surprise and grabs hold of a knife from the counter, waving it at Anna. 'Get over there, next to him, where I can see you both.'

'Evie,' Anna yells.

'For God's sake,' Seb says.

'I mean it.' Her voice is cold. 'Shut up.'

Anna exchanges a glance with Seb.

'Do as she says,' he tells her, without taking his eyes off the knife.

'Mummy.' Rosie appears in the doorway. Her eyes widen when she sees the knife.

'Get back in there,' Josie says. 'Sit at the table and don't move until I tell you to.'

'But ...' Rosie's lip trembles.

'Evie, Mummy's here.'

'Shut up,' Josie says, jabbing the knife at Anna. 'Have you told him what you did?'

'He knows everything,' Anna says, eyes fixed on Rosie. She is standing awkwardly, still holding her hip.

'Good. Now that he knows what you're capable of, he can see through your pretences. See what a criminal you are.'

'Let's be sensible here,' Seb says. 'We all want what's best for Evie and we just need to know that she's all right, that you haven't harmed her.'

'Rosie, her name is Rosie.' Spittle flies from her mouth. She doesn't care.

Seb nods. 'I know. Habit, I'm sorry. Rosie.'

'Of course I haven't harmed her. She's my daughter.'

'No she isn't. Evie darling, Mummy's here. Are you all right?' Anna inches towards Rosie. Josie pokes the blade towards her.

'Shut up, I said!'

'Stop waving that knife about.' Seb steps forward. 'You won't use it.'

'Oh won't I? You don't get it. I *will* hurt this woman if she tries to come near my daughter again.'

'Mummy ...' Rosie starts crying.

'Take her in the other room, Seb. I have a few questions to ask Anna. Like why she stole my child.'

'I—'

'Get in there, or I'll hurt her. Believe me, I won't hesitate to stick this into her.' Josie's voice is loud, and Rosie cowers against the wall, whimpering.

'Go, Seb,' Anna says, her voice shaking. 'Look after Evie. Go with Daddy, there's a good girl. The lady is playing a game.'

'Come on,' Seb says, ushering Rosie away. 'Everything's OK, don't be frightened. I won't let anything happen to you.'

'Why did the lady shout?' Rosie asks Seb as they disappear.

Josie is still holding the knife towards Anna.

'Can't you stop waving that at me? I'm not going anywhere. I need to sit. My hip is hurt. Let's both calm down.'

'Don't tell me to calm down. I have every right not to be calm. You stole my child. You could go to prison.'

'You didn't report it. You didn't care enough. You can't just change your mind suddenly after all this time. She doesn't even know you.'

'And whose fault is that?'

'All you ever did was complain about being pregnant, about not wanting a child. I'd been trying to get pregnant for years, I'd had rounds of IVF that got my hopes up, took all my savings and cost me my relationship. I poured out my pain in that hairdresser's chair because I thought you were a caring person who would listen. You knew how much I loved children.' Anna takes a moment to breathe. 'I'd just had a failed pregnancy and you were going on and on about how you didn't want a child because it meant you'd have to give up your career and your social life. Do you know what it feels like to give birth to a child that is no longer alive? You're so self-centred; you couldn't care less about anyone but yourself.

'None of this was planned. Running off with her was the last thing on my mind, but I saw you in the park that day, pushing her along, chatting on your phone, not even noticing that she was upset, or that she'd dropped her toy penguin. I picked it up to put in the pram when you abandoned the pram to go and chat and laugh with your friend. You had your back to Evie, didn't even care what happened. Any decent mother wouldn't let their child out of their sight. I took a photo as proof. I wonder how long it took you to notice she'd gone. If you'd run after me you'd have caught up with me. I don't believe you even tried.

'I waited for you to come and get her, and you didn't even bother to inform the police. I did you a favour, admit it. Evie deserves better than that. She deserves a proper mother and that's what I am to her. Nobody could love and care for her more than I did – still do, always will.'

'Her name is not Evie.'

'She thinks it is, don't you see? She's had four years of being Evie. There's a little girl at the heart of this. Listen to her. Doesn't hearing her crying and upset break your heart? It splits mine in two. We have to think about how she feels, what she wants, what is best for her. I love her so much.' Anna's voice cracks and she leans against the wall for support, rubbing her hand over her hip. 'That's all that matters.' She swallows hard, tears filling her eyes.

'But you've brainwashed her into thinking she's yours. If I ring the police, let's see who they think is in the wrong. A social worker would have her away from you like a shot.'

'But I love her. I've loved her ever since I set eyes on her, and I can't bear to lose her.' Tears spill from Anna's eyes and she wipes them away with her fist. 'Do you think they'll let you take her back after what you did? They'll put her into care and neither of us will have her. You didn't want her then. Why do you suddenly want her now?'

'He hasn't told you, has he?' Josie can't help smirking. 'What has changed now is that I'm not on my own any more. I'm sure you love Rosie, but Seb does too. He was forever going on about her – almost made me jealous.' She laughs. 'I'll admit I wasn't ready to be a mother when she was born, but now that I've got a partner who loves me, I can do any—'

Anna cuts Josie off by charging towards her, stumbling and crashing into her. Josie lashes out with the knife, nicking her on the side of her head. Anna screams, grabbing her ear.

'Seb!' she yells.

Seb rushes into the hall, but Josie is ready and pushes past him into the living room. Rosie is standing in the middle of the room, and she throws her arm around the child's waist, swooping her up, then turns so that her back is to the window and holds the knife in front of her.

'Put her down,' Seb says. 'You've got what you wanted. I'm here, aren't I? You're scaring her.'

Josie lets Rosie slide down so her feet are on the ground, but keeps her arm around her waist, trying to stop her wriggling.

'I knew you'd see sense, that you wouldn't share my email with her. Tell her what you've decided; we owe her that much. Then she can leave the three of us in peace. You want to be with me and Daddy, don't you?' She nudges Rosie.

'I want Mummy.' Rosie strains against her arm, reaching towards Anna. Josie holds her firmly.

'I *am* your mummy. She's confused, poor kid. See what you've done. Tell her, Seb.'

Seb looks uncomfortable, which endears her to him even more.

'We both want what's best for Rosie; we're all on the same side really. Tell her about the email.'

Seb looks at Anna. 'Jo emailed me when you were asleep in the car. She's asked me to go and live with her and Rosie, and I've agreed. I'm sorry.'

Josie can't help grinning. She's almost won. The stars don't normally align for her in this way, and she gazes at Seb, looking into his eyes for that spark they always shared. He approaches her, but he's speaking to Anna.

'I'm sorry, but I can't condone what you've done. I love this woman, and I want to be with her. It will be a fresh start for the three of us.'

'No!' The word is a wail bursting from Anna's mouth, and Josie almost feels sorry for her.

She relaxes as Seb turns to look at her, easing her hold on Rosie, who shifts away from her; but his eyes aren't loving, they are narrow slits, and he's opening his mouth in an ugly way, charging at her, shouting, 'Anna, grab Evie.' Anna rushes at her too, and angry heat engulfs her and she slashes the knife against Anna's raised hands, blood spurting. With her left hand, she manages to grope behind her and push the door open, taking Rosie out onto the balcony. Rosie is screaming and kicking her feet against Josie's legs. The blade of the knife glistens red as she holds it in front of her.

'Anna!' Seb shouts. He turns to Josie. 'You've hurt her.' His face is full of concern. 'Put Evie down, please, you've gone too far.'

Josie sees what this is. He's tricked her, he doesn't want her. Her chest is tight and it's hard to breathe. He prefers Anna with her bloody hands and mascara-streaked face – even like that he prefers her.

'You called her Evie. You're not coming with me, are you?'

'Please, Jo, give her to me. You're frightening her.'

He doesn't even care. All he cares about is the child, who is kicking her now and trying to break free of her grip. 'Daddy, Daddy—'

'Stop it!' she yells, her voice like a burst of thunder, gripping Rosie harder. 'If you don't shut up snivelling, I'm going to hit *her*' – she points towards Anna – 'really hard. And if you don't stop that hideous noise, I'll throw *you* down there.' She leans sideways, one arm still around Rosie's waist, forcing her to look over the balcony.

Rosie's body goes rigid, shocked into silence, only little noises coming from her, like a mewing kitten. Anna screams; Seb yells 'No!', followed by a horrific silence.

Noises of traffic from the street down below filter into the sudden stillness as Seb and Anna gaze at Josie in horror.

'Please, please, please,' Anna cries, tears pouring down her face. 'You can't hurt her. Hurt me instead, please.'

'You're terrifying her, Jo,' Seb says. 'If you love her as you say you do, you wouldn't be doing this. Think for a minute. You'll go to prison, is that what you want? Prove you love your daughter and step away from the edge. Let her live her life.'

Josie's eyes flick between Anna and Seb. She's read this all wrong. Or has she? Seb cheated on his wife, yet he's never lied to Josie. He's clever too. It's Anna who's being tricked here, otherwise he'd have shown her the email and they'd have come here united. She saw the way Anna burst in behind him, taking him by surprise.

'We can be a little family like you suggested, but now that you're threatening Rosie, I'm starting to think I'm making a terrible mistake. Put her down on the floor, at least do that; I won't try and take her from you. I just want to talk, but nothing can happen until you let her go. If you care about her, if you are her real mother as you say you are, you'll prove it to me, to both of us. The authorities will be on your side, of course they will. Anna knows that what she did was wrong; she wants to apologise and put it right somehow. I told her you were a reasonable person, I wouldn't love you otherwise, and that maybe we could come to some sort of arrangement, even if it's just for Anna to be able to say goodbye. So please, do the right thing and put her down.'

Seb pulls his mobile from his pocket and drops it on the floor.

'Anna, your phone, do the same,' he says, without turning to look at her.

Anna can't hide her shaking hands from Josie's unflinching gaze as she drops her mobile to the floor. The screen cracks.

CHAPTER FORTY

ANNA

The slightest wrong move could make Josie react, and Anna tries to stand rigid beside Seb, but a violent trembling has taken over her body. It's not the sharp pain from the hip, or her throbbing ear, or the cut to her hand that is making her shake, but a terror that Josie will drop her daughter to her death. She holds her hand up in front of her to staunch the bleeding, lips squeezed tight, terrified that she will antagonise Josie. Any wrong move and Evie's life and therefore her own will be finished. If Evie goes over that balcony, she will follow straight behind her. Life would be impossible and unbearable without her.

The balcony is so ordinary – a grey concrete box, identical to the one adjacent, potted plant in the corner, pigeon droppings on the wall – but the sight in front of them is incomprehensible: a woman threatening her own child. In this moment, Anna understands that this is the crux of the matter: Josie will never love this child. Anna did the right thing by taking her, and she would do it again a hundred times over.

Josie is blinking constantly, eyes darting between the two of them, her face and neck blotchy and red. The look in her eyes is wild, as if she's been overtaken by an evil force and can no longer see reason. Seb presses a warning hand against Anna, the slightest move, pushing her slightly backwards so that he is closer to Josie and holds her attention.

Anna senses from Seb's touch that he is on her side, despite the words coming out of his mouth. He will say what Josie needs to hear and do whatever he can to stop her harming Evie. She has to trust him. She drops her phone when he tells her, and now there's no chance of calling for help. In this little triangle, they are the only three adults in the world. Only a few feet separate her from her daughter, but it might as well be an ocean.

CHAPTER FORTY-ONE

SEB

Anna's mobile makes a clattering sound as it hits the floor, and the screen shatters. She's so close behind him she's lightly pressed against his back, and he can feel her trembling against him. He wills her to stay strong; one false move could literally send Jo – and Evie – over the edge. She doesn't know Jo like he does; he's been afraid all along of that dark streak he could sense in her.

'Now you let go of the knife,' he says.

Jo hesitates before lowering it to the floor, letting it drop.

'You can't have her. If I can't have her, no one can.'

'Jo,' he says. They lock eyes and he pleads with her to do the right thing. Evie is wriggling but has pushed her face against Jo's shoulder so that she doesn't have to see the drop down to the concrete in front of her. She's making little sobbing noises, her chest going up and down. 'Please don't frighten her any longer. Put her down and we can talk. No police, I promise. Unless you want to, of course. You call the shots here.'

'How do I know you're serious?'

'It's always been you, you know that. That's why I couldn't face seeing you, why I had to cut you dead. Being forced to confront you at the school fair ... it was all getting out of control. Even without the phone calls Anna had guessed, and I was going to have to reveal what I had done, what we had done. Finding out that Rosie is yours after all makes a fairy-tale ending for me – but seeing her here in this predicament makes me want to throw myself over the balcony in her place, if that's what it will take for you to let her go. You can have what you want – we both can – if you put her down and we sort this out like the adults we all are. There is no blueprint for this situation; it's a one-off and we can decide where this story goes next.' He softens his voice and takes a small step forward. 'You can have what you want: me and our daughter.'

Anna gasps as if she's been stabbed. A little smile flickers around Josie's lips, then she lowers Evie slowly to the ground. The minute her red sandals hit the floor, Seb lunges forward and grabs her to him, feels her heartbeat fluttering against his chest. The surprise makes Josie fall back against the wall.

'Evie,' he says. 'You're safe now. Go to Mummy.'

CHAPTER FORTY-TWO

ANNA

Anna hears Seb's words and freezes, invaded by panic. The confidence she felt moments before evaporates. After his lies and deception, is this what it's all been about? Is he really in love with this woman and together they are going to steal her daughter? Josie gave birth to this child. That's what will decide the outcome if the case goes in front of a judge and a decision has to be made by an independent party. But she has also threatened Evie's life and held her over a balcony. Anyone who can do that should never be around children. She doesn't deserve to be a mother. Seb loves Evie; he has just saved her life. His feelings for this little girl, whoever she belongs to, are genuine. Will he do the right thing?

'Evie,' he says. 'You're safe now. Go to Mummy.'

He puts her into Anna's arms.

CHAPTER FORTY-THREE

ANNA

ONE YEAR LATER

Evie has grown so much taller over the last year. She's made a new group of friends since she started school, and her voice has taken on the soft lilt of the local accent. She runs ahead now, following the winding coastal path, the cliff edge several feet away so she's not in any danger. Not any more.

Seb and Anna walk behind her in companionable silence. Every so often Anna glances at him, taking pleasure in the lack of tension in his shoulders, the frown lines ironed from his face. The strain of the previous year has taken a physical toll on both of them, but the country air has restored colour to his face, and his lean frame is filling out again. He's the Seb she first met, before she inflicted her terrible secret on him. She isn't sure she'll ever be able to forgive herself.

Anna will never forget the moment before Seb grabbed Evie from Josie's arms, when she didn't know which way this story would go. Was she about to say goodbye to this child she had loved since the moment she first saw her? It comes back to her vividly when she least expects it, and she has to stop what she's doing and calm herself down. The panic attacks are frequent, but she's getting better at handling them. At other times, like now, when Seb touches her arm, she's back in those seconds when he passed Evie to her and the little girl buried her face in Anna's sweater. Will Evie ever forget that view of the concrete below, or is it an image that will haunt her dreams for years to come, without her remembering what she is so afraid of?

'How could you threaten a child like that?' His voice was low, measured so as not to alarm Evie, although Anna knew he'd like to roar at Josie, to make her understand how he could never forgive her for this. 'You deserve to be punished for what you have done to her. Take her away, Anna,' he said without removing his eyes from Josie. 'Get her away from this woman. She may have given birth to her, but she doesn't deserve her.'

Josie crumpled in front of him, bursting into tears as she slumped against the balcony, pulling her knees to her chest and hiding her face.

Evie clung to Anna like a baby koala as she stepped back into the sitting room. 'I won't let anybody hurt you ever again,' Anna said, stroking her daughter's hair.

'What shall we do?' Seb spoke in a low voice. 'We can't just leave her like this.'

'You don't owe her anything. We have to get Evie out of here, away from her.'

Josie raised her head. 'She's still my daughter.'

'You threatened to kill her,' Seb said. 'You'll need help first before we let you anywhere near her again.'

'No,' Anna said.

Josie jumped to her feet and Seb held up his hands, unsure what she would do next. Tears poured down her face.

'What have I done? I don't know what came over me there. How I could have done that? I'm so sorry.' She took a step towards Anna. 'Please don't call the police. Everybody will know and I'll lose my salon.' She wiped her face with the back of her hand. 'You wouldn't understand.'

'Stay away from us,' Anna said. 'If I thought you weren't capable of looking after a child before, you've confirmed it now. There is no doubt in my mind whatsoever. If you ever come near us again—'

'Stop,' Seb said. 'This isn't helping. You're not going to hurt her again, are you?' It was clear that Josie was sorry; she was like a punctured balloon, horrified by what she had done.

Josie shook her head, biting her lip. 'I wish I could go back and undo what just happened.'

Anna went into the hall and hovered near the front door. Seb followed her.

'We should call the police,' he said. 'Report her.'

'You can't,' Anna said, her voice thick with tears. She was holding Evie away from her and speaking quietly so that she wouldn't hear. 'Once they find out the truth, they'll take Evie away from me, from us. She'll be put into care. I'll never see her again. She would hate that, and she wouldn't understand. How can we do that to her after what has just happened? She needs me to make it better for her. I'm the only mother she's ever known, no matter how it came about. You must understand that.'

'Don't call the police.' Josie stood in the doorway, a dark shadow against the light sky in the background. 'It was a moment of madness. I frightened myself. I didn't know I was capable of that. You have to look after her, Seb. You're the one who saved her. You're the only truly honest one of the three of us. Anna and I have both committed a crime, but we're living with what we've done. In a way, what just happened has made me see how Anna has been living, every day shrouded in fear that her secret could be exposed. Now it's my turn. I promise I will do whatever it takes – move far away from you and never contact you again, anything you want. Whether you choose to stay with Anna is none of my business, but she's been a good mother to Evie; I can see that even if I didn't want to. I hope one day you'll be able to forgive me. If you can't ...' She shrugged. 'I get it. I doubt I'll ever forgive myself.'

Anna goes over the scene repeatedly, unsure whether they have done the right thing in breaking contact with Josie, her whereabouts no longer known to them. But Seb trusts her to keep her word, and Anna would trust Seb with her life.

She lets him go in front as the path narrows.

'Stay closer, Evie,' he says, never letting his daughter stray from his sightline.

Anna didn't expect to listen to anything Josie said, but her insight in the aftermath of that terrifying evening has resonated. Not immediately, but in the days and weeks that followed, as they tried to rebuild their life, Anna recognised the strength in Seb, and how his actions did indeed speak louder than words.

'The divorce papers will come through next week,' he says when they've arrived at the pub and are sitting at a table outside, Evie working her way through a packet of crisps as if she hasn't eaten for weeks. The terror of what happened has made him re-evaluate everything. No longer fearing that her daughter will be snatched from her has changed Anna too. She's more relaxed around her, lets her go and play with her friends, stay with her grandmother; and when Evie is with Seb, it allows Anna to appreciate the time she has with her even more. She didn't need to be so strict with her over what she now sees as pettiness; not having the perfect diet one hundred per cent of the time doesn't make her a bad mother. A perfect mother is an illusion, as it should be.

Anna nods, sips her tea, looking out to the distance, where she can just about see the sea. The country air helps her breathe easily as she learns how to navigate this new life of theirs. Her house is a project that will keep her busy for months, but she's determined to do the work herself. Only Evie's room is freshly painted and furnished, and she's going to come over and choose which toys she wants there. She knows this is her second home; her main residence is with Seb. Anna marvels at this solution they have come to, and that she is happy with it. What she did by snatching Evie was almost as unforgivable as what Josie did. Seb is the parent that Evie needs.

'It's the right thing to do,' she says.

'Daddy,' says Evie. 'Mummy looks happy.'

They laugh, and he ruffles her hair.

EPILOGUE
JOSIE

I had an epiphany standing on that balcony, clutching my daughter – *my* daughter – who kicked and squirmed until she saw the concrete paving below. I expect her stomach rolled like mine does when a car goes over the brow of a hill – I say 'expect', because I can only guess at what she feels. I've had that intimacy stolen from me, her inner thoughts, her chatter, her likes and dislikes. We only had a snatched few hours together, and you can't base a relationship on that enforced togetherness. She doesn't know about me, about the truth, about the lies.

Time froze on that balcony. Me, the child, the bloody knife in my hand; him saying the words I'd been waiting to hear, and her beside him, hearing the same words and looking as if the bloody knife had been plunged into her chest. My moment of triumph.

Or so I thought.

I thought I'd won.

I'd planned this all so carefully, but I saw the concrete too, and I felt the swoop of my stomach as I saw her, arms flailing, dropping to the paving below, red spilling out around her. I couldn't do it. I snatched her back from certain death. I saved her because I love her, you see, despite the wriggling body and the kicking legs, the bruises and hurt she inflicted on me. All that is superficial. Give it time.

She's my daughter.

Mine.

He spoke those words I wanted to hear and I seized victory, couldn't resist a triumphant look at Anna; seeing her fall apart in front of me made it all worthwhile. That was enough punishment for the crime she'd committed. I lowered the knife, dropped it to the floor. I wouldn't need it any more; she was broken. I kept my daughter close, until he explained how we could carry on without informing the police. What could she do after all? She was the wrongdoer, the thief. I was the one holding the trump card.

I was just reclaiming what was mine.

And he was reclaiming me.

I lowered the child to the floor, and she ran into his arms. He loves her, anyone can see that. But then he broke the spell. His eyes didn't speak to me with love. They told a different story, and he called her Evie.

Evie. Not Rosie.

Told her to go to Mummy.

Mummy.

He didn't mean me.

I promised them I'd stay away, and I did. Of course I did. It's not in her interests to go to the police – she's a criminal. And I doubt I'll ever forgive myself for what I've done.

I've closed the Ludlow salon; it was never the right place for me – I only had one reason for being there and that situation is resolved now. Manchester is my focus now; I'm back to scouting around for possible sites for a new premises. This time I won't be distracted by a little girl crossing the road who look just like me.

She's with Seb now, he's her father and I hope she'll be happy, that my actions haven't caused her any lasting damage. Motherhood isn't for me, I think I've always known that, whereas Anna was born to be a mother.

My daughter is in safe hands.

A LETTER FROM LESLEY

Dear Reader,

I want to say a huge thank you for choosing to read *Every Little Lie*. If you enjoyed it, and want to keep up to date with all my latest releases, just sign up at the following link. Your email address will never be shared and you can unsubscribe at any time.

www.bookouture.com/lesley-sanderson

Writing *Every Little Lie* was such an enjoyable experience for me. I became very involved with my characters and loved getting the story down. I hope you enjoyed reading it too, and if you did I would be very grateful if you could write a review. I'd love to hear what you think, and it makes such a difference helping new readers to discover one of my books for the first time.

Thanks again for reading my book.

Lesley Sanderson

KEEP IN TOUCH WITH LESLEY

www.lesleysanderson.com

facebook.com/lsandersonbooks

twitter.com/lsandersonbooks

instagram.com/lsandersonbooks

ACKNOWLEDGEMENTS

I want to thank my editor, Therese Keating, who was been a great support through writing this book – from the early stages of plotting through the editing stages this book has been my favourite to work on so far. I'd also like to thank my wonderful agent Hayley Steed who, as ever, was with me from the early stages of plotting this book and who is always available to me for a friendly word, despite her soaring success, and for also helping to make the experience enjoyable.

Thanks to Louise, for all the writing chat and support. To Vikki, Ruth and Rona for being such great writing friends. To Nariece and Sally for the book appreciation trio. To everyone involved in the Lucy Cavendish prize, a continual support to me.

To all my other friends and relatives, and to Paul for enduring the home office situation – I'll get back to writing in cafés one day!

9 781800 199958